PENGUIN BOOKS

SAHYADRI ADVENTURE: KOLESHWAR'S SECRET

Deepak Dalal gave up a career in chemical engineering to write stories for children. He lives in Pune with his wife, two daughters and several dogs and cats. He enjoys wildlife, nature and the outdoors. His books include the Vikram–Aditya adventure series (for older readers) and the Feather Tales series (for younger readers). All his stories have a strong conservation theme.

This book is the sequel to *Sahyadri Adventure: Anirudh's Dream*.

A
VIKRAM–ADITYA
STORY

SAHYADRI ADVENTURE
—KOLESHWAR'S SECRET—

DEEPAK DALAL

PENGUIN BOOKS
An imprint of Penguin Random House

PENGUIN BOOKS

USA | Canada | UK | Ireland | Australia
New Zealand | India | South Africa | China

Penguin Books is part of the Penguin Random House group of companies
whose addresses can be found at global.penguinrandomhouse.com

Published by Penguin Random House India Pvt. Ltd
4th Floor, Capital Tower 1, MG Road,
Gurugram 122 002, Haryana, India

Penguin
Random House
India

First published by Tarini Publishing 2010
Sahyadri Adventure: Koleshwar's Secret was published by Silverfish, an imprint of Grey
Oak Publishers, in association with Westland Publications Private Limited 2013
This edition published in Penguin Books by Penguin Random House India 2022

Copyright © Deepak Dalal 2010
Back cover illustration: Reproduced by permission from Sooni Taraporevala,
front jacket of *Home in the City: Bombay 1977 – Mumbai 2017*
(HarperCollins Publishers India, 2017)
Inside illustrations: Anusha Menon
Geographical inputs and map illustration: Dr Sanjeev Nalawade
Map sketching assistant: Pradnya Apte

ISBN 9780143449430

Typeset in Adobe Caslon Pro by Manipal Technologies Limited, Manipal
Printed at Replika Press Pvt. Ltd, India

www.penguin.co.in

For my dear departed mother and father—wonderful parents who blessed my unusual career choice.

It had been twelve days since Koleshwar. Twelve days since Anirudh had fallen into a coma. Although there had been no moments of consciousness, Anirudh had tossed and turned often in his hospital bed. On occasion, he had even spoken, uttering names or speaking aloud, as if he were caught up in a dream. But his restless turning and utterings had ceased the last few days. He lay in bed, deathly still . . .

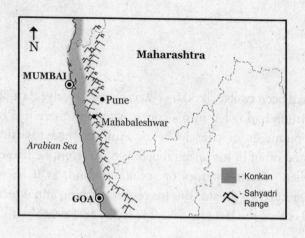

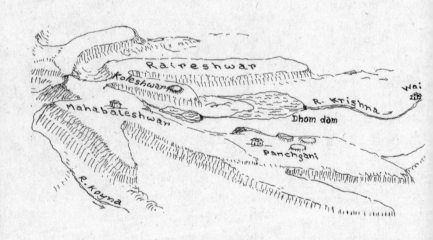

Sketch of Mahabaleshwar Region
(Not to scale)

TREACHERY

It was his father who had seeded a fascination for clouds in Irfan. His early memories brimmed with his father's love of the masses of smoke-like puffs that shadowed Bombay's monsoon skies. Mohammed Aziz had always longed for the touch of their silken tresses as it reminded him of his home in the Sahyadri.

The very thought of touching a cloud had mystified Irfan. How could one touch a cloud? They flew so high in the sky. Even when they descended during the monsoons, they floated well out of reach. But Mohammed Aziz would speak of his home in Mahabaleshwar, which was taller than the monsoon clouds, and where during the rains, one lived in clouds, breathed clouds, walked in clouds and slept in them too. Irfan had been born in the clouds, his father said. He had crept out of his mother's womb on a wet monsoon day when the cloud was so thick, it was a dense sea. Although Irfan had weathered three Mahabaleshwar monsoons, he had no memory of the feel of a cloud and could only guess at what his father talked and dreamt about.

Not surprisingly, clouds had captivated Irfan since his early years. And finally, on a tall Sahyadri mountain, on which an immense bank of vaporous mist rested, he had entered a cloud. Its nebulous touch had pierced his innermost being, triggering memories buried inside his consciousness. At once, he sensed a familiarity with the smoky haze that embraced him. Childhood memories he didn't know existed were awakened. Fuzzy images blurred his vision and long-lost fragrances filled his senses. A beloved face took form before his eyes: a feminine countenance, dark and beautiful, with adoring eyes and hair that streamed in a soft veil. It was a face he associated with love and joy and contentment. The image had dimmed when Irfan reached out to touch it. Diffusing into a shadow, it had wrapped itself around Irfan, sliding into the empty spaces inside his heart, filling them with a warmth and contentment that only a mother could bestow in her infant.

His father was by his side when they had entered the mists, and a great joy had overcome him. Even though Mahabaleshwar still lay a few days' march ahead, the moist clasp of the cloud elevated his spirits and he had jubilantly proclaimed that he was home.

Now, two days later, Irfan was in the clouds again, but the serenity and happiness they had lavished on him were gone. In its place, a numbing chill was fanning dread and panic within him. Irfan was in a forest on a mountainside that sloped steeply upward. His world was shrouded. The trees were like giant tombstones and there was an eerie cemetery-like silence. Spooky though it was, the forest was nowhere near as frightening as the kind of fear that inhabited every nerve and cell in his body.

Murky shadows plodded beside him, most barely hip-high. They stumbled along on four legs, weighed down by heavy chests strapped to their flanks. Two upright shadows marched amongst the burdened animals, one stooped, the other thin and erect. The stooped shadow was Rustom, his face red from the exertions of the climb. The other was Tabrez, their companion during the voyage, the youngster who wielded a catapult as if it were an extension of his arm.

Irfan scowled in irritation when Tabrez suddenly halted. There was a pressing need to keep moving, yet this was the third time Tabrez had pulled up.

Tabrez faced Irfan, sweat dripping from his dark features. 'We've gone far enough,' he panted. 'They could need our help. The further we go, the longer it will take for us to respond.'

Irfan glowered furiously. 'Father would have asked us to stay if he needed our help,' he snapped. 'He doesn't want it. He wishes for us to safeguard the mules and their chests instead. Stop questioning his orders. You are wasting time; we must go on.'

Tabrez glared at Irfan. He opened his mouth, then snapped it fiercely shut. Swearing, he kicked viciously at a bush beside him, prompting a mule to bray loudly and back away. Irfan swore. The mist shielded them from their pursuers, but noises like these carried far and could betray their presence. Unleashing another kick, this one propelling wet mud harmlessly from the ground, Tabrez stomped away.

Irfan clenched his fists, striving to calm himself. Anger drained precious energy he could ill afford to lose. The swift-paced climb was exhausting. The heavily laden animals were tiring, and Tabrez's half-hearted efforts at urging them along only escalated his and Rustom's exertions.

A gut-wrenching fear scorched Irfan's insides. After weeks of hiding in mountains and forests, they were finally on the home leg of their journey. But barely an hour earlier, a band of horsemen—four in number—had been spotted far below, speeding their steeds up the slope. Though distance rendered identification difficult, their garments and style of riding had confirmed them as Englishmen.

Wallace had tracked them down.

'It is Wallace,' Irfan's father had declared. 'It is him, I know. We took great pains to cover our tracks, yet he has found us.' Mohammed Aziz had spat as he stared down the slope. Muttering darkly, he had speculated on the possibility of betrayal.

Shahid, the sailor, had suggested making a break for the mountains. Wallace would never find them if they hid in the crevices of their lofty cliffs. But Mohammed Aziz had shot the plan down as it involved abandoning the mules.

'We cannot escape them,' Mohammed Aziz had said. 'We must prepare for battle.'

Mohammed Aziz had settled upon a plan. Their group totalled seven in number: three youngsters—Rustom, Irfan and Tabrez—and four adults. The youngsters were to race to the top of the mountain with the mules. The slope terminated in a ridge, he had explained. Beyond, dipped a valley nestled between two towering mountains with immense plateau-like crests. The plateau on the right was Mahabaleshwar and the one to the left was known as Koleshwar. The boys were to head to Koleshwar, an uninhabited wilderness, and hide the mules in its forested slopes.

The adults would take cover in the trees and ambush Wallace's party. The Englishmen would certainly have the edge with superior firepower. Mohammed Aziz's entire company possessed only two firearms, but they were equipped with swords and spears, and their strategy of surprising the enemy would work to their advantage.

Tabrez had vociferously opposed Mohammed Aziz's plan. He saw no need to split the group. He could take down two of their pursuers himself, he had claimed. Working as a team, they could defeat the Englishmen and continue their journey thereafter. But Mohammed Aziz's only concern was Wallace's treasure. His chief objective was to deny the Englishman the fruits of his ill-gotten bounty, and he was willing to die to fulfil his goal. Mohammed Aziz had believed that Tabrez would be more useful with the mules and their precious burden. It was crucial that the animals be spirited away and concealed on Koleshwar's slopes. Once that was accomplished, they could return, but no further than the ridge above. From there they were to assess the outcome of the battle. Inshallah, the Englishmen would be defeated, but if Wallace prevailed, they were to flee with the mules into the mountains, do whatever they possibly could to prevent him from recovering his misbegotten cache.

Irfan needed a vent for his smouldering anger. Brooding helped distract his mind from the impending battle and its possible heartbreaking consequences. He fixed his thoughts on Tabrez as he hurried up the slope, specifically the transformation of his genial personality to its present churlish, ill-natured state.

The change had taken place shortly after Irfan's jubilant union with his father. They had been reunited in a forest not far from where Tabrez hailed. The next day, Tabrez had been sent on a mission to requisition mules from a nearby village. Irfan and Rustom believed that it was on Tabrez's return—when the animals he herded in were burdened with chests of cargo from Wallace's boat—that his temperament had turned. Several of the chests had jingled and clinked suggestively, and Tabrez had immediately wanted to see what was stored inside them. But no one had enlightened him, and Mohammed Aziz had warned him against tampering with the locks that sealed them. From that day, his cheery disposition had faded.

So marked was the shift in Tabrez's conduct that everyone had noticed. Shahid had even inquired as to what the matter was, but Tabrez had refused to reply. Rustom and Irfan were certain that the sealed contents of the chests were to blame. Although no one discussed the mysterious baggage, it was common knowledge that the chests contained riches—a treasure of perhaps immeasurable value. It was for their safekeeping that they led the lives of fugitives, travelling clandestinely and secreting themselves in forests. None in their company had been affected by the presence of Wallace's cache—none except Tabrez.

The mules wearied quickly. Irfan and Rustom worked tirelessly, prodding the animals with sticks, cajoling and urging them forward. Mists clung to the mountainside like an enveloping sea. The poor visibility forced them to band the animals together, for fear of losing them in the shrouded forest. Tabrez made only a pretence at helping. He often stalled their progress, climbing lethargically and lingering at the rear. He kept casting glances down the slope, his mind distracted by the skirmish that would soon take place below.

Rustom had topped the crest of the hill when the muffled blast of a musket exploded below. Abandoning the animals, he raced to Irfan's side as more explosions followed. Irfan's breathing turned ragged as he gazed into the mist. He started to tremble and sway. Rustom reached out, steadying him.

Tabrez turned on them, nostrils flared, eyes wild. 'I am going down!' he yelled, gazing challengingly at them. Cries wafted through the mists, guns boomed. 'Don't try to stop me. People are being killed below.'

'Wait!' exclaimed Irfan. 'I'm coming with you.'

'You!' he scoffed. 'What can you do?'

'It is my father down there. Rustom, you look after the animals.'

Rustom grabbed Irfan's arm. 'Irfan . . . no!' There was terror in his voice.

Irfan tried to jerk his hand free, but Rustom refused to let go. He turned angrily. Then he saw the desperation on his friend's face.

'Rustom . . . I have to go. My father is down there.'

Rustom swallowed, eyes shining and filled with dread. 'No. Not without me. I will come with you.'

Irfan shook his head. He spoke gently. 'This is not your fight, Rustom. I won't let you endanger yourself. Stay with the mules. Abandon them if we don't come back. Run and save yourself.'

Tabrez swore impatiently, stamping his foot. 'Come on! There is no time to waste.'

Tears spilled from Rustom's eyes. 'No . . . no,' he sobbed. 'It can't end like this, Irfan.'

Irfan clasped Rustom's hand. 'It won't,' he cried. 'I will be back. I promise.' He crushed Rustom to his chest. 'You are my treasure, Rustom. My life! The best friend I've ever had. Goodbye.'

Tabrez was running down the slope. Irfan cast one last look at Rustom and plunged after him. The incline was wet, steep and slippery. Irfan skidded often, saving himself by clutching at branches and bushes, most of them sharp and thorny. His hands bloodied quickly. He hurtled down the mountainside, Tabrez a few strides ahead. In a matter of minutes, the mists thinned and they found themselves at the sifting edge of the clouds.

Tabrez pulled up. A rocky knoll jutted skyward to one side of the trail, its crown peaking above the trees. He scrambled up the wet, black rock. Irfan followed, panting heavily.

A wind teased the mist, engulfing the knoll with cloud one moment and sweeping it away the next. During clear intervals, a wet forest drifted into view, interspersed with rocks and grassy clearings. Apart from birds hovering in the sky, the only sign of life was a pair of horses in a clearing halfway down the hill. A light rain pattered softly. Leaves rustled in the wind.

'The ambush must have taken place where the horses are,' whispered Tabrez.

Irfan battled a wave of hysteria. 'Where are the men?' he cried. 'I can't see my father. Did he survive?'

'We can't tell from here. We won't know unless we get closer.'

'Wallace's men could have won.' Distress rose in Irfan, churning like bile in his stomach.

Tabrez acknowledged the possibility. 'They could have. We have to be careful.'

Tabrez led the way, moving slower now, his tread soft. He had unsheathed his catapult. Irfan drew his sword. It was long and curved at its tip. His father had presented it to him shortly after their reunion in the Konkan forests. Irfan had never wielded a weapon combatively but was ready to do so if the need arose.

The damp earth muffled their footfalls. Tabrez barely disturbed the litter of leaves carpeting the slope. Irfan was mulish in comparison, his heavy feet snapping twigs and dislodging stones. They descended quickly. Lower down the incline eased, and on a level stretch of forest, when the horses came into view, Tabrez halted.

'Wait here,' he whispered when Irfan drew up alongside. 'You can be heard a mile away. We can't take chances . . . Wallace could have won. I'll go see and come back for you.'

Irfan did not argue.

Tabrez departed, slipping noiselessly through the underbrush. The sky was dark and it was raining. Although

9

they had emerged from the mists, the heavy canopy and grey skies ensured visibility remained poor. The gloom deepened as the rain increased in intensity. Irfan sheltered beneath a tree, head bowed, waiting.

Minutes later, Irfan leapt to his feet on hearing a shout. It was Tabrez. He wasn't visible, but his voice was clearly audible. His words brought joy to Irfan. 'Wallace and his men are dead. You can come out. Your father is well.'

Irfan sprinted forward. The horses backed away as he sped past them. Tabrez was waiting for him deep inside the forest. He turned away as Irfan approached, hurrying through a jumble of trees and rocks. Irfan followed, pestering him with questions, but Tabrez's only reply was that he would soon see for himself.

Around a bend, they came upon two bodies lying in the mud. One was a foreigner with light hair. Irfan caught his breath when he laid eyes on the other.

Shahid.

Tabrez spoke harshly. 'Keep walking,' he ordered. 'Shahid is dead, but your father awaits you ahead.'

Irfan stumbled along, blinking tears. There were more bodies in the undergrowth, sprawled lifelessly, limbs stretched at impossible angles. Irfan kept his head down, unable to muster the courage to look at them. The trees thinned, the gloom lessened, but Irfan still did not look up.

They were walking on bare rock when Tabrez halted. He spoke roughly. 'There's your father.'

Irfan raised his head and went deathly still.

Mohammed Aziz lay sprawled on the ground, propped awkwardly against a black rock. One hand cradled a shoulder, fingers dark with blood.

Two men stood beside his father, both European. The shorter wore a dark tweed jacket. Although his blond hair was dirty and tousled, there was a parting down the middle. His face was finely boned, and his lip was curled in a leer.

'Thought you would escape me?' sneered Wallace. 'I said I'd track you and your thieving father down. Promised you, didn't I?'

Raw anger flooded Irfan. A visceral rage exploded inside him. He charged forward, wrenching his sword from his belt. Something smashed into him from behind, sending him crashing to the ground. The fall jerked his sword loose. It was snatched away before he could reach for it.

Tabrez knelt beside him, the sword held lightly in his hand.

Irfan's gaze was incredulous. 'You!' he mouthed, voice filled with loathing.

'Me!' smirked Tabrez, backing away.

Wallace laughed uproariously. 'Yes, him!' he said, mimicking the repugnance in Irfan's voice.

Irfan swung his gaze from Tabrez to Wallace, his face a mask of hatred.

Wallace's fingers caressed the butt of his holstered pistol. 'Your comrade has been useful. Very useful. I had expected your dog of a father to slink back to his hole at Mahabaleshwar. It was at Mahad that your friend here informed me otherwise. The forests of Koleshwar were a good idea. I hadn't thought of that I must admit.'

Irfan swore, attempting to lunge at Tabrez.

'Don't!' warned Wallace, yanking his gun free. He trained its muzzle on Irfan. 'I can blow your brains out if I want. Just one flick of the trigger, that's all it will take.' He lowered the muzzle and smiled. 'But I don't want to do that. It would spoil my fun. You and your father must live so I can savour my victory.' He lifted the muzzle again, face hardening. 'But don't force me—'

Irfan held back, staring murderously at Tabrez.

Wallace's companion was a tall, bearded Englishman with shifty eyes and a scar on his forehead. 'Collins,' said Wallace, addressing the man. 'There's rope in my saddle bag. Bring it here and tie the boy so he can't move.'

Collins departed.

Wallace turned away from Irfan. Pirouetting slowly, he inspected the area.

They were in a rocky clearing, at the edge of the mountain. A sharp abyss loomed a few feet from where Mohammed Aziz was propped. The area was strewn with boulders. Except for one blackened stump of a tree—decapitated, possibly by lightning—there was no vegetation in the clearing.

Wallace's eyes settled on the stump. 'That trunk should do,' he said. He gestured at Tabrez. 'Take the boy there,' he ordered. 'Secure him to it.'

Tabrez pushed Irfan forward.

The stump protruded only a few feet from where Mohammed Aziz lay. 'Father,' cried Irfan, running towards him. But Wallace stepped in-between, pistol raised.

'Get back,' he commanded.

Tabrez grabbed Irfan, steering him roughly to the tree stump.

'Rope him tight,' ordered Wallace. Then he smiled crookedly. 'See, I'm tying you next to your father. Not out of compassion, if you are stupid enough to think so, but because I want you to see him die.' He laughed evilly. 'Your father is dying, you know, bleeding his black heart out. There are two bullets stuck in him. One in his shoulder, the other in his thigh. He's going to bleed to death and you're going to watch him, you little devil.'

Irfan's head dropped. Black hopelessness crushed down on him. He did not resist when Collins and Tabrez forced him to the ground and trussed him to the blackened stump.

Wallace surveyed their handiwork when they were done. Like his father, Irfan was sprawled on the ground, his legs splayed in front. But unlike his father, who was unfettered, Irfan was leashed securely to the tree, unable to stir.

'Good job,' commended Wallace, rubbing his palms. 'There's still one more task.' He smiled wickedly at Irfan. 'Yes, your friend with the mules. Collins, take our young Indian comrade with you. Find the boy with the mules and kill him. Check that the stolen chests are all there. Then hobble the mules and return. I will wait here with this pitiful man and his son.' Wallace smirked. 'I'm looking forward to a private session with them.'

Collins nodded at Tabrez. 'Come along,' he ordered. 'Let's get the job done with.'

'STOP!' shouted Irfan. He gazed pleadingly at Tabrez. 'Don't kill him.'

Tabrez stared, eyes dark and stony.

'Spare him,' appealed Irfan desperately. 'Spare Rustom. He is your friend.'

Collins was already striding away. Tabrez turned and followed the Englishman.

EXTREME RETRIBUTION

A stupefying dread had taken hold of Rustom the moment Irfan had rushed down the slope. Unable to deal with Irfan's shattered mental state, Rustom had let him go. But even as the clouds had swallowed him, Rustom had regretted letting him have his way.

Irfan's reckless decision to rush to the battlefield was the opposite of what Mohammed Aziz had desired. They had been sent away for their safety. Mohammed Aziz had sought to keep them out of harm's way. Irfan's thoughtless actions were contrary to his father's wishes. And what could he hope to achieve anyway? If the Englishmen had won the encounter, they would kill Irfan too.

Rustom found himself questioning his own role. What was he doing on the cloud-wrapped mountainside? He hadn't embarked on the harrowing journey from Bombay to tend mules. He was here to be with Irfan—to protect him, to give his life for his friend if the need arose. How could he sit idly while Irfan could possibly be dying below?

15

Rustom had quickly turned restless. Unable to control his mounting unease, he decided to act. The mists were a hindrance, concealing everything from view. All he had to do was descend below the cloud line, so he could observe for himself. His decisions would be informed then. Awareness could help save Irfan, and perhaps his own life too. But the mules would have to be taken care of first. A bundle of rope was strapped to one of the animals. He could hobble the creatures so they wouldn't stray far.

Though Rustom worked fast, hobbling consumed precious time. When he was done, he hurried down. He emerged from the mists beside the same knoll Irfan and Tabrez had. He climbed it quickly, disturbing a herd of spotted deer grazing nearby. The horses Irfan had seen were still in the clearing below. But now, in addition, vultures were circling the sky above a patch of forest not far from the horses. A prickly chill spread through Rustom. There were dead men down there. The vultures had come to feed.

The knoll commanded an excellent view of the area. Further descent was dangerous, so Rustom decided to wait there. The sky was dark and grey. A light rain fell like a mist. Nearby a troop of langurs fed quietly in the trees. Far below, three large animals emerged to graze on a patch of clear hillside. Rustom knew at once that they were gaur. The rhino-sized animals were common in these forests. They had passed several herds, some numbering hundreds, during their journey. It was while he was distracted by the gaur that Rustom spotted movement.

He pressed himself to the ground as two shadows strode out of the forest, not far from the horses. A surge of relief shot through him on identifying Tabrez. But relief switched to horror when he saw that his companion was an Englishman.

Were his eyes playing tricks? It didn't make sense. Where was Irfan, and what about the others? Tabrez was accompanying the enemy! Realization flooded Rustom. They had been betrayed. Tabrez was a traitor.

Rustom suddenly felt vulnerable, exposed on the knoll. Tabrez and the Englishman were striding up the hill, their purpose painfully clear. Panicking, he started to descend, then halted. The langurs. His movements would disturb the monkeys. That would draw attention to the knoll. He was in any case hidden from their view. Movement risked detection. He chose to stay put.

Tabrez!

Fierce anger blazed inside Rustom. Irfan and he had doubted his loyalty. They had even conveyed their misgivings to Shahid and Mohammed Aziz. But Shahid had brushed their doubts aside. He had said he had known Tabrez since he was a child; his father was a trusted friend. Yet Tabrez had betrayed them. But how? When could Tabrez have informed Wallace? The answer came unbidden to Rustom. At Mahad—the town at the foot of Mahabaleshwar. Mohammed Aziz had sent Tabrez to the city to gather information on Wallace's movements. It was obvious now that Tabrez had spilled information instead of acquiring any.

Tabrez was leading his English comrade away from the knoll and Rustom understood why. They intended to circle and come upon him from an unexpected direction. Rustom smiled grimly. Little did Tabrez know that his quarry was down here watching him. The mists soon absorbed them, obliterating their presence, like a curtain drawn across a windowpane. Rustom waited briefly, then descended.

The forest drew a roof over Rustom as he slipped down the slope. Its tangled canopy veiled his view of the sky. But fallen trees provided breaks, enabling him to glimpse the vultures and bear towards them.

Rustom was certain that Irfan was alive. There had been no gunshots since the battle. Tabrez must have turned Irfan over to Wallace, and he was being held captive somewhere in the forest. It was clear also that if he was to rescue Irfan, the best time was now, before Tabrez and his companion returned. Rustom was homing in on the vultures because they were guiding him to the scene of the battle. He hoped to find firearms amongst the dead. A gun might tilt the scales in his favour.

Rustom hurried forward, the wet earth muffling his footsteps. Soon the vultures were before him, several on the ground, and an equal number perched on branches. Rustom halted. His eyes swept the forest gloom. Except for the birds, the area was empty. He started forward once more. Long snake-like necks craned in his direction. The birds stared, unsure of what to make of him. Some hopped away, others flapped their wings, squawking.

Without warning, a blast-like explosion destroyed the forest peace. Rustom froze. The effect on the birds was more pronounced. A cacophony of shrieks and squawks erupted from them, alarming Rustom far more than the boom of the firearm. The bedlam was heightened by the frantic flap of wings as the vultures rose in a flailing mass. Rustom dropped to the ground as the heavy birds teetered in disarray, crashing into one another in their frenzied rush to get airborne.

Someone had fired a gun. The blast had detonated above, from high on the mountain, the area where Tabrez and the Englishman had gone. Tabrez did not own a gun. The Englishman did. Rustom racked his brains wondering why the Englishman had discharged his weapon. There were two possibilities. The first was an attack by a wild animal. There were bears here, and tigers and leopards too. The second was an altercation between Tabrez and the Englishman. Rustom rejected the second possibility, settling on the wild animal theory.

Whatever the cause, the gunshot simplified Rustom's task, as it had scared away the birds. He gingerly approached the area where they had congregated, flinching when he saw the bodies. Faces had been mutilated by the vultures. Clothing helped him identify the remains of his companions. Rustom gagged in horror when he saw Shahid's coat draped on one of the bodies. Two more of Mohammed Aziz's team lay dead, sprawled beside the corpses of two fair-skinned men. Rustom searched the forest for Mohammed Aziz, but there were no additional bodies. Could it be that Irfan's father had survived? Rustom prayed that he had.

Muskets and pistols lay scattered amongst the dead men. Shahid's fingers clutched a pistol. A musket lay beside one of the fallen Englishmen. Both Englishmen had pistols tucked in their belts. Rustom decided against muskets. They were too unwieldy. Pistols would suit his purpose. The pistol in Shahid's fingers had certainly been discharged, but the ones in the belts of the dead Englishmen might still be loaded. Rustom had never handled a gun in all his life. He had no idea how to load one. Nor could he tell whether they had been discharged or were armed. The fact that the dead Englishmen's guns were still holstered gave him confidence. The men had probably been killed during the ambush before they had time to draw their pistols. Working quickly, he plucked the Englishmen's pistols and stuffed them in his belt. A sword with a curved blade lay on the ground. Collecting it, he turned his back on the bloodied battleground.

The gunshot devastated Irfan. Wallace laughed with diabolic glee. Mohammed Aziz's head dropped.

Tears streamed from Irfan's eyes. He didn't want to live even a minute more. It was for him that Rustom had made the supreme sacrifice. He wished Wallace would put a bullet through him. The burden was too much, impossible to bear.

Irfan's distress elicited great mirth from Wallace. 'I have news for you, master Irfan,' he cackled, rising to his feet. Holding up his hand, he raised two fingers. 'Two tidings my boy—one good and the other bad. I shall present the good news first.' He paused dramatically. Cocking his head, he whispered conspiratorially, drawing out his words. 'Your friend . . . is still alive.'

The world stood still for Irfan. He stared open-mouthed at Wallace.

Wallace rocked on his feet, enjoying himself. 'That gunshot didn't kill your friend. It killed the young man who betrayed you.'

Irfan felt as if he were in the clouds. It was as if an impossible weight had been cast off his shoulders.

'Collins had instructions to shoot the other fellow first,' continued Wallace. 'Aha, I see you are smiling. I'm glad that you are because it might be the last time you will. Now . . . the bad news.' Wallace grinned malevolently. 'The bad news will be the next gunshot. It will take care of your friend; return him to his gods.' Wallace burst into peals of laughter. 'So, save your tears for the next explosion.'

Irfan felt as if a new life had been breathed into him. Rustom was alive! Wallace's 'bad news' was of no consequence. Rustom would escape. He was too smart to allow himself to be killed. Allah would help him. Irfan closed his eyes and moved his lips in prayer.

'That's right,' jeered Wallace. 'Pray to your God. Beg for His forgiveness because all of you will soon be joining Him up there.'

The sounds of Wallace's mirth floated through the underbrush, guiding Rustom forward. The forest was dark and dense, in a permanent state of twilight. The trees banded tightly together, and vines and creepers snaked everywhere. There was no grass beneath the trees, but the leaf litter was several inches deep. Rustom stepped gingerly, bearing down with infinite caution. He moved with a minimum of sound, his breath echoing in his ears.

The gloom quickly lightened. The forest thinned and patches of cloud appeared between the trees. Through a mesh of leaves, Rustom saw that the mountainside terminated in a jumble of rocks. To one side, a towering rock face reached for the sky, its upper section obscured by cloud. Irfan and his father were at the base of the rock face, beside a mountainous heap of fallen rock. Irfan was well but, even from a distance, it was obvious that Mohammed Aziz's condition wasn't good. His head hung limply and a hand clutched a shoulder, which was dark and wet. Irfan was roped to the stump of a tree. Mohammed Aziz's hands were unfettered. It was clear from his condition that he posed no threat.

Both father and son were uncomfortably close to an abyss. The hillside fell away sharply just a few feet from where Mohammed Aziz lay. A vast void, packed with cloud, yawned at his feet. Wallace squatted opposite Mohammed Aziz on a waist-high rock, wearing a jacket and long boots. Wind fluttered his long blond hair.

Irfan was saying something. 'Friend has escaped . . . the mules . . . your treasure . . . gone.'

His words were drawing a sharp response from Wallace, whose handsome face was turning a shade of purple. Wallace shouted at Irfan. But Irfan continued, ignoring him. Wallace leapt to his feet, enraged. Crossing to Irfan he swung his hand, smacking Irfan a blow on his face. Mohammed Aziz raised his head and mumbled something. Irfan fell silent.

Wallace began to pace back and forth.

Rustom examined the clearing. Ahead, rock replaced soil. Trees thinned and the forest terminated well short of the cliff edge. Grass grew where the forest ended, thrusting from the rock in tall clumps. There were boulders strewn amidst the grass. The boulders were modestly sized, few of them chest-high. They provided cover of a sort. Not reliable cover, but they would have to do. To achieve his objective, Rustom would have to sneak within point-blank range of Wallace. Pistols were accurate only over a short range, and never having fired one before, he lacked the confidence of hitting a target, even at arm's length. This was a do-or-die affair. There would be no second opportunity. Wallace would see to that. He had to get it right the first time.

Rustom braced himself. Choosing his moment, he crept forward.

Rustom had stolen undetected to the first rock when there was a shout from the mountainside above.

'A curse on this miserable forest,' roared a voice. 'Wallace, can you hear me? The bloody fog has descended! I don't know where I am.'

'Over here!' responded Wallace. 'Not far now.' He cupped his hands to his mouth. 'The mules and my chests—did you find them?'

'All thirty chests are up there. I counted them.'

Wallace's shoulders lifted. He grinned triumphantly at Irfan. He cupped his hands again. 'Did you find the boy?'

'I killed the traitorous one,' replied Collins. 'But I didn't find the other. The abominable fog again. We need to be on our guard. The mules had already been hobbled, and I saw tracks on the way down. It sounds unlikely, but he could be somewhere in this awful forest, or down there beside you, searching for his friends.'

Wallace stiffened and placed a hand on his gun. He swept his gaze across the clearing.

Mohammed Aziz lifted his head. 'What are they saying, son?' he asked in a feeble voice.

'They did not find Rustom, Father. The man says he could be down here. Wallace is worried.'

Though it was an effort, Mohammed Aziz managed a smile. 'Rustom is a good boy. I was wrong about him.'

'He could still rescue us, Father. There is hope.'

'There is no hope for me, son. There are bullets inside me and I have lost much blood.'

There was a terrible sadness inside Irfan, yet he forced himself to speak words of hope. 'You will be well, Father. Rustom will rescue us, then we will treat your wounds.'

Mohammed Aziz smiled again. 'I was wrong about a lot of things,' he whispered. 'Wrong about Rustom. Wrong about Forjett. Wrong about you. I was blinded by anger.'

'There was a reason for your anger, Father. It was justified. We have been over this before. You have forgiven me. We love each other—'

'Yes,' breathed Mohammed Aziz. 'Yes, we are father and son again. It is good. I can die a happy man.'

'Stop the chatter, you two,' interrupted Wallace harshly.

Irfan sneered at the Englishman. 'You deny a dying man. You are afraid even his last words can harm you.'

Irfan expected another blow, but surprisingly Wallace's face cleared instead. He grinned. 'Die he will, and you with him!'

Wallace seemed more relaxed now. His hand had dropped from his gun. His eyes no longer scanned the clearing.

'I will kill him,' muttered Mohammed Aziz. 'I still have strength. I have saved it for him. With my last breath, I will take him with me.'

Irfan bowed his head.

Fog was rising above the rim of the abyss. The wind gusted a breath of cloud across the clearing, then swept it away.

Wallace inhaled deeply. 'COLLINS!' he roared. 'Where are you?'

The reply was much louder this time; from behind the foliage. 'Almost home,' yelled the Englishman.

Irfan blinked. A figure had flashed between the rocks. At first, he thought it was an animal, then his heart leapt.

Rustom!

'Father,' said Irfan, struggling to keep his voice normal. 'There is help at hand. Rustom is here. The angrez murderer has not seen him. Don't look up. Do nothing that might alert him.'

Mohammed Aziz sighed. 'Allah has been kind. I will be avenged now.'

Rustom was surprised at his calm. Neither the impending duel nor the likelihood of death affected him. He felt no different than if he were at the docks in Bombay, scrutinizing a ship's manifest. Even the imminent arrival of Collins failed to perturb him. The news of Tabrez's demise hadn't saddened him. Instead, he had computed grimly that it eased his task, nudging the odds in his favour. His enemies were down to two.

It was vital that he remain undetected. He had to manoeuvre himself to a strategic location, good enough to shoot both men from. Wallace was near the cliff edge, still too distant for accuracy. There were rocks near him. He crouched, waiting for an opportunity to steal forward.

Wallace whistled. He leaned on a rock, his back to the abyss. He faced the forest, leaving no scope for Rustom to steal forward. Mist was pouring into the clearing in waves. The wind had dropped, but it still ruffled the grass, furrowing its blades one way and then another.

Rustom heard the sound of shrubbery being parted. A shadow emerged at the edge of the clearing. Wallace looked up in the direction of the disturbance. Rustom bit his lip; he was trapped between the two Englishmen. Bowing low, he drew both the pistols from his belt, one in each hand.

'Phew!' snorted Collins, stumbling into the clearing. 'Dratted thorns. They've ripped the legging of my pants.' He walked forward brushing his trousers.

'You sure about the chests?' queried Wallace, as Collins materialized ghostlike from the cloud. 'Not a single one missing?'

'Exactly thirty,' grinned Collins. 'I counted them twice over.'

Wallace rubbed his hands. 'Good,' he whispered. 'GOOD!' he repeated, shouting victoriously. He thrust his hands to the sky. 'It's over! I'VE WON!' He rounded gloatingly on Irfan and his father. 'All that remains is to deal with these two. A task I have dreamt of for weeks!' He stepped towards them, a murderous light shining in his eyes.

Collins was moving briskly. There were no boulders between him and Rustom, only grass. The mist had withdrawn. If he looked up he would see Rustom.

Wallace advanced on Irfan and his father, licking his lips.

Rustom pushed himself to his knees. Placing a pistol on the ground, he steadied the other on Collins. Collins hadn't detected him yet. Rustom hoped he wouldn't till he was only an arm's length away. At that distance, even he couldn't miss.

But Collins suddenly froze. His hand fell to his holster. 'What on earth . . .' The Englishman left his sentence incomplete as he swept his gun from his holster. Rustom pulled his trigger. His gun was squared on the Englishman's chest. His aim was slightly off, a little high. His bullet pierced Collins's heart. The force of the explosion jolted the weapon from Rustom's hand. He reached for the other pistol and whipped about to face Wallace.

Wallace turned on hearing Collins shout. His face blanched as he saw his comrade fall. By the time he looked up, Rustom was on his feet, facing him, gun in hand.

Wallace stepped back, screaming as Rustom pulled the trigger. But there was no deafening explosion, no smell of gunpowder—only a harmless click.

Blood rushed back to Wallace's cheeks. Drawing his gun, he laughed as Rustom repeatedly pulled the trigger.

'What a turn of events,' he crowed. 'Surprising?' he asked, cocking an eyebrow. He gestured with his gun. 'Maybe surprising for you, but not for me. God is on my side, you see! It is good to believe in him, and I am blessed that I do. Look what he has done for me. My best plans couldn't have conjured a situation like this. My money is safe. No need to share it with anyone now that Collins is no more. And I have all three of you where I want you.'

The man cackled, laughing maniacally.

'You first,' said Wallace, waving his gun at Rustom. 'You are the dangerous one.'

Behind Wallace, Mohammed Aziz was rising.

Wallace trained his gun on Rustom.

Rustom worked his mind furiously. 'Wait!' he begged. 'You believe in God. I am a Parsee. Allow me to prepare for my death.'

Wallace stood still. Only his facial muscles twitched. Behind him, Mohammed Aziz, unable to stand properly, was inching forward.

Laughter pealed suddenly from Wallace's lips. 'Be my guest,' he chuckled. 'Yes, you must make peace with your God. Do what you must. I am in no hurry.'

Rustom fell to his knees, clasping his hands together. He shut his eyes and moved his lips in fervent prayer.

Irfan sat utterly still. Mohammed Aziz was only a couple of steps behind Wallace. What could his father do, wondered Irfan? Mohammed Aziz was almost bent double, on the verge of death.

But there was a gleam in Mohammed Aziz's eyes that Irfan couldn't see. With a heart-wrenching effort, he straightened himself.

Sensing something, Wallace half-turned.

Mohammed Aziz's hands snaked forward, wrapping like bands of steel around Wallace. The Englishman twisted, pushing Mohammed Aziz back. Grunting in agony Mohammed Aziz held on, allowing himself to be pushed but holding fast to his bearlike embrace.

As Mohammed Aziz stumbled backwards Irfan understood his father's intentions. 'NO, FATHER . . . DON'T!' shrieked Irfan.

Mohammed Aziz stood at the edge of the abyss. Wallace's energies were focused on his gun hand, struggling to free it. Then he realized the danger. He screamed as he and Mohammed Aziz tottered on the edge. Wallace abandoned his exertions for his gun. He strained forward, intent only on distancing himself from the abyss. Crablike, Mohammed Aziz hung on to his victim. Allah had answered his prayers. He had granted him one final opportunity to avenge himself and nothing, not even death, would prise his fingers loose. His chest was on fire. His leg was buckling, but power flowed in his arms. Summoning every last shred of his strength, Mohammed Aziz pulled Wallace, stepping back. One foot pressed on solid rock, but the other flailed on air. Wallace voiced a terrible high-pitched shriek.

'FATHER!' screamed Irfan.

Rustom dashed forward, but he was too late. Mohammed Aziz had consummated the justice he had sought all his life. He slid off the edge in slow motion, his wife's murderer wrapped tightly in his arms. The sea of swirling cloud claimed them, swallowing their spinning bodies. The clouds parted for an instant and Rustom saw that Mohammed Aziz's hands still clutched the doomed Englishman, not letting go even as he plunged to certain death. The clouds coalesced once more and there was nothing except the howl of the wind.

THE CLOUD FOREST

For some time now, a feeling had been building within the bystander that the dream was drawing to a close. Flashes of luminosity had crept into its imagery, disrupting its flow. And the familiar darkness, the space he retreated to during nightmarish sequences of the dream, had vanished altogether. When he pulled back next, in the aftermath of the tragedy of Mohammed Aziz's death, instead of darkness, a burst of dazzling light had erupted about him. Glittering images appeared, shimmering and sparkling everywhere, dipping and cartwheeling, like a school of playful dolphins. The images were impossibly bright and fuzzy, but with time they banded together and started to resolve. He spied a white object overhead. Flat propeller-like arms projected from it, generating a current of air that wafted down on him. It was some time before the bystander realized what he was staring at.

A fan!

Its design was different from the pankha of the dream. It was driven by a superior energy, far more efficient than the simple rope that energized the pankhas he had grown familiar with. He sucked in a breath. A shadow lurking nearby sprang forward when he inhaled. A face appeared, trembling with hope and joy. A voice impinged on his consciousness.

'ANIRUDH!'

The face . . . the voice. Memories hurtled through his brain. He struggled, attempting to rise and darkness seized him again.

The final leg of the dream was dominated by forest, cloud and rain. It was as if a giant cloud had taken charge of the world, sweeping away the blue skies and banishing the sun. Rain fell constantly. Sometimes it let up, moderating to a drizzle, but those moments were rare. Mostly it rained hard and often for days on end.

Mr Hunter—Irfan's teacher—had spoken of Noah's Ark and of the Christian belief that the heavens had once leaked so much water that the earth had flooded. It rained so heavily on the plateau of Koleshwar that sometimes Irfan wondered if the earth was indeed being swamped and that the only hope for survival was to ride out the storm in a boat, the way Noah once had.

They sheltered from the rain inside a cave. Rustom and Irfan tended a fire there, ensuring it blazed through the day and night, keeping them warm and dry. Like the rain, the smell of wood smoke became a part of their existence—a memory associated with the gloom and wetness of a Sahyadri monsoon.

But more omnipresent than the rain was the smothering presence of cloud. Experiencing exactly what Mohammed

Aziz had said of his beloved mountains, Irfan and Rustom breathed clouds, walked in clouds, and slept in them too. As weightless as air and as fine as satin, the mist hung upon them like a veil, so diaphanous that except for a mild dampness they hardly felt its touch, but so layered that it masked the light of the sun, enveloping them in a world of permanent half-light. Their existence alternated between the darkness of the night and the lustreless glow of day. Morning, noon and evening were impossible to tell apart, each suffused with an indistinguishable twilight-like glow.

And as if the clouds weren't enough, a wild and luxuriant forest added to the gloom. Trees clustered as thick as hair follicles on the plateau of Koleshwar. They were uniformly short, extending sideways instead of upwards. Their branches were crooked and squiggly, lacing together in a labyrinthine mesh, shadowing the meagre light the mist let through.

Not every inch of Koleshwar was overlaid by forest. There were sections of the plateau where the trees gave way to meadows and vast fields of rock. In these open spaces, clouds swirled in thick grey curtains and herds of deer and gaur grazed silently. The animals were numerous, moving in large herds. Often, packs of jackals attacked the deer, taking away the young or bringing down the old. On occasion, tawny wolves hunted in packs, and twice they spotted a tiger.

Carnivores were a constant source of worry for Irfan and Rustom, and they retreated to their cave if they sensed even a whiff of their presence. The fire they tended there was a crucial defence against possible attacks. A leopard once halted outside their cave but did not enter. Its gaze had lingered on them and the fire and after a while, it had moved on. Bears also came to investigate the cave, but they growled and backed away when they sensed the smoke and spied the leaping flames.

The cave was a source of security for Irfan and Rustom. It was their shelter and their home. But it wasn't just the fire they relied upon. An additional safeguard protected the cave, so they believed. A holy man—a sadhu—had lived in the cave. Withdrawing from the world outside, he had spent his days there in prayer and meditation. Without a fire for protection, he had passed several months unharmed in the cave. It was said that his prayers had exalted and sanctified it. Irfan and Rustom wholeheartedly believed so.

It was to the sadhu that they owed their lives. After Mohammed Aziz's death, they had rounded up the mules and herded them to the valley at the foot of Koleshwar. There, in the midst of a thick forest, they had unburdened the animals and set them free. Working fast, they had hidden Wallace's treasure. Nervous that they would be discovered, they had hastened up Koleshwar's slopes in thick mists and pouring rain. The rain had fallen relentlessly for several days, and the sadhu had found them lost on the plateau, sick and cold and starving, and on the verge of death. The sadhu had carried them bodily to the cave and, with the help of a young village boy, had nursed them back to health.

The sadhu wore only a loincloth and, in the evening when it grew cool, he wrapped a shawl across his upper body. Although his bleached hair indicated an advanced

33

age, the texture of his face was like that of a newborn, with not a wrinkle or line marring its smoothness. A snow-white beard hung from his chin and his brows were thick and furry. His eyes were round and dark and when Irfan stared at them, he felt he was gazing into a restful sea.

The sadhu never spoke. They learnt from the village boy that the holy man had taken a vow of silence years before. The village boy's name was Dagdu. He was a quiet, sober-faced youngster, about their age. His skin was dark, the same shade as Irfan's, and though he was small, he was exceptionally strong. He lived in a village at the foot of Koleshwar. He tended cattle on the lower slopes of the mountain, herding them out to graze during the day and returning at nightfall. His parents considered it their religious duty to feed the sadhu, and so, he trudged up the mountain early each morning with fresh food cooked by his mother.

On learning of the boys' plight, Dagdu's mother generously increased the quantity of food she sent up. Dagdu also spent more time on the plateau. Directed by the holy man, Dagdu collected leaves and herbs that the sadhu crushed and stirred into their food. He also brought fresh water for them, gathered wild fruit and cut firewood.

Irfan and Rustom recovered quickly under their care. Shortly afterwards, to their consternation, the sadhu moved to another cave deeper in the forest. Dagdu explained that the sadhu needed to be by himself. Allaying their guilt, he made clear to them that the holy man's move was influenced only in part by their presence. The sadhu frequently changed his place of meditation, he said, migrating across the plateau with the seasons. Their arrival had only speeded his move. Sensing their nervousness, Dagdu calmed the boys, assuring them that they would be safe in the cave. No animal would trouble them, he said. The sadhu had blessed the cave for them.

Dagdu told them that Koleshwar was an immense plateau located at the divide between the Konkan and the mountains. It was so vast that even a strong man would take an entire day to cross it from end to end. At the plateau's eastern boundary stood a fort called Kamalgad. The western edge of the plateau—where they were camped— was a forested wilderness where no one cared to live, except the sadhu. Although there were villages scattered around the base of the mountain, on account of the forests, people rarely ventured up. Hunting parties sometimes visited, but hardly ever during the rains.

Though Dagdu readily volunteered information, he never sought any. Matters regarding the boys—elemental facts, like their identity, or where they came from—were no concern of his. Dagdu's simplicity and guilelessness suited the boys. When they asked him not to speak of their presence on Koleshwar to anyone, he readily agreed. He even assured them his parents would remain silent.

Dagdu's concept of hardship was very different from that of the boys. He thought nothing of climbing and descending the mountain each day. Forest, rain and landslides were simply obstacles to contend with. As far as Dagdu was concerned, dwelling in a forest was a natural activity, no different from tending cattle or planting rice

35

before the monsoon. He couldn't imagine the daily stress it induced in the city-bred boys.

It was the nights that were especially difficult for Irfan and Rustom. They dreaded the time when the misted gloom of day faded to the impenetrable fastness of night. Crickets heralded the dark hours, shrieking their falsetto as all traces of light withdrew. Frogs lent their babble to the cricket chorus, their crooning and croaking overpowering the performance of the insects. The slimy creatures bounded everywhere, thronging in puddles and streams. Several entered the cave, inquisitively exploring the area. The frogs did not bother the boys, but the snakes that sometimes followed them did. A bewildering variety of snakes—green, black, brown, striped and hooded—crept in from the darkness, pursuing frogs and swallowing them whole. Rustom was unafraid of the scaly creatures and tried hard to convince Irfan that the reptiles meant them no harm. Although there was truth in Rustom's observation, nothing could suppress Irfan's fears. He huddled in terror beside the fire till Rustom turned them out of the cave, intimidating them with sticks, in the manner Dagdu had taught him.

It wasn't just snakes and frogs that the boys had to deal with. During the dark hours, a flood of other creatures swarmed disconcertingly into the cave. There were long centipedes that bristled with a legion of flailing legs; there were snake-like worms as thick as a thumb; there were lizards and scorpions and beetles, and an army of revolting creatures that could bite, sting or induce a horrible rash.

Yet, if measured in units of terror, the rush of creepy crawlies was a mere pinprick of alarm when compared with the horror of the bloodthirsty carnivores that prowled the dark. Every night they would wake shivering from their sleep when screams erupted from trees. Often the undergrowth would quiver as large creatures treaded outside. Eyes would spark in the light of their fire, driving a chill into their hearts. Often, in spooky silence, the eyes stared steadfastly, holding still, like stars. Sometimes the eyes would multiply, perforating the darkness with scattered orbs of menacing incandescence. At times they caught glimpses of spotted tails and low-slung bodies. Once, a striped creature, surely a tiger, settled itself just beyond the light of the fire, gazing unnervingly at them for hours. Yet, in spite of the undesirable attention their cave drew, not once did a predator pass its threshold. Something deterred them—either the fire or the holy man's spell. Rustom and Irfan were convinced that it was the sadhu's blessings.

It wasn't that the nights were always filled with fear and doom. There were moments of wonder and joy too. Fireflies transformed the bleakest hours of darkness, stringing together a show that never failed to uplift their bruised spirits. The little creatures were everywhere in the night, tempering the darkness with pulses of radiance. But they reserved their magic for the late hours, when the mist and silence smothered the night. Always, the show started with a scintillating burst of light. An entire tree would glow with a thousand synchronized pulses of light. A millisecond later the neighbouring tree would erupt in brilliance, but only for an instant. Immediately the next would flash and then the next. The trees would each prickle, as if suddenly spattered with stars. The inflorescence would leap from tree to tree, in the manner of a spike of brilliant light speeding through the forest. The firefly diversion was a heavenly balm. Like a drug it calmed their fears, easing them into a troubled slumber.

Time hung heavily on the boys' shoulders. Except for one unfinished chore, there was no work to occupy them. Wallace's chests still lay where they had left them, in the forested valley between Koleshwar and Mahabaleshwar. Although well hidden, the boys weren't comfortable leaving them there. The wilderness of Koleshwar was a far better place as it was virtually free of human intrusion. But the chests were as heavy as stone. Hauling them uphill even one at a time would be a backbreaking effort. In the slush and pouring rain, the task was near impossible. So they deferred it, waiting for conditions to turn favourable.

With not much to do but stare out of the cave, they soon became familiar with the creatures they shared the forest with. An event that entranced them was the crafting of entire colonies of exquisitely designed nests by birds with bright yellow heads. In a matter of days, a hundred sock-shaped nests dangled before them with the yellow-headed birds and their mates flitting in and out of them.

Irfan and Rustom quickly developed favourites amongst the creatures of the forest. One of these was an animal they never tired of looking at—the giant squirrel, a furry creature the size of a large hare. The golden-brown animals wandered the canopy, constructing sprawling nests and chattering shrill calls. When it came to birds, without doubt, the most impressive winged creature was a big black-and-white avian, larger than even the brown monkeys that inhabited the forests. It wasn't a particularly graceful bird, especially in the trees, where it hopped clumsily from branch to branch. And it had a ridiculous dagger-like beak, which was disproportionately large measured against the rest of it. But it was in flight that the bird was at its awe-inspiring best; when it soared wraith-like in the mists, imperiously trumpeting its call—a guttural roar that boomed and echoed across valley and forest.

On the ground, they saw shy, mouse-like deer, only a wee bit larger than porcupines. There were ghorpads, fearsome lizards with webbed feet that raided nests, swallowing eggs and hatchlings. There were black langurs, brown macaques, mongooses, fox, wild pigs, rats and an intriguing variety of wild cats.

It was during their forest existence—as they grew familiar with their wild environs—that the dream started to break up in earnest. Visions of the white room and the ceiling fan appeared again. A face materialized—the same that had flashed earlier. It belonged to a middle-aged woman. Her skin was fair, she wore spectacles and she was asleep in a chair. He tried often to take her name, but each time her image faded and he strayed back to the cave and forests. The dream switched wildly between the placid comfort of the room and the wind and cold of the mountain. Sequences began to rupture. Continuity and narrative were lost as the dream shed its momentum, beaming disconnected scenes like a disjointed film.

Seasons changed, projecting pictures of incredible beauty. Mists waned and the rains receded. A watery sun steamed the drowned landscape, breathing fresh life. Birds welcomed the burst of warm effulgence, flitting and singing with frenetic enthusiasm. Flowers bloomed, daubing entire hillsides with flamboyant colours. There was an invasion of butterflies. Tens of thousands of the delicate creatures fluttered like buttercups in the grasses. The skies conjured countless rainbows. Every hour fetched a fresh rainbow. They soared across the skies, sometimes singly, sometimes in pairs and sometimes they arched one within the other. Once, at night, after a burst of rain, the skies cleared and a rising moon projected an arc of light across the sky, exactly as a rainbow. White as the stars and delicate as gossamer, it was a moonbow, an imitation rainbow, a shimmering refraction of the light of the moon.

Troubled far less by the elements, Rustom and Irfan ventured far. They recovered Wallace's chests, hauling each one painfully to the plateau and burying them near a small banyan tree rooted a short distance from the jungle track that led to the valley. Rejoicing the exit of the rains they explored every inch of the plateau. They traversed its wide boundaries, peering down into valleys and admiring the formidable range of mountains unveiled finally by the clouds.

Sometimes Dagdu accompanied them, furnishing names for the plateaus and valleys and craggy summits. The long and narrow plateau topping a steeply-sloped mountain to the north was Raireshwar. It was on Raireshwar he said that the great king Shivaji had taken his oath of swarajya. He named two distant peaks Torna and Rajgad. They were forts, he said.

The dream reverted once more to the room. The same lady appeared. She was standing now and beside her were two men, both clad in white, the hue of their coats matching the colour of the room. The lady was mouthing a word that pierced the tissues of his brain.

'Anirudh!'

The word had a familiar ring to it. Confusion seized him. His head swam.

He was with Dagdu and Rustom again. Kinjalghad was the nearest fort, just across the valley to the east, said Dagdu, pointing out a tall mountain with an amazingly flat crown. There were other forts, Pandavghad, Pratapghad . . . all of them had once belonged to the greatest king of all time, the mighty Shivaji.

'Anirudh!' impinged the voice again.

He saw faces, a flash of white, but the dream dragged him back again. There was a curious shimmer to the dream now. Its imagery sparkled with fizzing pinpricks of light, like shooting stars.

Rustom and Irfan were at the edge of the plateau once more. It was evening and it was late. They should have turned back for their cave, but the sheer spectacle of the mountains and sky had stalled them. The sky was an incandescent red to the west, but elsewhere it was a pale blue, screened here and there by a patchwork of stringy, racing clouds. Across from them, a minute's traverse for an eagle, was the sprawling plateau of Mahabaleshwar, its cliffs and forests rising island-like above an ocean of whirling cloud. A long channel yawned between Koleshwar and Mahabaleshwar. It was the deep mountain hollow that

41

spawned the River Krishna, the valley where they had first hidden Wallace's treasure.

Clouds swamped the Krishna Valley, inundating every inch of it. Like a sea they washed against the cliffs of Koleshwar and Mahabaleshwar, spilling here and there over outcroppings of black stone. If it were possible to walk on cloud, Irfan could have crossed on the surging vapour to Mahabaleshwar, his hometown, the place of his birth.

A tempest-like wind was howling in the valley, riotously attacking the cloud, lifting it, whisking it and speeding it in satin waves across the dark, brooding cliffs of the plateau. The wind deafened the boys' ears. Bitingly cold, like the ice they had once enjoyed in Bombay, it cut through their clothing, yet they lingered, enjoying the evening.

It was Rustom who first noticed the leopard. The animal squatted in eerie silence at the edge of the forest, barely a hundred yards away. The animal sat so still that Rustom would not have spotted it if it weren't for the sunlight that flashed on its speckled hide. The leopard's gaze was fixed on them.

The boys were armed with spears, yet they rose nervously. They swept their gaze about them, seeking a safe sanctuary. To one side rose a small hillock of rock. Everywhere else there was tall grass and stones. They were stranded between the forest and cliffs.

A rain-fed stream flowed to one side, not far from where they sat. Brandishing their spears, they backed towards it. The raging wind was performing tricks on the stream, arresting its flow as it swept off the cliff edge, suspending it in mid-air. It then bodily lifted its water, twirling it back in a massive arc and spraying it back on the mountain.

But the cycle of wind and water was lost on Rustom and Irfan. As they stood uncertainly, blinking back the fine mist of wind-propelled water, the leopard stirred and rose. It advanced several paces and halted, watching them.

The white light appeared again. The voice impinged on his consciousness once more.

'Anirudh!'

But he brushed away the voice, willing the dream forward.

The wind had ceased howling. It had dropped to a breeze. They had scaled the hillock of rock and crossed to its far side. The leopard had followed and was descending the rock. As Irfan helplessly watched the leopard, Rustom crept on hands and knees to the cliff edge. He shouted excitedly and Irfan, eyes on the leopard, crawled to his side.

The cliff fell away dizzyingly. A sweep of cloud screened the valley below. Rustom pointed at a narrow ledge that led downwards. Irfan gazed at Rustom with an expression querying whether he was mad. But Rustom pointed once more, this time at the leopard. The animal was advancing on them, its intent clear.

Irfan clutched his spear, his heart throbbing wildly. The animal was barely hip-high, but its neck was thick and its shoulders were strongly muscled. With their spears, the two of them together could hold off the animal, but in his heart, he wasn't sure.

Rustom decisively settled the issue, choosing retreat over resistance. Turning his back on the cloud-swamped valley, he lowered himself to the ledge, shouting at Irfan to follow. Irfan hesitated, but the leopard started forward, quashing his indecision. His legs shook as he clutched wet rock and lowered himself over the edge. Rustom waited several feet below where the sheer wall of the mountain turned a corner. The cliff was wet and slimy. Tufts of grass pockmarked its black surface. Irfan clutched them as he descended. The ledge grew broader. The rock face was soaked and the air was heavy and wet. At the corner Irfan turned, looking back. The leopard stood at the edge of the cliff, staring down at them.

Rustom had disappeared round the cliff bend. The wind tore at Irfan when he negotiated the bend. He blinked, struggling to keep his eyes open as a blinding mist of water was driven into his face. Rustom was crouched beside a crack in the cliff surface. Rustom pointed at the hole and stepped inside. Irfan followed, reasoning any place was safer than the knife-edged face of the cliff.

'Anirudh!' surfaced the voice again.

Anirudh blinked the voice away, struggling to stay with Rustom and Irfan.

Though daylight penetrated the cave's entrance it was pitch dark inside.

Rustom was calling.

Two names—Irfan and Anirudh—united in his consciousness. The fizzing pinpricks of light, very much a part of the dream now, glowed brightly in the darkness of the cave.

The cave wall was wet. There was mud on its uneven floor. Rustom called once more. Irfan couldn't see him, but his voice indicated he was nearby. Irfan halted suddenly. His foot had slid on something on the ground. His heart stood still as something slithered against him.

'RUSTOM . . . saap . . .'

The two names came together again.

'IRFAN!' shrieked Rustom.

'Anirudh . . .' called another voice, much gentler.

The blackness spun. He felt himself falling. There was a flash of excruciating pain.

The voices came together once more: IRFAN—ANIRUDH.

The starlike pinpricks began to expand. Darkness slipped away, taking with it the cave, the terror, the pain . . . and Rustom too. The luminous specks continued to grow, swelling rapidly till they coalesced in a glittering wall of white radiance.

A fan rotated gently above him and a face, the same he had seen before, was staring at him, eyes filled with tears and tenderness.

'Aai!'* cried Anirudh.

---

* 'Mother' in Marathi.

BOOK III
MUMBAI

MUMBAI

If one were to judge a city's popularity by the increase in its inhabitants, Mumbai's skyrocketing population would surely propel it to the ranks of the most successful in the world. Where just a few centuries earlier, thousand was an appropriate unit to keep track of its residents, now only tallies in millions make sense. Figures ranging from 15 to 20 million are bandied about, and though no one has a true measure, it is fashionable today to declare that Mumbai's numbers exceed the population of the entire continent of Australia—a comparison that boggles the mind.

It isn't easy to imagine that a tongue of narrow coastal real estate, tiny enough for a jet aircraft to cruise over in a minute, is home to more people than a continental landmass many times the size of India. Yet, astonishing though the estimate is, many thousands continue to swell Mumbai's ranks, pouring in each day, reinforcing a facet of the city, its lure of wealth and a better life, that has endured unaltered since the time of the British.

Neither the revolution that restored it to its native rulers, nor the obliterating change in its geography, nor its suffocating lack of space, has diminished Mumbai's appeal. The city still beams its ray of hope, luring hordes of newcomers with the promise of a brighter future. The city of gold, some have called it; the city of dreams, say others. So complete is its spell on its inhabitants that those born in its embrace rarely leave, and those that emigrate into its ever-expanding borders are invariably hooked for life.

For outsiders, entry to the metropolis arouses strong emotions. There is an assault on all the senses. The air reeks with a unique organic smell: a combination of the sea, the earth and the stench of human habitation. Noise overwhelms the ears, particularly the bedlam of traffic and the clamour of densely packed humanity. The eyes are seized by a baffling variety of human tenements. Buildings, shanties, skyscrapers, offices and factories jostle each other along narrow roads, grudgingly yielding space to mosques, temples and the occasional Parsee agyari. The sheer scale of the city numbs the mind. It generates powerful passions. People either love it or despise it. There are no in-betweens.

Vikram's father, Mr Govind Singh, belonged to the camp that disliked the city. But that had not always been the case. When he was younger, Govind Singh had dearly loved Mumbai. The city had been far smaller then and he had shared a personal relationship with it, an easy familiarity and deep intimacy. But since that honeymoon period, the city's population had exploded and his sentiments had undergone a dramatic change.

His bitterest complaint was against the city's leaders, the men and women trusted with its development and upkeep. A war had been waged against the city's open spaces, he said, commanded ruthlessly by politicians and hand-in-glove city fathers. Where there had once been parks and gardens, now slums and skyscrapers flourished, multiplying unchecked, like weeds in an unkempt garden. The result was a city with critically depleted lungs, smothered by an unrelieved monotony of grey, its citizens condemned to a congested, polluted existence.

There was another diametrically opposite opinion of the city that Vikram was familiar with. That of his uncle, Mr Satish Nair, a long time resident of Mumbai who belonged firmly to the club that loved the city. 'Not true,' he would counter. 'Congested yes, and in the extreme. But several green areas remain, despite the best efforts of politicians and greedy businessmen. And I don't entirely agree with the observation on pollution either. Being an island city helps. Strong sea winds cleanse the city's atmosphere daily. It's not so bad actually.'

Satish was steadfast in his support for Mumbai. 'People complain,' he often said, 'but they continue to live here and enjoy their lives. I wouldn't live anywhere else, even if I were paid to. Yes, there are problems. The traffic is terrible and life can be hard if one has to commute long distances, but isn't that the same in all Indian cities?' He would conclude always with an expansive wave of arm. 'Bombay . . . Mumbai, call it what you want, it doesn't matter. What does matter is that it is a great city. Don't you ever forget that.'

For Vikram, opinions on the city were irrelevant as Bombay held a special place in his heart. It was the city where his mother had spent her childhood. It was in Bombay that his mother and father had met and fallen in love. It was the city of his birth. It was also the place where his mother had died.

Bombay was firmly on Vikram's itinerary this holiday. His visit had been scheduled at the end of his holiday, when his father, who now lived in Delhi, was due to fly down for a family reunion with his uncle and aunt.

But a call from Anirudh brought his plans forward.

'I need you to come down,' Anirudh had said.

'Aren't you coming back to Poona?' Vikram had queried. 'Your dad is expecting you.'

'It's Mom who is returning tomorrow,' Anirudh had replied. 'There's a meeting at her college that she has to attend. She wants me to return with her, but I don't want to.' Anirudh's frustration had carried over the phone, a sign that his illness hadn't smoothed his stormy relationship with his parents. 'Mom's giving me a hard time, refusing to let me stay back. She's insisting that I must have someone to accompany me back home. If you come down, I can stay here a couple of days more and then we can return together.'

Vikram had hedged. 'Is it important?' he asked. 'There's a lot happening here.'

By 'a lot' Vikram was referring to skydiving. Conditions had turned favourable with the monsoons easing over Pune. More importantly, an aircraft was available. Ishwar's business partner was flying in with their plane during the week. So, understandably, Vikram had been reluctant to leave Pune.

But Anirudh had persisted. 'I need you to come,' he had repeated. 'There's something I want to talk to you about. Something personal that I can't speak about in front of the others.'

The plea in Anirudh's voice, coupled with a fair amount of guilt, had clinched Vikram's decision. The guilt stemmed from the fact that Vikram hadn't met Anirudh since he had regained consciousness. Except for his parents, no one had as he was in a naval hospital in Bombay. His father had since returned to Pune and Anirudh had been scheduled to return with his mother. Then Anirudh had changed his mind and Vikram found himself on a train to Bombay.

The journey was an enjoyable one through pleasant countryside and fields heavy with rice. The colour green dominated the landscape: from the mountains to the valleys, and in the fields, where it deepened to a brilliant emerald shade. The ghat section—where the train dropped from the Deccan Plateau to the flat expanses of the Konkan— was spectacular, with deep valleys, gorges, waterfalls and an endless series of tunnels. On the Konkan, there were villages and more fields. As the journey progressed to the coast the villages grew larger and grimier. After a while, the fields disappeared altogether and a solid line of tenements, most of them squalid, lined the tracks. Racing through an ocean of humanity, the train finally pulled up at its destination.

The chaos and bedlam of Bombay pummelled Vikram like a monsoon gale when he stepped out of the spacious

53

interiors of the station. As a portal to one of India's largest cities, the square outside the station was hopelessly under-designed for the passenger traffic that flooded like a torrent through it. The driveway was choked with cars, locked bumper-to-bumper. A storm of noise equivalent to the roar of a battlefield assaulted Vikram's ears. Cars honked, drivers yelled, coolies swore, and traffic policemen ineffectually waved their arms and tooted their whistles.

Vikram breathed deeply, taking in the warm humid air. This was Bombay as he knew it: bustling, crowded, chaotic. Yet, refreshingly, unlike other cities of its size, it was sociable, amiable and friendly too. The undercurrent of threat he associated with large cities was for the most part absent here. Bombay certainly wasn't a city he loved, but it was one he felt comfortable in. Maybe his fondness was because of his mother, for if he were to equate any place with home then Bombay came closest.

Experience and familiarity had long since taught him that the city's mess and commotion were usually no more than skin-deep. There was a method to its madness. Weaving past the stationary vehicles, he crossed to a queue of people standing patiently beside a sea of yellow and black taxies. Sure enough, after a short wait, he was directed by a sweating policeman to a rusted vehicle badly in need of a paint job, and sped out of the chaos of the station by a pleasant-faced young man who drove with the skill and aggression of a rally driver.

Anirudh had said he was at a building at Colaba, on the third floor, in a flat that belonged to his grandmother. Vikram had no difficulty finding the place: a quiet building society, tucked away from the main road and bordering the sea to one side. Deciding to exercise his limbs, he climbed the stairs to the flat.

Anirudh's mother, Smita Dongre, greeted Vikram with a smile and a warm hug. Ushering him inside she introduced him to an old lady with long white hair having breakfast at the dining table.

'My mother,' she said.

The old lady was dressed in a bathrobe. Her eyes were lidded, half-closed. She smiled briefly and returned to her meal.

'Mother is a creature of the night,' explained Smita. 'Reads till the early hours of morning and rises late. She's been like that since I was young. Unfortunately, Anirudh has inherited this habit of hers. He's still having his bath. Come to the balcony, we'll wait there.'

A surprisingly pleasant view greeted Vikram when he stepped on to the balcony. Several trees had been planted in the building compound and their leafy crowns were level with where they stood. Through gaps between their branches, the expanses of Bombay's famed harbour were visible. Reflecting the sky, the harbour waters were dull and grey, and there were ships anchored in the distance. A collection of faded rugs was spread on the balcony's earthy brown tiles and in the centre was a cane sofa-set. Smita settled Vikram on the sofa and a young lady dressed in a bright salwar kameez placed lemon juice and biscuits on the table.

'Please,' said Smita, indicating the refreshments. Her hands came together as Vikram helped himself. She wrung them unconsciously and Vikram recollected that the gesture was a sign she was worried.

'Anirudh is fine now,' she said, flashing a smile that failed to reach her eyes. 'Thirteen days it took him to recover—' she gulped, lowering her head, 'thirteen terrible days.'

'Fooled everybody, didn't he?' said Vikram, sipping sugary lemon juice. 'The doctors too. They were all confident he would recover soon, weren't they?'

'Yes, he confounded everyone,' acknowledged Smita Dongre. She shuddered. 'It was horrible. As the days slipped by, I started to resign myself to the fact that I had lost my boy. Then . . . just like that, as if waking from a deep sleep, he pulled out. The doctors were as surprised as we were.' She laughed a mirthless laugh. 'Then they thought he would take a long time to recover, but he astonished them again by bouncing back in little more than a day, showing no ill effects of his trauma at all. He's as good as new . . . as if nothing ever happened to him. I can tell you that the doctors are a puzzled lot.'

'Never mind the doctors,' said Vikram. 'It's a relief to know he's fine.'

Smita managed a smile. 'Yes, my son is fine . . . and that's all that matters.' She wrung her hands again. To Vikram, it seemed that her actions and her words were contradictory. Something didn't feel right; something was troubling Anirudh's mother.

She continued in a halting voice: 'There are things that the doctors don't know . . .' Vikram stared keenly and Smita dropped her gaze. 'No one knows except me.

Even Anirudh's father has no idea.' She looked up again and Vikram saw that her eyes were shining. 'My Anirudh has never had many friends. It has been a problem for him since he was a child. Aditya and he have known each other since they were toddlers, yet they have never struck a real friendship. It's Anirudh's fault. He doesn't trust people easily. Even with us, his parents, he maintains a distance. You, Vikram, are one of the few people he trusts.'

Smita paused. Then balling her hands into fists, she continued: 'Anirudh called you here because he wants to share with you what happened during his coma. It's something very personal. My Anirudh has undergone a strange experience. He had a dream. I don't know if it's right to call his experience a dream, because what he underwent is realistic and lasted thirteen days—much longer than any dream can last. What he has described for me has left me deeply disturbed. I'd be lying if I don't admit that I'm horribly nervous and confused. His story is so strange that people would say he was hallucinating. That's why he hasn't told anyone, not even his father. You will be the second person he will talk to, and if he doesn't open up to his father, you might also be the last. He will expect you to keep what he tells you a secret. You will understand why when you hear what he has to say. If people get to know about it, they will say he has gone mad and I wouldn't blame them because, to the rational mind, his dream would seem ridiculous, implausible . . . a fantasy. But I believe him. Maybe not the entire dream, a substantial portion could be the fabrication of a traumatized brain. There are threads, however, that are frighteningly real.'

Vikram stared at Smita. Not a word of what she said made any sense to him.

A tired smile creased Smita's cheeks. 'I can see that you don't know what I'm talking about. You will have to wait till Anirudh comes. You have the whole day free, I hope?'

'Two entire days,' replied Vikram. 'Both today and tomorrow. Except for the evenings, that is. I'm spending the nights at Malabar Hill, at my uncle's flat.'

'Do you have to?' asked Smita Dongre. 'You said they're out of town. Why don't you stay here with Anirudh?'

Vikram smiled and shook his head. 'It's already been arranged. The caretaker is expecting me.'

'If you change your mind, you are welcome to stay. I want you to be with him.'

A loud voice intruded, startling both of them.

'There you go, Mom! Babysitters for me—that's all you think of. You might not have noticed, but I've grown up, you know. Hey, Vikram! Great to see you again.'

Vikram looked up.

Anirudh was striding towards him, a welcoming grin on his face. Though Vikram tried not to, he couldn't hold back a flicker of surprise. In spite of his mother's bulletin of a hale and hearty son, he had expected a paler and weaker version of the Anirudh he was familiar with. But the grinning boy striding towards him—though noticeably slimmer—was red-cheeked, clear-eyed and healthy.

The friends hugged. Anirudh clasped Vikram hard, not letting go.

'I'm going to leave you boys,' said Smita, when Anirudh finally released Vikram. 'I stayed behind only for you,

Vikram. The car is ready downstairs. I'll send it back the day after to bring both of you home.'

'There's no need,' said Vikram. 'There are trains and buses.'

Anirudh made a face. 'Mom doesn't believe I'm well enough yet.'

'The car will come,' insisted Smita. 'It will be here by morning. I expect the two of you to reach NDA by lunchtime.'

She bid goodbye to her mother, hugged each of the boys, and after extracting a promise from Vikram to look after Anirudh, she departed.

Returning to the balcony, the boys leaned against its balustrade. The awkwardness between friends who meet after a long time lasted a few minutes during which they exchanged small talk and banter. Vikram inquired about Anirudh's health and he replied he was fine. The bump where he had fallen on his head had reduced, and he wasn't wearing a bandage any more. There was no dizziness, no pain, nothing. He was perfectly healthy.

Vikram updated Anirudh on their friends. 'The NDA term has started and Kiran is back to the grind. We hardly get to see him now. Chitra is disappointed with Aditya and me. She was hoping we would spend time at the Snake Park with her, but that hasn't happened.' Vikram grinned. 'She's particularly upset with Aditya because he has always said he wants to learn how to handle snakes. But you know how it is. The wind has been blowing up a storm on the lake and we've been sailing and windsurfing. And when not on the lake we've been riding and playing squash and tennis. It isn't easy to leave a place like NDA and travel into the city.'

'Dad says the weather's clearing and the wind has dropped. Those aren't exactly the conditions Aditya likes.'

Vikram grinned. 'That's what's angering Chitra even more. You're right. With the wind gone the 'sailing' excuse doesn't hold. But she doesn't understand that the change in the weather has opened up skydiving for us. And we even have a plane available now. Uncle Ishwar has promised us jumps. If you are up to it, you can join us too.'

Anirudh shook his head. 'I've had more than my fill of excitement these past few days. In any case, Mom wouldn't let me even if I wanted to.' He changed the subject. 'What news on Salim? Mom told me that he and Chitra are pushing off somewhere.'

Vikram frowned. 'Haven't you spoken to Salim? He's your buddy, isn't he?' Then his brow cleared. 'Oh yes! You said he doesn't come to the phone when you call.'

Anirudh scowled. 'He's such a nerd! The man is wallowing in guilt. Mom says he's blaming himself for what happened to me.'

'There's truth in what your mom says, isn't there? I mean it was he who was being chased. You were the innocent one and it was you who ended up suffering. You might not know, but Salim didn't eat for two days after your fall. Your dad forced him finally, standing over him with a stick.'

Anirudh sighed. 'I can understand his guilt. But I'm fine now, and yet he won't take my calls. Mom makes excuses for him, but it's clear that he's avoiding me.'

'His guilt trip is obvious. He leaves the room every time there's a call from Bombay.' Vikram laughed. 'If you think of it, it's possible that this outing with Chitra is another excuse to put off meeting you.'

'Of course it is!' exclaimed Anirudh. 'It's childish, I tell you. He can't avoid me forever. Where are he and Chitra off to in any case?'

Vikram grinned. 'What do you think? Come on, use your head. Snakes, of course! You should have guessed that one. It all began on Chitra's last visit to NDA, when she showed Salim pictures of a snake. Some kind of snake called a shieldtail. Apparently, it lives underground most of the time, surfacing only during the monsoons. After examining the photos, Salim said he had seen plenty of them on the Koleshwar plateau, and Chitra, as you would expect, was so thrilled that she almost had a fit. She begged your dad to grant Salim leave so he could go with her. You know Chitra, when she's fired up about something, nothing can stop her. But your dad refused. He's a tough one. Can't blame him actually, because if Salim had left then, there would have been no one to run the house, as your mom was here with you in Bombay. So Chitra called your mom, and it was she who finally gave the okay. Since your mom's returning today, she assured your dad that she will take charge of the house. Chitra and Salim leave first thing tomorrow.'

'Salim is thrilled, I'm sure,' said Anirudh. He stared sourly at the sea before turning to Vikram. 'What's been happening about those men who chased us? I asked Mom, but she kept changing the subject. Was there an investigation? Has Salim finally spoken to the police?'

'There was an investigation,' confirmed Vikram. 'Your dad ensured that. Your father is an excitable man, and that's putting it mildly. He would have drawn blood then and there if those men chasing us had been around. He wanted revenge. He whisked Salim to the police station—not the Poona police station, but the station at the town of Wai, near Salim's village.

'Salim wasn't very communicative with the police—no surprises on that one. He wasn't kidding that night when he told us he is afraid of cops. He refused to utter a single word in front of them. He was terrified of your father too, which I don't blame him for, as by then your father had lost patience and was mad enough to kill someone.'

'Poor Salim,' commiserated Anirudh. 'Dad's temper is awful. I should know. I've been at the receiving end often enough.'

'Your mom stepped in though,' continued Vikram, 'which was a good thing. She took Salim home to NDA and talked calmly with him, and it was to her that he finally opened up.' Vikram paused, wrinkling his brow. 'But hold on. You know all this. Salim said you knew his story.'

'Salim did speak to me,' affirmed Anirudh.

'That car journey . . . You two sat by yourselves most of the drive. He must have told you everything, and a lot more, I'm sure.'

'Yes,' replied Anirudh. 'But I still want to hear what he had to say.'

Vikram shrugged. 'Fine,' he said. He leaned back on the sofa pillows. 'You know, of course, that it was Salim those men were chasing, not us. We just happened to get caught in the crossfire, both at Torna and Koleshwar. That was the obvious part. The question was, "why"? Why would anyone want to chase Salim, especially with that kind of murderous intent? Salim's story, the explanation he gave us, was the kind of stuff out of a movie script . . . something straight out of your wildest dreams.

'The Koleshwar plateau, where you knocked yourself on the head and passed out, has always been a part of Salim's life. He told us that since childhood he has taken his cattle up there to feed. He has hunted small game on the plateau and has collected firewood from its forests. Although he never lived there, his brother did. He told you that, didn't he?'

Anirudh nodded. 'That was his youngest brother. He quarrelled with their father, who then threw him out of the family home. So the brother—angry and bitter—built himself a house far from everyone else, high on Koleshwar, with only the forests and wildlife for company. That was where you found Salim and me when we sped ahead of you and the others.'

'Yup,' nodded Vikram. 'You and Salim were waiting there, I remember, looking very solemn . . . paying your respects to his departed brother. It was the place where you said you felt deeply moved, as if you knew the brother who had lived there.'

'There were many strange sensations going on inside me that day,' said Anirudh. 'That was one of them.'

Vikram nodded sympathetically. 'Salim visited Koleshwar regularly, especially in the dry season when the plateau was the only place with grass, and he would take his cattle there to graze. Last month, just before the rains began, there was a heavy pre-monsoon shower in the area and the ground turned to slush. One of his buffaloes got stuck near a cliff and he had to clear a path for it. While doing so, his sickle hit something metallic. He dug the thing out. It was a solid metal box, rusted with age, which after some hammering with his axe, he managed to open.' Vikram paused. 'He told you what he found so you don't have to hold your breath, but boy we all did. He blew us away with what he said. There was stuff inside made from gold and jewels.'

Anirudh grinned. 'He thought he was dreaming. He is desperately poor and what he had stumbled on was a fortune beyond his wildest imagination.'

Vikram nodded. 'Yes, he told us that he sat there for an hour, unable to move or think. When his excitement finally settled, he decided to hide the treasure. He couldn't risk taking it down to the village because people would rob it off him if they came to know.'

'Did he tell you where he hid it?' asked Anirudh.

'He did,' said Vikram. Then he frowned irritably. 'I don't get it. If you know the story, then why am I repeating it for you?'

Anirudh's eyes twinkled. 'Did he tell you that he divided the treasure and hid it in two different places?'

Vikram started. 'No,' he said, gazing at Anirudh. 'No! He never said anything like that.'

Anirudh chuckled. 'So you see why? He told me everything, Vikram. He didn't hold anything back from me. I want to know what kind of story he told you. How much it differed.'

'This is news to me. The man was hoodwinking us . . . and we fell for it. Wow!' Vikram whistled. 'But . . . he could be having you on too, Anirudh. It's possible that he is a lot smarter than any of us gave him credit for. He could have found two boxes or more of the treasure and told you he only found one. There's no way anyone can tell.'

Anirudh shook his head. 'What I know is the truth. Salim would never lie to me.'

Vikram stared. 'If you say so. But I'm not convinced.'

'Let's assume he won't lie to me,' said Anirudh. 'Go on. What happened next?'

'I have to modify my story now . . . adjust it to accommodate that dramatic twist of yours. So . . . instead of depositing his treasure in one place, he divided it and buried it in two caches, except for two gold coins that he slipped into his shirt pocket. Also, instead of discarding the rusted treasure box, he strapped it on the back of his buffalo.'

'Villagers are great recyclers,' said Anirudh. 'They never throw away anything that could be useful. He thought the box would serve him well as a storage dabba. Unfortunately for him, that decision proved to be his undoing.'

'Yes. In spite of its rusted state, he decided to carry it home. But as he emerged from the forest he unexpectedly came upon two strangers. Meeting anyone on Koleshwar is a rarity, and if Salim ever did, it was always villagers. But these men weren't villagers. They weren't interested in him and would have left him alone if they hadn't noticed the box strapped to the buffalo. The men halted Salim, very rudely he said, and forced him to unstrap the box and open it.

'Although there was nothing inside, the men were fascinated by the box. By then Salim had started to get an odd feeling about the men. He grew really frightened when they ordered him to empty his shirt pockets. He thought of abandoning his buffaloes and making a run for it, but before he could the men grabbed him and ripped the pockets from his shirt and the gold coins came tumbling out. The coins electrified them. One of the men, a tall one with curly hair, went berserk. He started to thrash Salim, asking him where the rest of the treasure was. Salim endured the thrashing, but then the man pulled out a knife and threatened to cut off his nose. That put an end to Salim's resistance, and he led them to where he had buried the treasure.'

'One half of the treasure,' corrected Anirudh.

'Yes, one half,' acknowledged Vikram. 'It's beginning to make sense now. You see they kept beating him even after he showed them the treasure, and that didn't sound right. Would you carry on thrashing a man who has led you to a cache of gold and jewellery and precious stones? I didn't understand then, but now, after what you told me, I can see why.'

'The men weren't stupid,' said Anirudh. 'What he dug up for them barely filled half the box. Even a dummy would have figured out that he had hidden the other half somewhere.'

'Dad has always told me to watch out for simple faces,' said Vikram. 'Simple faces don't necessarily imply simple minds, he says, and he's right. Salim's honest, guileless mug hoodwinked us all. But Salim's attackers were far smarter than us. They didn't trust him one inch and thrashed him accordingly. The tall man was merciless, Salim said. He would have killed him, he told us. It reached a point where Salim started to fear for his life. But then Salim turned lucky. While they beat him, he fell beside the treasure they had forced him to excavate.'

'And once again he showed why he isn't exactly dumb,' said Anirudh.

'Yes, what he did next showed presence of mind,' acknowledged Vikram. 'He grabbed at whatever of the treasure he could and flung it far into the forest. It was only a few ornaments and coins, but as it was all gold and precious stones—every coin and necklace was of immense value. The prospect of losing even a single item of their grand find horrified the men. Abandoning Salim, they plunged after the scattered jewellery, and seizing his chance, Salim ran for his life. The men cursed and gave chase. But Salim was fleet-footed and kept ahead. At this point, to Salim's horror, he discovered that the men had guns. They fired bullets at him, but it was dark and they were running, so accuracy mustn't have been possible. They finally gave up, but they swore they would come to his home and catch him there.'

'Their rage and shouting further terrified Salim,' said Anirudh. 'They warned him they wouldn't rest till he showed them where the rest of the treasure was. Even worse, they believed that there were other boxes on the mountain. They threatened to kill him if he didn't show them where the other boxes were located.'

'That's greed for you,' marvelled Vikram. 'They already had a half-box of all that precious stuff, which fell into their laps, like a gift from heaven, and all they thought of was that they wanted more. That's serious greed. Poor Salim. Their murderous threats convinced him that they meant business. So when he reached his home in the valley he decided it wasn't safe staying there, and he caught the night bus out. His idea was to keep away from the area for a while, wait for things to settle down.'

'That's right,' said Anirudh. 'Disappearing wasn't a problem as he's a bachelor. No one was going to miss him. Once again, he chose intelligently. What better refuge could he have found than a secure armed forces set-up like NDA?'

'That was good thinking,' said Vikram. 'I'll give him that. But he miscalculated the determination of the men chasing him. They tracked him to NDA, but as it is a secure area they held back. They struck at their first opportunity, on Torna, when we were alone on the mountain. If you ask me, Salim showed poor judgement in volunteering to be our guide. Maybe Torna was okay, but taking us on a tour of his village, just after fleeing from it, wasn't exactly a sensible decision. Those men had a genuine reason to hunt him. Half a box of gold and jewellery is as powerful an incentive as any. Men would kill for far less. Returning to his village was stupid.'

'Salim was driven by other reasons,' said Anirudh.

'Like what?' asked Vikram. 'I can't think of any. Not if my life is at stake.'

'He had his reasons,' said Anirudh. He kept silent, choosing not to elaborate.

'And you don't want to tell me.' Vikram shrugged. 'That's fine by me.'

Anirudh made to protest, but Vikram shushed him.

'It doesn't bother me,' he assured. 'There were a lot of things you and Salim chatted about in the car, most of it private, I'm sure. Stuff I don't need to know. But enough of that. Let's get back to Salim's story.

'There were two men who beat up Salim on Koleshwar. One was the tall man with curly hair, the sadist, according to Salim. The other was a short man with a balding head. The short man wasn't one of the gang that attacked us. But Salim confirmed that the tall man did—both on Torna and Koleshwar. On Torna, he was the one who led his companion away after my stone bounced off the man's head. On Koleshwar he was the one who led the attack on us.'

Vikram broke off here, posing a question to Anirudh.

'Did you see a house, a really nice bungalow, at Salim's village?'

Anirudh stared, not understanding what Vikram was getting at.

Vikram explained. 'I'm not sidetracking here if that's what you think. The house is important to the investigation. It's located at the head of the valley below Koleshwar. It was once a beautiful bungalow, but now it's falling apart. We saw it when we followed you and Salim as you raced to the top of the plateau. It looked very different from the village huts. Did you see it?'

Anirudh shook his head.

'That's what I thought,' said Vikram. 'You and Salim were super-charged that day, rushing to get to the top. I'm not surprised you didn't see it. The reason I asked is because later, we found out that the men who attacked us were living in that bungalow. They were gone, of course, by the time your dad and the cops went to look, but neighbours said that men fitting our description had been staying there for a week or more. The villagers said the bungalow wasn't permanently occupied, but people, mostly from Bombay, used it on weekends or holidays. The owner rarely visits, but friends come to stay. The police then checked the land records and discovered that someone called Chaggan Patil, a gentleman from Bombay, owns the bungalow. They found his address and went knocking on Chaggan Patil's door somewhere in Bombay's suburbs.

'Patil flatly denied having anything to do with the men who attacked us. He said he had no idea who the men were and that he had been in Bombay on that day and could prove it. The police kept questioning him, asking what those men were doing in his house. They thought it strange that he did not know who used his bungalow. Patil started to get angry then. He argued, saying that how was he to know as he rarely visited. This is true, as Patil was last seen in the village more than a year ago. But the police continued to question him, at which point Patil made a phone call. To cut a long story short, Patil has political connections. He spoke to someone who then contacted the local Bombay police. Shortly afterwards, the phone rang in Patil's office. It was a senior Bombay police officer and he asked to speak to the policemen from Wai accompanying Salim. The senior officer told his junior colleagues that Patil was an honest, law-abiding citizen. He summoned his colleagues to his office the next day and spoke at length to them, telling them that Patil was above board and that they should abandon the line of investigation.'

Anirudh looked in disbelief at Vikram.

'I know what you're thinking,' said Vikram. 'But there is nothing on Patil except that he owns the place where the men had lived. He has not stayed at his bungalow in the village for a year. Not only that but the villagers also say he has visited only a handful of times in the last ten years. So the policemen returned empty-handed and the investigation lost steam.

'The main reason it cooled off was concern over your health, Anirudh. Everyone's attention shifted to transferring you to Bombay. Your mom and dad travelled with you, and no one has followed up since. Maybe the policemen have made headway, but they haven't contacted us, so we have no idea. Your dad is back in Pune now and I know he intends to make calls, but as far as I know, he hasn't yet done so.'

Anirudh was clearly disappointed. 'That's no progress at all. We're back where we started. No names, no clue to the identity of the men who attacked us . . . nothing.'

'You are being a bit harsh, aren't you? They've made a start. They have sketches. There is an alert in the region for the men and they are staying away from the area—they haven't visited since. These things take time. The police are giving it their best shot.'

Anirudh fell silent.

He leaned on the balustrade, staring out across the harbour. The sun had broken through the clouds, and the murky water glittered as if capped with a million mirrors. A naval warship was chugging out to the open sea. Cruising past it, in the opposite direction, was a cargo vessel. Long and low, like an enormous torpedo, it coasted inland to unload its containers at one of Bombay's numerous docks.

Anirudh swept a hand across the balustrades. 'Did you know that once upon a time canoes used to ply this harbour?'

'Possibly,' said Vikram. 'But that must have been ages ago. You are speaking historically, aren't you, of some bygone era?'

Anirudh went on as if he hadn't heard. 'There were so many canoes on the water that it was impossible to count them. Every day, they would bring vegetables and fruits from the mainland opposite. The canoes were useful in other ways too. They helped unload cargo vessels and also ferried passengers from ships that docked in the harbour. It was all very different back then. If you looked at the harbour you would see hundreds upon hundreds of mastheads sticking out of the water, like a stack of toothpicks. In those days it was mostly sails that powered boats. I wish you could have seen the sails. They were a colourful sight, especially when they were puffed by the wind. There was not a single vessel as drab as that cargo carrier on the water. Ships looked like ships, if you know what I mean . . . they had character.'

Though he thought the comparison unfair, Vikram remained silent. He wasn't sure what Anirudh was getting at.

'Remember how I led us to that cave on Koleshwar?' continued Anirudh. 'It was bizarre, wasn't it, knowing how to get there even though I had never been on that mountain before? Did you ever wonder how I did it?'

Vikram snorted. 'Wonder! That's the understatement of the year. Your navigation on Koleshwar was so unerring that there was no way it could have been guesswork. It was as if you had some mystical knowledge of the plateau. I asked your parents, but they said that except for Sinaghad where you drove to its summit, you have never climbed a mountain in the Sahyadris. No rational logic could explain your precise knowledge of Koleshwar's terrain. In some ways, that day on the plateau was the strangest of my life. It's not every day that someone who is a close friend has a supernatural experience; it was scary, if you ask me.'

Anirudh flashed a smile. 'Supernatural describes it exactly. The extraordinary thing is that I was as clueless as you that day, Vikram. Honestly, I had no idea how I knew where to go. There was this map sitting in my head, like one of those navigational aids in cars. The information was all just there. For you it was creepy. But to me, it didn't seem in the least odd. I didn't question the source of my knowledge. It just seemed natural.'

Anirudh laughed. 'I see I've only managed to confuse you more. Maybe I should put it another way. Let's say, I have an explanation now. Not a thorough explanation, but something that makes sense of this madness. Given the

73

bizarreness of all that has happened, the explanation came to me in an equally unreal manner . . . in the form of a dream. I'm not sure that I should term what I underwent a dream, because it wasn't the ordinary kind of dream we experience at night. It was a story that came to me. Even "story" is not right. How do I put it . . . during those thirteen days I wasn't asleep. Instead, I lived another life. An existence sparked alive inside me during my coma, and it ended abruptly in death when I woke. I have told only my mother about this dream and I'm going to tell it to you now. I trust you, Vikram. This is for your ears only. I know you won't repeat it to anyone else.'

Anirudh gestured to the cane sofas. 'Sit. Make yourself comfortable. This is going to take time.'

Vikram was possessed of a rational mind. For him, dream and reality were two separate entities whose trajectories couldn't possibly cross. Never in his wildest imagination could he have envisioned them coming together. But Anirudh's quiet storytelling, relating a perfectly plausible story, laced with sound historical fact, turned his sane, ruled-by-logic world, upside down. Vikram sat spellbound. Anirudh's descriptions were graphic. He wove verbal images of Irfan's story. Starting with the encounter with Rustom he steered Vikram through the highs and lows of Irfan's tumultuous existence.

Vikram was hooked from the start. The hours slipped by without either of them noticing. It grew warm and stuffy as morning yielded to afternoon. Later, a refreshing rain fell, but Vikram paid no attention to it. Enraptured, he sat like a child engrossed in a bedtime story. The sun broke through after the rain, steaming the balcony and the garden below. It grew stuffy once more and both the boys sweated. But Anirudh kept talking and Vikram imitated a statue to perfection. He absorbed Anirudh's words, he opened his heart and soul to them, and at the end, he shed unbidden tears at Irfan's abrupt demise.

Anirudh rose and excused himself. Vikram did not notice him leave. It was a while before he noticed anything at all. Very slowly, his mind emerged from the shroud the dream had encapsulated it in. Reality returned, registering in a fittingly practical manner with a deep gnawing in his empty stomach. With a start, he realized it was evening. Crows were crooning in the trees, settling in for the night. Lights had been switched on in the tiny garden below. Anirudh's grandmother, stick in hand, was shuffling slowly across a patchy lawn with the lady in the bright salwar kameez by her side.

'Aaji takes a walk every evening,' said Anirudh, sauntering on to the balcony with a plate of sandwiches. 'It's one of her few pleasures. The other is reading, for which she stays up late every night.'

Vikram reached gratefully for a sandwich. 'Have you told her?' he asked.

Anirudh laughed. 'No. Aaji lives in her own world. She wouldn't believe a single word. Only Mom and you know. I'm not telling anyone else. They'd think I'm crazy.'

Vikram swallowed his sandwich. 'There's no doubt your story stretches the imagination,' he said, reaching for another.

'Mom did not believe it, and I see that you aren't convinced either. I don't blame you. If someone else had undergone what I did, I'd be questioning his story. Disbelief is only natural. Here, have another sandwich.'

Anirudh waited while Vikram wolfed a few more.

They settled on the sofas again. There was a faint glow in the sky, but the harbour waters were dark. The murmur of traffic filtered in from the main road behind. The evening was cool and still.

Anirudh spoke after Vikram had exhausted the sandwiches. 'My dream had a lot to do with the old Bombay Fort. It no longer exists, but its original location isn't far from here. You've lived in Bombay so you know where the Churchgate Railway Station is, right?' Vikram nodded. 'Then you would know the Fort Area—that's what they call it now. It's only a two-minute walk from Churchgate. Mom and I went there yesterday. We didn't go just for a casual stroll. It was Mom who suggested the outing.' Anirudh paused, a smile stealing across his face. 'Mom never let on, but it was obvious she was testing me. Mom's a student of history. She knows everything there is to know about the Fort. And she also knew that I knew nothing about the Fort.' Anirudh laughed. 'My history is so terrible that I wasn't even aware of its existence before the dream. Mom had an agenda, a simple but clear-cut one. Her test was for me to locate the Fort in the midst of the mess of all the buildings and roads and traffic. The reason I say her test was clever is because if you have to come up with an instance of the complete eradication of a historical monument, then Bombay's Fort is a perfect example. Not a trace of it remains today, not even a single wall. Mom expected me to fail her test. In her heart, she wanted me to fail . . . my dream frightens her.'

'I should think so,' said Vikram. 'Your dream would frighten anyone.'

Anirudh smiled again, eyes twinkling. 'Distressingly for Mom, I passed her test. And it wasn't that I passed it ordinarily. I aced it. You should have seen Mom's expression as I traced where the Fort walls had once stood. At first, there was denial, then there was disbelief, finally, there was undisguised terror, as if I had set off a bomb. The parent in her was devastated, shattered. Yet, at the same time, another part of her, her scholarly self that constantly sought knowledge, was aroused. Her jaw dropped when I showed her where the moat had once existed. I had to support her as I identified the exact locations of the Church Gate, and the Apollo and Bazaar Gates. I walked her along the streets inside, many of which are the same as before, recalling their original names. Poor Mom. She was dazed. She couldn't decide whether to be frightened or to laugh.'

'Your mother is disturbed,' said Vikram. 'She doesn't want to believe you, but she does. Not all of your dream—only threads that she feels are true.'

'Mom's a tough nut to crack,' sighed Anirudh. 'She simply doesn't want to accept that her dear son had such an experience. She's searching . . . desperately . . . for excuses to shake off the possibility. She knows I now have outstanding knowledge of the history of Bombay. She believes that the dream in some inexplicable way helped me acquire it. But that's about it. She says the characters in my dream, except for Forjett and other historical personalities, are figments of a traumatized imagination. When I tried to convince her, she asked for proof and she was very relieved when I couldn't produce any. How could I? Everyone in my dream lived a hundred and fifty years ago. It is absurd to expect me to produce documentary evidence that they existed in flesh and blood. I found Mom's reaction upsetting. The dream was real for me, but it seems to me that everybody is going to doubt me the way she does. Are you going to be like Mom?

Vikram paused for thought before replying.

'You want the truth, don't you?' he said finally. 'No beating around the bush. The truth is that I don't know what to think. To you, the dream is as real as the sun or the moon. But as an outsider, I can't accept what you say as absolute truth. I want to believe it is true, but to convince myself, I need some sort of proof too. I'm not saying I doubt you, but at this point, all I can say is, maybe. Maybe Irfan, Rustom and the others existed. But then again, maybe—'

'—maybe they didn't,' said Anirudh, completing the observation left hanging. 'I take no offence, Vikram. I'm disappointed, but I understand your reasoning. It isn't easy for me to be objective about something so intensely personal, but when I force myself to be so, I have to admit that it seems likely that Irfan, Rustom and the others did not exist.'

Anirudh steadied his gaze on Vikram. 'This is going to surprise you. I called you here to Bombay not just to share my dream with you. That was only part of it. There's more.' Anirudh hesitated. 'How do I put it? I'm not sure, Vikram. I can't say for certain . . . but I have reason to believe I have proof that the characters in my dream are all true. I believe there is evidence that they aren't just inventions of my imagination. I'm hopeful I can prove all of them were once flesh and blood. It is for this that I requested you to come here.'

A crow arrived, dropping silently on the balcony railing. In the garden, children shouted as they played. Vikram returned Anirudh's gaze but did not speak.

'It's been a long day for you,' said Anirudh. 'I've spent most of it filling your mind with the inconceivable. You are saturated, the blank look in your eyes says it all. We'll take a break. Mom needed a full day to get over the shock of the story. It's late now in any case. Aaji will come up for her dinner and then the maid will leave. We'll continue tomorrow. I hope you can spare the day for me.'

Vikram rose to his feet and stretched. The crow flew away, springing from the railing with a whir of wings. Anirudh had guessed correctly. Vikram's mind was reeling, like it had been strained through a sieve. He yawned. 'My uncle and aunt return tomorrow evening,' he said, covering his mouth with his hand. 'I'm free till then.'

Anirudh placed an arm around Vikram's shoulder as they turned away from the balcony. He switched on the lights when they entered the living room. 'I'm busy in the morning,' he said. 'A relative is coming to meet Aaji for lunch. Mom insisted that I be around. I should be able to leave by one o'clock when they sit for their meal. Is that okay with you?'

Vikram paused at the door. 'Will that leave us enough time?' he asked.

'More than enough,' smiled Anirudh, opening it. He squeezed Vikram's shoulder. 'It was good of you to come. I'll always remember.'

'And I'll never forget either,' said Vikram. 'My head is spinning. You're making a habit of this, Anirudh.'

'Wait till tomorrow,' grinned Anirudh. 'If you think this was startling, tomorrow will strike you dumb.'

Vikram laughed. 'You are enjoying this, aren't you?'

'You guys had fun for thirteen days while I lay unconscious,' said Anirudh, as Vikram turned to the stairs. 'It's my turn now.'

THE OVAL

Calling the next morning, Anirudh arranged to meet Vikram at Bombay's Oval Maidan at 1.00 p.m. Vikram arrived early as the bus from Malabar Hill covered the distance to Churchgate Station faster than he had anticipated.

The skyline of Bombay, dominated as it is by the concrete crests of buildings, takes a dip at the Oval, descending all the way to ground level, and grass, in a pleasing swathe of green, displaces the tar and cement of which most of modern Bombay is composed. The Oval is one of Bombay's scarce recreational areas, but an unusual one as it is neither a park nor a garden in the traditional sense. The only trees on its massive expanse are along its periphery and there is no pretence of landscaping with bushes or ornamental plants. The other half of its name, 'maidan', suggests that it is a playground, and it is exactly that—a huge, sprawling playground.

One of the reasons why the Churchgate area was amongst Vikram's favourite sections of Bombay was that the Oval was just one of a trio of maidans there. Two other sweeping reaches of green, the Cross Maidan and the Azad Maidan, connect up with the Oval, joining forces in a brave stand against the encroaching human tenements that have overrun the city. Together, the three maidans are a haven, a green lung in a gasping city.

The charm of the Oval Maidan is heightened by the absence of high-rise buildings in the area. On one side the maidan is lined with short, elegant buildings, and on the other by the magnificent complex of the High Court and University edifices. The architecture in this part of Bombay, especially the University and the grand railway terminus nearby, is inescapably loud in part, yet there is an overall magnificence that enthrals so completely that the viewer is inclined to forgive the decadent revelry of its builders.

Vikram couldn't help being struck by a special feeling whenever he visited this part of Bombay. In spite of a rash of commercial establishments and the constant buzz of traffic, a unique charm persisted here. Compared to the rest of the city, its architecture is regal, its spaces large and open, its roads wide and lined with trees.

Unaware of the area's history, Vikram had thought it odd that such a fine concentration of Bombay's proud buildings should be compacted into one single area while the rest of the city was in truth little more than an endless urban sprawl. But Anirudh had solved the puzzle for him. It was here that Bombay's historical Fort had once stood. This then was the original Bombay. This was the nerve centre of the seven mosquito-infested islands from which the city had sprung. It was from here that the fledgling city had spread its wings, expanding its borders, and emerging finally as the commercial capital of independent India.

The massive clock of the Rajabai clock tower, the tallest feature of the University, chimed pleasantly as Vikram strolled beneath its brown steeple. Vikram admired its refined opulence as he strolled along the sidewalk that bordered the Oval Maidan. A sturdy steel-wire fence stretched like a wall around the Oval. Only two gates broached the fence, allowing passage for pedestrians. Anirudh had selected the gate opposite the University to meet Vikram.

As he waited, a brass plaque caught Vikram's attention and he read with interest the information etched on its polished surface.

According to the plaque, Vikram was standing in a historical section of Bombay, with resplendent Gothic architecture on one side (the University and surrounding buildings) and graceful latter-day Art Deco architecture adorning the far side buildings.

But it wasn't the commentary on architecture that riveted Vikram's attention; rather it was the reference further down to the maidans. The plaque stated that the three maidans, together with the adjacent Cooperage, had once been part of Bombay's renowned Esplanade, the recreational ground whose existence he had learnt of the previous day.

As Vikram peered at a diagram showing the layout of the erstwhile Esplanade, he sensed someone leaning over his shoulder.

'Yup,' chirped a familiar voice. 'The plaque's got it right.'

Turning, Vikram saw it was Anirudh.

'This is it,' he said. 'You are standing on the Esplanade of my dream.'

There was a broad smile on Anirudh's dark features. Grabbing Vikram's arm, he pulled him through the gate on to the wide expanse of the Oval. A tiled path led forward, providing a level surface for pedestrians. Although the path thronged with pedestrians, the green reaches on either side were virtually empty in comparison, with only scattered groups of youngsters playing cricket or chasing footballs.

'I have sandwiches in my backpack,' said Anirudh, steering Vikram off the busy path. 'The same chutney and vegetable ones you enjoyed yesterday.' He halted on an empty patch of grass midway down the Oval. 'Let's have lunch.' Unhitching his backpack, he settled on the ground.

The sky was overcast, but there was no threat of rain. Although humid, the conditions were pleasant as a mild breeze swept the area. Groups of people relaxed nearby, chatting or stealing an afternoon nap. Further out, several congregations of youngsters, clad in shorts and T-shirts, indulged in more hectic activity. The massive spread of the Oval absorbed their exuberant shouting. All Vikram could hear was the faint bustle of traffic from the roads that fringed the maidan's periphery.

Vikram sat cross-legged. Plucking a blade of grass, he stuck it in his mouth.

'I'm confused,' he said, looking around him. 'You said the Esplanade was on the sea. You spoke of a beach with rocks and sand and crabs. Where's the sea, then? I only see buildings.'

Anirudh grinned. 'The sea broke right here. I'm not kidding; right where we are sitting. Everything west of here,' he said, waving a hand, 'those buildings that you see, have been erected on land that has been reclaimed from the sea. Churchgate Station, Marine Drive, the cricket stadiums—all that space was underwater in Irfan's time.'

Vikram stared at the mass of buildings to the west. 'It's hard to believe,' he said.

Anirudh extracted a sandwich dabba from his backpack and placed it on the grass.

'You are talking about hard to believe.' He made a snorting sound. 'Spare a thought for me. Everything I see is hard to believe. My brain spins so fast sometimes that if I don't sit down, I get scared that I will fall. I don't know what the truth is any longer—the dream or what I see with my eyes. I'm still trying to make sense of it all.'

Anirudh turned to his friend. 'You are the clever one, Vikram. Come on, then. Set something straight for me. Solve a mystery that I crave an answer for. Explain to me why I was chosen for the dream? It could have been you or Chitra falling in that cave. Then one of you might have had the dream. But instead, I lived the dream. Why me?'

Vikram opened the dabba and helped himself to a sandwich.

'I don't think there's anyone who can give you a satisfactory answer,' he said, chewing appreciatively. 'But we can try. I was up most of last night just thinking of your story. I analysed your Irfan; compared him with the Anirudh I know, and I found striking similarities. For instance, you both loved horses. Irfan was an excellent rider, and you are born to the sport. Next, both of you are paranoid about water, Irfan far more than you, I would say. Also, neither of you made friends easily: Irfan never had many, and I know you don't. Correct me if I'm wrong, I'm guessing here as I have never seen Irfan, but you and he must have looked the same too.'

'Irfan was a mirror image of me,' confirmed Anirudh. 'You could say he was fleshier, but that's a minor detail.' He dressed differently, of course, wearing the clothes of those days, mostly loose robes and a cap or turban. There's one big difference between us, though. His fingers and toes weren't bent like mine. They were normal, no kinks. Otherwise, everything was the same; even his complexion was dark, like mine.' Anirudh paused. 'There's an additional likeness that you missed. Both of us suffered difficult relationships with our fathers—Irfan's even rougher than mine.'

'I missed that one,' acknowledged Vikram. 'But that backs up what I've been thinking. You might not like what I'm suggesting, but I'll say it in any case.' Vikram looked keenly at Anirudh. 'Just hear me out. Don't take what I say to heart; this is only an opinion.'

Vikram hesitated. Though his eyes held Anirudh's, his gaze turned inward, as if unsure where to begin. He spoke at last, his tone defensive. 'It is possible, Anirudh, that Irfan is simply a creation of your imagination. We all have strange dreams, of ourselves in different places, in different situations, sometimes as different people . . . and often these dreams are very realistic. It is likely that during your coma you were dreaming of yourself. Irfan could simply be a reflection of you. It might have all seemed real to you, yet the entire experience could be nothing more than a dream.'

Anirudh's shoulders dropped. A weariness fell upon him. 'It's as I feared. You are no different from Mom. Even you doubt me.'

'I didn't say I doubt you,' said Vikram. 'I was simply speculating. I told you to hear me out, nothing more.'

Anirudh raised his hands, as if defeated. 'This scepticism is getting to me. You and Mom can have your point of view, but I refuse to accept it. I've listened to what you had to say, now it's your turn to hear me out. I want you—at least for now—to believe that my dream is true. Imagine that Rustom and all the others existed. Can you do that for me?'

'Sure,' said Vikram.

'In my dream, Irfan died, right?'

Vikram nodded.

'My dream ended on his death. So, obviously, my knowledge of all that happened during Irfan's time ended with his demise. You agree that I have no idea what happened after?'

Vikram nodded again.

'Everything after Irfan's death is just guesswork. Even Rustom's survival. Although I am certain he did survive, to convince sceptics like Mom and you, I have to prove that he did. Proof is crucial, not just for you, but for the sake of my sanity too.'

Anirudh paused, helping himself to a sandwich. 'That's what we are going to do today; investigate the proof. The matter will be settled by evening. One way or another we will know.'

Swallowing his sandwich, Anirudh continued. 'There is something else that we talked about yesterday. Something you said that got me thinking. You spoke about that abandoned house in the village below Koleshwar. That pretty cottage. The one that could not have been built by villagers.'

Vikram nodded.

'My parents called last night, and I asked Dad about the police investigation.' Anirudh made a face. 'It's just as you said, the inquiry's going nowhere. And Dad, of course, threw a fit on my asking. When he was done with ranting about the inefficiency of the police, I asked him about the house in the village. He repeated what you said . . . that it belonged to that man—Patil. Then I asked him for the name of the fancy house. At first, Dad didn't understand what I was getting at. I told him that we all give our homes a name. Flats in cities only have numbers, but homes, especially bungalows and cottages, always have a name. Dad had no idea what the name of the place was, but then he said something that got my blood pumping. He said the villagers called the house "Parsee Ghar". I asked him whether the house had ever belonged to a Parsee gentleman. Dad said he had no idea. He only knew that the house was known locally as Parsee Ghar—this even though it is owned by a Hindu named Patil.'

Vikram absorbed the information. Then he asked, 'Does Salim also call the place Parsee Ghar?'

Anirudh heaved a sigh. 'What do I say about Salim? He still refuses to speak to me. So, I told Mom to talk to him, and he confirmed that the place is called Parsee Ghar. He is not sure why, but his grandfather had once said that Parsees had lived there. It was a long time ago, he said. He knows for sure that the house predates everyone in the village. The general belief is that Parsees had once lived there, and it is they who had constructed it. Now you explain to me, Vikram, what is a Parsee house doing in a remote village like Salim's?'

They consumed sandwiches, deep in thought. On the path, Vikram spotted a channa-wallah. Excusing himself, he crossed and bought two packets of singh, and handed one to Anirudh.

'My favourite snack,' beamed Vikram. He slid brown peanuts from a conical paper wrapper on to his palm and munched enthusiastically. 'Can't resist the stuff when it's available. Now . . . about the Parsee Ghar. I am sure that there is no doubt in your head that it was Rustom who built it.'

Anirudh spoke with deep conviction. 'It is Rustom and none other.'

Vikram slid more peanuts on to his hand. 'I don't want you to misunderstand, but let's consider what you are saying from another point of view. An impartial observer would accuse you of jumping to conclusions that suit you.'

'To hell with impartial observers!' snapped Anirudh. 'There's nothing partial or impartial about this. I KNOW!

I know Rustom survived. I know for sure that if that house was built by a Parsee, then it was built by Rustom. And hear this . . . there's more. It's not just the house. Wallace's treasure is also proof. When Irfan died, all of Wallace's riches came into Rustom's possession. Where do you think Salim's gold came from?'

'I'll give you that,' said Vikram. 'The treasure is a huge thumbs-up for your dream. Makes it more believable. Salim could have stumbled upon a stash left behind by Rustom—that's of course assuming your dream is true. But then why would Rustom have left the treasure, or even bits of it, buried up there on Koleshwar? No one in his right mind would leave anything behind. If Rustom, as you believe, returned to Bombay, he must have taken every last bead, necklace and coin with him.'

'You are an intelligent guy, Vikram,' said Anirudh. 'But you are being far too clever here. How can you have any idea how Rustom's mind worked? There could have been circumstances that forced him to leave the treasure behind. God knows. He might have kept it buried on purpose, maybe for his children . . . that is if he had any. Rustom's affairs are a mystery to us, and we can't really know how his mind worked. All I'm saying is that in addition to the Parsee cottage, the presence of gold on Koleshwar is a pointer that Rustom is not an imaginary person, but someone who had once existed in flesh and blood.'

'Okay,' said Vikram. 'The Parsee Ghar and the gold on the mountain are credible pointers. I agree. But that's what they are, just indicators, they don't in any way establish proof.'

'Boy, you are a hard nut to crack,' said Anirudh, shaking his head. 'But just you wait, you will crack today. And, if you want to know, there are more pointers.'

Vikram looked inquiringly, but as Anirudh made to speak, Vikram's phone rang.

'It's Aditya,' said Vikram, peering at the number flashing on his phone.

'Don't let on you are with me,' said Anirudh hurriedly. 'Not a word of the dream or what we have been speaking of.'

Lying to Aditya was distasteful, but for Anirudh's sake, Vikram did. When, after exchanging pleasantries, Aditya asked for Anirudh, Vikram replied he wasn't with him.

'When am I ever going to get to talk to the guy?' complained Aditya, venting his frustration so loudly that even Anirudh heard him. 'He never takes my calls or returns them. He's behaving the same with Chitra. It's as if he's trying to avoid us.'

'He is a bit stressed,' said Vikram. 'Anyone would be after such a long coma. Just chill and don't be hard on him. Give him time, he'll be back to his normal self.' Vikram changed the subject, inquiring about Chitra.

'She took off this morning with Salim to search for those shieldtail snakes of hers. The timing of their trip is good for Salim, as the rural police had sent a message asking him to report to them at Wai. You know how he is with cops. And it turns out he had kept their summons a secret! He had been avoiding the issue, but Chitra's presence will give him the confidence to face them. They head to Koleshwar once they are done with the police.'

'Didn't she persuade you to come along?' asked Vikram.

'She tried.' Aditya laughed. 'But there's too much going on here, stuff that will cheer you too. The plane is available tomorrow. We're jumping, man. The reason I called is to find out what time you will be returning. Uncle Ishwar wants to know. He'll schedule the jump accordingly.'

Vikram's heart leapt. 'Wow! Awesome, bro. We're leaving Bombay in the morning tomorrow, ten-ish or so. Schedule the jump for the afternoon. After 3:00 should be fine.'

'Perfect,' said Aditya. 'Uncle Ishwar prefers the afternoon too. Got to go now. He's pushing me hard. There's another skydiving theory class on now. It's downright unfair that you get away lazing in Mumbai. Tell Anirudh that I'm looking forward to meeting him, even though he's avoiding me. Say I need some tips on polo, maybe that will get him talking. Don't be late tomorrow or we'll jump without you.'

Smiling, Vikram bid goodbye and disconnected.

'You are in demand, Anirudh,' he said, pocketing his phone. 'Everyone wants you back. Aditya too.'

Anirudh did not respond. Turning, Vikram saw him staring out across the Oval, a dreamy look in his eyes. Nudging him with his foot, he snapped Anirudh from his reverie.

'Sorry,' grinned Anirudh. 'I was trying to remember how far the sea would come, but it isn't easy as landmarks from that time are all gone.'

'There's the place called Bandstand.' Vikram raised his hand, pointing. 'Isn't that where the band would play in your dreams?'

Anirudh's eyes flashed. 'You're amazing, Vikram. You just supplied me the bearings I was searching for. How could I have been so stupid? Should have thought of it myself considering Mom and I stopped by the other day and I had taken a look. And I was thrilled because the bandstand is just as it was in those days. It's one of the few monuments that has survived from Irfan's time.'

Anirudh stared south, across the road to the cloistered area of the bandstand. 'Back then it stood at the edge of the sea. My guess—using the bandstand as a reference—is that we are sitting where the beach was. Our feet would be wet. On a monsoon day like this, we would have been in danger of being swept away.'

Anirudh laughed at the incredulous expression on his companion's face.

'Sounds crazy, doesn't it? But that's how much the city has changed.' He leaned back. 'The view Irfan saw from here is etched like a hi-res photo in my mind. I can see sand, rocks and waves. The sea stretches before me to the far horizon. Malabar Hill rims my view to the north and there are thick forests on its slopes. The sky is blue, the sea is calm and there are fishing boats, sails fluttering in the wind. There are lots of birds too, most of them seagulls, and I can feel the wind. I smell the sea and taste salt.'

All Vikram could see were buildings. The incessant buzz of traffic and the steady movement of people rendered it impossible to conjure a vision of the sea or fishing boats. There was no salt in the air, only a whiff of exhaust fumes.

Anirudh gestured with his arm. 'Irfan loved his evenings at the Esplanade and so did Rustom. It wasn't just them—everyone who lived in the Fort came here to enjoy the wind and the sea. There was always a festive feel to the area.

On most days, there would be a band playing. The English would gather near the bandstand, their expensive carriages and horses drawn nearby. The rest of us—Parsees, Hindus, Bohris; the non-European populace—roamed everywhere. The area at our disposal was vast. Imagine all the maidans merged, throw in even the University, the court buildings and the Prince of Wales Museum behind—that should give you an idea of the expanse of the Esplanade. Even Marine Lines was part of it. There were tents there, pitched in neat lines. Rustom loved to walk along the sea, especially beside the tent lines . . .'

'Is that why they call the road there, Marine Lines?' interrupted Vikram.

Anirudh gazed incredulously at Vikram. 'Oh my God! You're a genius, Vikram. The sea and the line of tents . . . it makes sense . . . that's why the street is called Marine Lines.'

Vikram grinned. 'Not bad, huh? But the credit is all yours. That was just a guess, based on your descriptions. Now . . . before Aditya's call interrupted us, you were saying something about proof that Rustom had existed.'

'Yes,' said Anirudh, blinking, the distant look vanishing from his eyes. 'Yes! The proof.'

There was a yell and a muddy football bounced towards them, rolling to a halt just metres away. Vikram rose and kicked hard, looping it to a barechested man with mud-caked legs. Smiling his thanks, the man booted it back to where his equally muddy mates were waiting.

Vikram turned and saw that Anirudh had risen too.

'Let's move on,' said Anirudh, strapping his backpack to his shoulders. 'There's a possibility of rain, and there are things I want to show you.'

'The proof?' asked Vikram.

'Soon,' smiled Anirudh. 'I want to show you the Fort first. Come on.'

THE FORT

A short amble from the Oval, during which they passed an unusual number of people dressed in black—lawyers, working at the courts, Anirudh said—and strolled down arcaded corridors, brought them to an oval-shaped arena with a skyline made up of elegant colonial buildings. Vikram was familiar with the place as it was a well-known crossroad. Maps called it 'Hutatma Chowk', but Vikram knew it as 'Fountain'—the name taxi drivers and a majority of Bombay's citizens preferred. And indeed, a fountain stood before them, the very one for which the area was famous. It was a tall, elaborately carved structure. There were domes moulded into each of its four sides, and strong, graceful figures reclined at every corner.

'This is it,' said Anirudh, pointing at the fountain. 'Exactly where the Flora Fountain stands today is where the Church Gate of old stood. There was a proper military-style gate here, and if you were on the Esplanade, you would enter the Fort from this Church Gate. From here the Fort walls, black and stony, looped away on either side.'

Vikram stared, trying to imagine a Fort and a gate, but failed.

Anirudh tugged his arm. 'Come, I want to show you around what was once the walled Fort town.'

As usual, the Fountain area was busy, and since it was lunchtime, it was even more crowded than usual. Weaving through the throng, Anirudh guided Vikram to a wide tree-lined road that split a cluster of buildings.

'You've entered the Fort,' said Anirudh, as they strolled between graceful buildings, whose facades, even though they were screened by signboards, still managed to convey a stately elegance.

'What happened to the Fort and its walls?' asked Vikram, edging to one side of the road to allow a determined-looking lady to pass.

'I knew you'd ask,' grinned Anirudh. 'My dream has no answer as the Fort still existed when Irfan and Rustom fled Bombay. So the explanation I have is Mom's, not mine. According to her, the walls were brought down a few years after Irfan and Rustom left the city. The British were absolute masters of the land by then as they had quelled our war for independence. The Maratha forces had also been subjugated a few decades earlier and so with the absence of any real threat there was no need for the fortifications. The walls were a terrible nuisance in any case. They blocked light and fresh sea breezes and created unhygienic conditions. People would have rejoiced when they brought the walls down.'

Vikram tried once more to imagine turrets, towers, fortifications, and an encircling black wall and failed again.

It was only people and cars and crows and buildings that he saw.

'They called this road Church Gate Street in those days,' said Anirudh. 'Makes sense as it was the main thoroughfare to the Church Gate. It was never as busy as this, of course, but during festivals, when the entire city turned out to enjoy the Esplanade, it could get crowded too.'

A short distance ahead, Anirudh raised his hand and pointed.

'There it is. Look ahead. The church still stands exactly as it did all those years ago. The very church that gave its name to the Church Gate.'

At the point where the road broadened, there was a squat stone structure with a church steeple protruding chimney-like from its roof. Remarkably, despite its antiquated origins, the church was in excellent condition. It was evident that its patrons had lavished love and care on it over the ages.

'It's called Saint Thomas's Cathedral now,' said Anirudh. 'For a long time, its steeple was the tallest structure in this part of Bombay. Can you believe it?'

The statement seemed so absurd to Vikram that it was laughable, as even the buildings that surrounded it, which weren't by any means tall, dwarfed the historical steeple.

They passed the church and soon came to a wide circle ringed by handsome buildings, with a neat compact garden at its centre.

'You don't have to tell me,' said Vikram. 'I know this place, Horniman Circle. I've always liked the garden here.'

'Then you would have liked it even more in the old days,' said Anirudh. 'This was a huge open area back then. They called it the Bombay Green. This'—he swept a hand around the circle of buildings—'is where the old Green used to be.'

Having failed at his earlier attempts to envision images of the past, Vikram made no effort to visualize the open expanse of grass that Anirudh spoke of. He admired the encircling buildings instead.

'None of the buildings stood here in Irfan's time,' went on Anirudh. 'This was such a large open expanse that it was like a maidan inside the Fort itself. If you recollect the start of the dream . . . it was here on the Green that Rustom and Irfan's friendship took root. There was a well here, remember? The well beside which Rustom sat sobbing the day after the robbery?'

Vikram nodded.

'It's still here, in the garden. Come, I'll show you.'

The garden was fenced, but on the Church side of the circle, there was an entrance. Vehicular traffic was light and they crossed easily to the gate.

'This is one of the few places in the city that still bears the name of an Englishman,' said Anirudh as they entered the garden through a pair of stately wrought-iron gates. 'When the British laid out the city, they named every road, every corner, every landmark, after themselves. So, quite naturally, after Independence, the government went about setting the record right, changing English names to Indian ones. Horniman is one of the exceptions. Mom says that although he was a white man, he sided with us in our struggle for freedom. So, in recognition of his services, our government named this circle after him.'

The Horniman Garden was a pleasant, leafy place, with an abundance of trees, modest expanses of lawn, groves of bamboo, and a fine central pond. As it was lunchtime the garden was crowded with office goers either grabbing a bite or dozing in its quiet environs. Anirudh steered Vikram from the central path across a strip of lawn and halted beneath a stand of bamboo.

He pointed at a raised concrete platform.

'The well,' he said and laughed at Vikram's confused expression. 'No need to look so startled—it is a well! In the old days, it was circular and it looked like a proper well. They pulled water out with buckets then. Now, we have pumps. It's amazing, isn't it? The same well . . . it doesn't look the same, but it's still here . . . from Irfan's time . . . and still full of water.'

Anirudh had no idea, but at that moment, beside the ageless water reservoir, something he wished for from the bottom of his heart finally came to be. A certainty settled on Vikram. A certainty that Anirudh's dream was true and not a hallucination. Since morning, as Anirudh had rolled out one historical fact after another, a feeling of conviction had been building inside Vikram, and as he imagined Rustom's tear-stricken countenance, his rapidly swelling acceptance crystallized to unconditional belief.

They strolled afterwards to the central pond where several ducks waddled lazily. Spying an empty bench on the path that circled the pond, they settled on it.

'Know what?' said Vikram, 'I'm beginning to understand what you are going through. Not fully, but enough to sympathize with you. It's hard to imagine a big maidan here instead of this garden with its trees and grass. And even after giving it my all, I couldn't picture a Fort and black walls, or any kind of gate, as we walked through that crowd at Fountain.' Vikram shook his head. 'You must be going crazy.'

'Finally!' exclaimed Anirudh, rolling his eyes. 'I was losing faith in you, Vikram, thinking that you were going to be like Mom.' He placed a hand on his heart. 'Phew! I can't even begin to describe to you how much better I feel now! You have no idea how accurate what you just said is. I am going crazy. It's like my eyes and head are disconnected, on two separate planets. I see one thing, yet my brain draws an entirely different image. But I'm coping now and it's getting better with time. The mad confusion of before is no more.'

Anirudh stared at the pond for a long time.

Vikram maintained a respectful silence.

Anirudh finally snapped out of his reverie. He turned to Vikram. 'Did you know there's a street in Bombay named after Forjett?' he asked.

Vikram looked up interestedly.

'It's true. There's a street down the road from Kemp's Corner, which has Forjett's name. Not just that, the entire hill there is named after him. Like Horniman, his memory too survived the renaming frenzy.'

'Surely they appreciated his efforts as the police commissioner,' said Vikram.

'True,' said Anirudh, 'He did a great job as the police chief. He turned the police force around. From a laughing stock, he made it a respected arm of the government. No one disputes that, but—' Anirudh paused. '—there were other things . . . things he did that were anti-Indian.'

Vikram stared.

'Remember Irfan's dad, Mohammed Aziz?'

Vikram nodded.

'Remember in the dream he was caught up in a plot to trigger an uprising in Bombay?'

Vikram nodded again.

'Forjett was aware of the plot. Using that beggar disguise of his, Forjett infiltrated the ranks of the plotters and foiled them. He arrested the conspirators, and the men were later executed. Forjett hadn't been joking when he told Irfan he would not protect his father and that the penalty for conspiracy was death. The unfortunate men—friends possibly of Mohammed Aziz—were strapped to cannons and blown apart. They were executed publicly on the Esplanade, the section of which is now the Azad Maidan. The name 'Azad' is a remembrance of the martyrdom of those men.

'You might think that the Indian population would have been against what Forjett had done, but no, it was the opposite. Bombay's Indian business fraternity actually rewarded Forjett for his efforts at unearthing the plot, and as a token of their thanks they presented him a large sum of money.'

Vikram puckered his eyebrows. 'That doesn't sound right. You don't reward the enemy.'

Anirudh shook his head. 'You are getting it wrong. In those days—at least in the eyes of the native business community—Forjett wasn't the enemy. The local businessmen were terrified of a possible uprising in Bombay. The very thought made their knees knock together. The stories of death and killings that trickled into Bombay from the north frightened not only the businessmen but also the entire population of the city. The people of Bombay didn't want their happy, prosperous existence disturbed. They were relieved when peace prevailed and their lives were unaffected. To them, Forjett was an upright officer and a well-liked man. And since he played a big role in ensuring the city was unaffected, the wealthy citizens of that time rewarded him.'

An elderly lady settled herself on the low wall that encircled the pond. Leaning forward, she cooed softly to the ducks.

'What happened to Forjett?' asked Vikram, looking at the birds who were now shooting towards the lady as she tossed crumbs from her meal into the pond.

'After the Fort walls were pulled down, Forjett was involved more in the reconstruction of the city rather than the policing of it. Mom says Forjett personally supervised the conversion of the Green into these buildings. He served for many years and was eventually pensioned off to London. The people of Bombay loved him so much that they once again rewarded him with money before he departed the country. He eventually died in London, an old man.'

Vikram clasped his knee and leaning back pulled it to his chest. 'I wonder whether Forjett ever thought about what happened to Irfan and Rustom after they left Bombay?'

Anirudh whipped his head around to stare at Vikram. 'Whoa!' exclaimed. 'Hold on there! Am I hearing this right, or what? If that question—Forjett wondering about Rustom and Irfan's fate—came from you, I take it that you believe my dream?'

'There's no way you could be making all this up,' conceded Vikram. 'Yes, I'm convinced. If I believe in your knowledge of the area, then it follows that I should believe everything else about your dream too.'

'A BELIEVER!' cried Anirudh, looking up at the sky. He turned to Vikram, eyes shining. 'The well! Do you realize that you have declared your faith in my dream here, beside the well—the same place that Rustom and Irfan cemented their friendship?'

'But we're already friends,' laughed Vikram.

'Yes, of course,' said Anirudh. 'But it was here that a friendship that lasted a lifetime began.'

'A rather short lifetime if you ask me,' said Vikram. 'Let's hope ours doesn't end the way theirs did.'

'What's death got to do with it?' Anirudh looked aggrieved. 'Rustom would never have forgotten Irfan. It was too deep a relationship. Irfan would have lived on in his memory.'

The lady feeding the ducks had departed and they were now waddling hopefully in their direction.

'Getting back to your question,' said Anirudh. 'About Forjett and whether he ever gave thought to Irfan and Rustom's fate, I have no idea, as my dream ended with Irfan's death. I can only say that he dearly liked them both, and that when Rustom returned to Bombay, he must have helped him as much as he could.'

'You are talking in riddles here,' said Vikram. 'Didn't you just say that your dream ended with Irfan's death? So then how do you know that Rustom came back to Bombay?'

'I just know,' said Anirudh. A mysterious gleam shone from his eyes as he rose to his feet. 'You will say that I'm guessing here.' He shrugged. 'You could be right. But we'll know soon enough. I told you that I have possible evidence. That evidence—if it exists—isn't far, just a short walk from here, near the Gateway. Come . . . it won't take long, let's walk there.'

As they stepped out of the garden, Anirudh directed Vikram's attention to a stately building with a magnificent sweep of staircase and towering pillars. It was the old Town Hall, he said, which had been converted to a library. It was called the 'Asiatic Library' now. He reminded Vikram that it was here, on the hall's hallowed stairs, on a warm evening 160 years earlier, that Forjett had informed a disbelieving Rustom that his uncle's stolen money had been recovered. The Town Hall had been a building of great prominence in the old days, said Anirudh. It was where people gathered for meetings and where important dignitaries made speeches. The famous African explorer, Sir David Livingstone, was one of many distinguished personages who had spoken there when he visited Bombay.

The Town Hall was one of few buildings to survive from Irfan's time. Most were gone, said Anirudh, lost to history, including the peculiar rounded structure on the old

Dockyard Road that had once been the Ice House, where ice imported from America in shiploads used to be stored and sold to Bombay's thirsty populace.

When they passed the quiet, unostentatious building that housed the office of the Bombay Natural History Society, it was Vikram's turn to explain. The BNHS was an institution half as old as the Fort itself, he said. It was renowned for its pioneering work on wildlife studies in the Indian subcontinent. The simple, squat structure with its iconic hornbill carving never failed to trigger sweet memories in Vikram, for it was here that his mother and father, both pursuing studies in wildlife sciences, had met and fallen in love.

A while later, after crossing a busy circle and stepping on to a wide thoroughfare that led to the sea, the massive arch of the Gateway of India loomed in front of them.

Anirudh skirted the Gateway's extensive courtyard, which was packed as usual with tourists, and led Vikram to a promenade that bordered the sea, providing an unrestricted view of Bombay's harbour.

The promenade was busy. People strolled along its pavement admiring its view; some reclined on its hip-high stone wall. To one side, little children fed pigeons, tossing handfuls of channa on the ground. Vendors roamed the cobbled length of the walkway, drawing attention to themselves and their wares. Vikram purchased packets of singh for himself and Anirudh before they settled companionably on the wall.

The harbour was in a decidedly angry mood. Reflecting the murky sky above, its waters were dark, almost black, and as if tormented by some alien force, they heaved and writhed, thrusting giddily upwards one moment and plunging frightfully the next. Though the harbour was famous as a safe anchorage, at that moment it seemed to Vikram that it was anything but safe.

For the second time that day, Anirudh swept his arm grandly.

'The harbour,' he said. 'The expanse of water that terrified Irfan.'

'I wouldn't blame him,' said Vikram. 'Just looking at it makes me sick.'

'True,' agreed Anirudh. 'But you know . . .'

'Yes I know it's not always like this.' Vikram interrupted his friend. 'But boy, is it scary now!'

'It was even worse on the night Irfan left Bombay.' Anirudh shuddered. 'Poor Irfan. Imagine being forced to confront your worst nightmare on a sea more dreadful than even this.'

The flotilla of pleasure craft that floated near the promenade wall was conspicuous by its absence, and so were the harbour boats that ferried tourists on joy rides. But further out, larger vessels tenanted the distant reaches of the harbour. The hills of the mainland were visible, but barely, like brush strokes on a leaden horizon.

Anirudh chewed his peanuts appreciatively. 'You must have guessed that by the time he took the voyage Irfan was coming out of his paranoia of the sea.'

'It makes sense,' said Vikram. 'Childhood paranoias fade with time. He wouldn't have survived the voyage otherwise, would he?'

109

'True,' said Anirudh. 'But he kept it a secret, never letting on; particularly to his father. He was afraid Mohammed Aziz would drag him off to Mahabaleshwar and never allow him to return.'

Although the harbour was scenic, its unstable surface made the boys queasy and after a while, they turned their backs to it.

The majestic Taj Mahal Hotel hovered before them, its stone walls grey and scrubbed scrupulously clean. Its tall domes sparkled against the stormy backdrop of the sky.

Anirudh turned his eyes from the Taj Hotel to the stately row of buildings that bordered the road.

'It's all so trim, tidy and beautiful now,' he said. 'In Irfan's time, there was nothing here except the sea and rocks.' He raised an arm, pointing. 'The Gateway,' he said, 'Exactly where it stands is where the Apollo Bunder was. There would be chaos when passenger boats arrived at the bunder. The poor travellers, especially the first-timers—the English men and women who had never left the shores of their country—just didn't know what hit them the moment they staggered on to the jetty. Coolies would swarm around them like flies, clutching at their bags, just as they do at the railway station nowadays, only it was much worse. Irfan and his friends would sit and watch as the poor bewildered travellers were conned and fleeced.'

'Didn't Forjett put an end to that?' asked Vikram.

'Forjett was a good man, but even he couldn't perform miracles. He did try. A frequent assignment for Irfan and Rustom was to report on the badly-behaved coolies and the con men that hung about the bunders. Action would be taken against them, but most returned in a few weeks and continued with their harassment. You know how it is.'

Vikram laughed. 'Some things don't change, I guess.'

'Yes . . . they don't.' Anirudh laughed. 'It's the same at the stations and airport today—rogues waiting to rip you off. But if anything it's travel that has undergone a major change since then. In Irfan's time, the sea was the point of entry for everybody. There were no airports; trains had only just begun. In every sense, the harbour was the Gateway of India. It's no wonder they built the monument here.'

Vikram gazed at the proud arch of the Gateway. Only symbolic now, it was a reminder of an age that had passed.

There was a 'whoosh' of sound as the entire flock of pigeons on the pavement took wing. They traced a circle before settling on the ground again. It was a little girl who had disturbed them. Waving her hands she ran joyously amongst the birds, laughing as they scattered about her.

'That evidence of yours,' said Vikram. 'It was here, you said.'

Anirudh grinned. 'Yes . . . the evidence.' He lifted himself off the wall. 'Come with me. I'll show you. Let's walk down the promenade.'

SEAWIND

They strolled along the cobbled promenade pavement. It was a pleasant walk with the expanse of the harbour spread before them and boats bobbing everywhere. They were halfway down when Vikram, who was admiring the buildings across the road, suddenly halted.

'Hey!' he exclaimed, pointing. 'That name ... Seawind. Isn't that the name of the place Irfan lived in?'

A polished brass plate was fastened to the gatepost of the building Vikram was indicating with the words 'Hotel Seawind' imprinted on it.

'Yes, that is the name of the house Irfan lived in.' Anirudh smiled. 'Nice coincidence, isn't it? Is there anything else that strikes you about the place?'

Vikram stared.

Only the upper section of the structure was visible as a stand of trees screened the lower floors. From what he could see, Vikram gained the impression of a fine, well-maintained building. The walls were painted a sparkling white. There were several windows, their frames polished deep brown. Green lintels overhung them. Potted plants were visible on the sills of the windows and some, the larger picture windows, were graced with quaint wrought-iron balconies.

'It's a nice building,' said Vikram, not sure what Anirudh was getting at. 'Well maintained too. Someone is doing an excellent job.'

'Look at the gateposts,' said Anirudh. 'Do you notice something about them?'

Vikram looked closely. The gateposts were each topped by a statue of a lion.

'Nice posts,' he commented. 'Those lion figureheads are cool. I'd love to have them in my house.'

'Do the lions ring a bell?' asked Anirudh.

'No,' said Vikram, clearly puzzled now.

'Remember, the mansion Irfan and Rustom visited, the one which Mario and Ajit were working on?'

'Yes, I remember,' said Vikram, still puzzled.

'There were lions sculpted on the walls of the pillars of that house—lions that fascinated Rustom. I told you that Rustom was bowled over by the entire house: the veranda, the garden, the fountain, and the lions. He swore that one day he would build a home just like that one.'

'Are you saying . . .?' Understanding dawned on Vikram. His expression turned incredulous, as if the stone lion had miraculously sprung to life. 'You are saying that Rustom built that house?'

'Did I say that?' asked Anirudh. 'I don't recollect so.' Then he smiled. 'One thing my dream has taught me is that strange things happen, and you'd be surprised how often they do. Yes, Rustom could have built this. It is possible. And if I can prove that it was indeed Rustom who did, then here is my evidence.'

Vikram sank to the promenade wall. He stared wordlessly at the gateposts and their proud lion heads. A wind stirred the trees, scattering leaves on the scrubbed pavement at the hotel gate.

'Seawind,' muttered Vikram. 'You are saying Rustom named the house he built after the one Irfan lived in.'

Anirudh shook his head. 'I haven't said anything,' he corrected. 'I'm only guessing . . . I have no proof that it was Rustom. Just about anyone could have built it. It may even have been Jehangirbhai—the Parsee who owned that monstrous mansion on Malabar Hill. That is of course if he ever recovered from spending all that money on that fancy home of his. All I'm doing is making a connection between the name 'Seawind' and the lion heads—both of which are from my dream.

'Mom brought me here for a walk on my first outing after recovering. It was my idea, actually. I pushed her into coming here. You see, I came here often as a child with my parents. Dad's office was close by. There was this strong memory in my mind of the hotel and its lion gateposts. As an infant, I remember being terrified of the lions. Even though they were made of stone I was certain they would leap on me and tear me apart. The dream jogged my memory as its lion statues were similar to those of my childhood; so I wanted to see for myself.' Anirudh paused, recollecting. 'There I was,' he continued, 'just recovering from my coma and then I saw the gateposts, exact replicas of my dream. I had a fit. Next, I saw the name of the hotel and my head started spinning so badly that I asked Mom to take me away. Poor Mom. She panicked. It wasn't fair on her, but I couldn't possibly tell her of the wild connections spinning in my brain.

'Later, I called for you. It wasn't just to share my dream that I insisted on you coming to Bombay. I also wanted you to accompany me to this hotel. I don't have it in me to go in on my own. I need an escort, a trusted friend with me. The two of us have to go in together. I have to see for myself whether Hotel Seawind was indeed built by Rustom or whether it's the wrong dream I'm chasing.'

Vikram's eyes were like balloons now. He gazed at Anirudh, as if seeing his friend in a new light. 'What . . . what is it that you are looking for?'

Anirudh shrugged. 'I don't know, Vikram. I have no idea. All I know is that I need time inside. I have to explore the place, I need to poke around, to search it for God alone knows what. You have to buy me that time, Vikram. Whoever runs the place isn't going to just grin and allow me to snoop around. I'm depending on you to manage that time for me. Talk to the man at the desk. Ask him rates, ask to see a room, tell him your father or uncle is coming. Spin him any kind of story. Just keep the staff off my back.'

Vikram looked thoughtfully at Anirudh. 'A father or uncle won't be enough. A single room is nothing for a receptionist. Won't interest him. I'll have to spin a story of a marriage in my family.' Vikram laughed. 'I'll request several rooms, maybe the whole hotel. That will make them sit up and pay attention.'

Anirudh slapped Vikram on his back. 'Now you're talking. See, this is why I needed you. Only you can help me with this.'

Vikram shook his head. 'Not true. Aditya is far better at this than me. He's the sort that can have the entire management of the hotel eating out of his hand.'

'Maybe,' said Anirudh, 'but I have more faith in you.'

On the far side of the road, a taxi pulled up beside Hotel Seawind. A formally dressed man of either Japanese or Korean descent emerged. Handing the driver a note, he hurried into the hotel.

Vikram looked inquiringly at Anirudh. 'Shall we?' he asked.

Anirudh suddenly turned nervous. 'Now?' His voice was dry.

'Right now,' said Vikram. 'No point hanging about. Come on.'

Vikram grabbed Anirudh's arm and yanked him along. They crossed the road, Vikram holding his friend, letting go only when they reached the pavement opposite.

The lion-crowned gateposts of Seawind Hotel loomed before them. As he mounted the footpath, Vikram noticed that the paving outside the hotel was of superior quality. The original municipality flooring had been stripped away and overlaid with expensive tiles.

Vikram walked confidently through the open gate. Anirudh followed on unsteady feet.

A pebbled pathway led inside. Even as they set foot on it, Anirudh halted, his jaw quivering.

'Look at the fountain on the lawn!' His voice, though a whisper, was sharp, like a hiss. 'I can't believe my eyes. It's identical to the one in my dream.'

To one side of the building there was a strip of grass, and set upon it was a large fountain. The centrepiece of the fountain was a magnificent stone lion sculpted into a spout, head thrown back, mouth snarling at the sky. Several smaller lion-headed spouts lined the circular frame of the fountain. A pleasant gurgle issued from the fountain as streams of water spilled from the jowls of the lions.

Anirudh wobbled, rocking on his feet.

Reaching out, Vikram steadied him.

They were in a courtyard decorated with potted plants. Ahead was a veranda, an unusually large one, with one half of its breadth taken up by a restaurant. The remaining was a reception area and lobby. At this afternoon hour, except for a young man at the lobby desk, the veranda was empty. The restaurant had a 'No Service' sign and the chairs in the reception area were unoccupied.

The young man at the desk was dressed smartly in black trousers, a white shirt and a tie. He looked inquiringly at them.

Vikram pulled Anirudh along. They crossed to the reception area, Vikram purposefully, Anirudh absently, his neck twitching birdlike, from side to side.

The young man wore a pair of heavily rimmed spectacles, and there was a badge on his shirt with the name 'Rahul Singh' emblazoned on it.

Vikram sauntered to the desk, smiling at Mr Singh.

Mr Singh smiled back brightly.

The desk was long and polished chestnut brown. A computer screen glowed on one side, and there was a vase with a spray of orchids on the other.

Vikram halted, resting his elbows on the desk.

'Do you have rooms?' he inquired. 'We would require them for September.'

Mr Singh turned to the computer screen. 'How many rooms would that be, sir?' His fingers tapped a keyboard below.

'A dozen or maybe more,' replied Vikram, not batting an eyelid.

Mr Singh paused.

'Marriage party,' continued Vikram glibly. 'My father has asked me to check out hotels in this area and find the best rate. We'll require the rooms for five days or maybe a week.'

Mr Singh looked up, appraising Vikram through his glasses. 'We can certainly work out a price for that kind of occupancy,' he smiled. 'Rooms aren't a problem. Maybe you would like to see them first. We can discuss rates later.'

Anirudh paid only half attention to Vikram and the attendant. The fountain, albeit a smaller one, was an exact copy of the one Rustom had marvelled at all those years ago. His head was ablaze. The evidence he sought was stacking up like a pile of bricks.

Anirudh trailed along as Mr Singh, effusively describing the features of the hotel, led Vikram past a room behind the veranda. Ahead, there were stairs and an elevator door. From the corner of his eye, Anirudh saw Mr Singh halt beside the door and press a button.

As his gaze flitted about, Anirudh's eyes did a flip once more.

On the glass panelled door of the room was a placard with 'MANAGER' printed on it in bold letters. It wasn't the designation that dumbfounded Anirudh, but the name stamped beneath.

Mr Percy Palkhivala.

Palkhivala!

No! No, there could be no connection with the Palkhivala of his dream. This had to be a coincidence. The speculation that the manager Percy Palkhivala might be a descendant of the tyrannical Palkhivala from his dream was absurd, stretching even his all-too-willing imagination to breaking point.

Anirudh abandoned the line of thought.

The elevator arrived, and without sparing as much as a glance at Anirudh, Mr Singh led Vikram inside. The door closed behind them leaving Anirudh unattended. Lady Luck seemed to be smiling on Anirudh. Singh's indifference was a heaven-sent opportunity for unimpeded snooping.

The walls of the elevator hall drew Anirudh's gaze next, as almost every inch of their surface was decorated with paintings. Canvasses of all sizes, encased in elegant frames, jostled for space on the walls. Anirudh's knowledge of art was abysmal, yet from the stark realism of the paintings, even he could judge they were from an earlier time, probably predating the building itself.

Interestingly, there was not a single landscape study amongst the paintings. All were portraits, and a glance was sufficient to confirm that the building had once been Parsee-owned.

Anirudh stared at detailed images of Parsee women and children, dressed in finery, the women displaying expensive jewellery. Curiously, alongside the Parsee profiles were canvases devoted to English women and children. Most intriguing was a mixed canvas with Parsee and English children posing together. A striking twist to the portrait was the swapped clothing of the children. The Parsee children were outfitted in European attire: a boy in a suit and a girl in a pretty summer dress; whereas the English children had donned Indian garb: a young girl wrapped in a sari and the boy sporting a typical Parsee costume.

Searching for likenesses, Anirudh strove to fit the solemn faces on the canvases with the images from his dream. He stared at the paintings till his eyes hurt, but was finally forced to concede that the resemblances he perceived were purely imaginary.

As he gazed at the walls it struck him that the collection was incomplete. There were no portraits of men, only images of women and children. Could there be more paintings on the upper floors?

Carpeted steps led upwards to one side of the elevator.

Anirudh hurried up the stairs and at the first landing he skidded to a halt.

An enormous portrait took up the entire wall opposite, the canvas much larger than any in the collection below. But sharp disappointment flooded Anirudh the moment he set eyes on it. The subject of the portrait was an Englishman, not a Parsee.

The Englishman was red-cheeked and tall and had piercing blue eyes. The sparse hair on his head was a light shade of brown, almost blond; huge sideburns covered most of his cheeks. Anirudh experienced a sinking feeling as he stared at the portrait. The building wasn't Parsee-owned after all. It was an Englishman who had constructed it. He was chasing a hopeless fantasy, guided falsely by his craving for connections with his dream.

He trudged up the stairs, head hanging in defeat. Arriving at the next level, he raised his head and froze in mid-step. His stride broke with such abruptness that he overbalanced and fell to the ground.

There was another portrait on the wall, only this time the recognition was instantaneous. He went numb all over, as if someone had thrown a bucket of ice water on him. He gasped painfully, his breath catching in his throat.

Rustom!

The likeness was unmistakable, the recognition instantaneous, even though the portrait in front of him was that of a grown man. The large dark eyes. The perfect nose. The same pale face. The artist had even faithfully reproduced his smooth, baby-like skin. Despite the years, the childlike features that characterized Rustom were intact.

Fierce dizziness struck Anirudh as he rose to his feet. His head spun and he had to lean against the wall to retain balance. The implication of the portrait was staggering. Incontrovertible proof that his dream was true. Rustom was no longer a hazy apparition from a dream. The portrait was the equivalent of a fossil find, instituting unshakable authority to his dream. This then was the evidence that he sought, the clinching authentication.

Anirudh goggled at the portrait.

A grown man, about fifty years of age, dressed in a jacket, tie and trousers, stared out of the canvas with a frank, friendly expression. Rustom's hairline had only fractionally receded. There were additions in the form of a moustache and sideburns of a fashion similar to the Englishman's. There was not a trace of the uncertainty and timidity that had once personified the boy from his dream. Instead, Rustom radiated composure, worldliness and wisdom. The face was a replica of the image that was dear and beloved to him—age and mellowing notwithstanding. This was the Rustom of his dream . . . Irfan's best friend . . . and his too.

The snap and hum of the elevator roused Anirudh from his stupor. Looking about him, he saw that he was standing in a broad corridor, so large that it resembled a hall. To one side was a wall with windows; on the other were several doors. There was another smaller framed picture on the wall opposite. The carpet muffled the tramp of Anirudh's feet as he strode towards it.

The lower section of the wall, from ground till hip height, was overlaid with tiles. Above, hung the frame. Instead of a painting, there was a photograph in this frame. It was an old black-and-white print but in surprisingly good condition. Its subject was a pair of men; both in traditional Parsee robes, with long rounded hats on their heads. The man on the left was Rustom, an older version than in the painting. Rustom's hair was totally white. He seemed shrunken and the skin beneath his chin sagged.

The man beside him was far younger; middle-aged, guessed Anirudh. In spite of their age disparity, there were noticeable likenesses, especially their dark saucer-like eyes, their clear-cut boyish features, and their noses, which were flawlessly formed.

Had Rustom started a family, wondered Anirudh? Was this his son? Were the children portrayed in the lobby Rustom's children? Could one of the Parsee ladies down there have been his wife? Anirudh leaned against the wall, his head whirring.

As he stood collecting himself, the elevator jerked to life again. It passed his landing, rising to the upper floors.

Something niggled at Anirudh. It was nothing to do with Rustom, or the photograph, or the paintings. Rather it was something about the wall and the tiles. As he stared at the tiles a conviction grew inside him that he had seen them before. They were embossed with the image of a lion, which on closer scrutiny proved to be a replica of the lions outside. It was as the elevator was descending, with Mr Singh's voice issuing from its door, that a bulb flashed in Anirudh's head.

The thought took his breath away.

No, it couldn't be. It was absurd to conjecture that Rustom had duplicated even this in his house. But the setting was identical. The size of the photo frame corresponded with the frame of his dream; the tiles on the wall were alike and their height tallied with the image in his head.

Anirudh's heart beat rapidly. A tingling sensation spread in his hands and feet. Vikram and Mr Singh had already returned to the lobby. He didn't have much time. If he wanted to test his hunch, he would have to do it now.

Anirudh stepped forward. His hands grasped the photo frame and lifted it off the hooks that held it in place. There was a film of dust where the photo had rested: dark and perfectly rectangular, a shadow on the wall. Anirudh brushed the dust away. His hands shaking, he ran his fingers carefully along the dusted section. There were two protuberances on the wall, hairbreadth projections about a foot apart; so minuscule that only a person aware of their existence would have noticed. Placing a thumb on each of them, Anirudh pressed. Nothing happened. Gathering his breath, Anirudh pushed hard, leaning against the protuberances.

This time there was a wrenching sound and Anirudh felt something move. A slit had appeared amidst the tiles. Anirudh pushed harder. There was a groaning noise, as if a creature asleep for centuries was reluctantly stirring, and then a set of tiles thrust forward from the wall, showering fragments of cement and paint on the carpeted floor.

A rectangular cavity, like a postbox slot, lay revealed behind the displaced tiles. Inside the cavity was a tray lying in a mess of dirt and lumps of dark, flaky material. It was clear that no one had sprung the mechanism in years, possibly decades. Anirudh brushed the muck away. Working quickly, his fingers encountered something wooden beneath the grime. Guessing from its outline that it was a box or chest of some sort, he grasped its edges and pulled. The box was heavy. Heaving it clear off the tray, he extricated it from the wall.

Fine dust billowed everywhere, like a cloud. Anirudh exhaled, hoping to keep the dust out, but when he was forced finally to inhale, it invaded his nostrils prompting him to sneeze violently. Clutching the box, he backed away from the wall, sneezing convulsively. Dropping the box on the ground, he pulled a handkerchief from his pocket and buried his nose in it, trying desperately to quell his explosive exhalations.

A voice called from somewhere.

Sneezing uncontrollably, Anirudh stumbled to the wall and grasping the protruding tiles, he pushed. There was resistance, but he countered it, pushing hard and the tiles slid back, falling in place with a discernible click.

The call was repeated and he heard the muffled thud of footsteps.

Panic-stricken, he stared about him. The wooden box lay on the floor beside the photo frame. Unslinging his backpack, he leapt for the box. Still sneezing, he frantically unzipped his pack and stuffed the box inside. Shouldering his pack he dashed to the wall and bent over the photo frame.

A stern voice barked behind Anirudh. 'The frame and the photo are hotel property. What may I ask are you up to?'

Anirudh jumped, turning guiltily, like a schoolboy caught in the act of stealing.

A short man stood on the landing beside the stairs. Though tears from his sneezing blurred Anirudh's vision, there was no mistaking the accusation on the newcomer's face.

Anirudh straightened himself, the frame clasped in his hands. He blurted the first words that came to his head.

'The photo had come loose, dangling to one side,' he croaked. 'I brought it down so I could put it back properly.'

Anirudh reached up and the frame strings snagged on the wall hooks on his first attempt. Taking care to centre the photograph, he faced the man, smiling sheepishly.

It was clear the man did not believe Anirudh. The look of disbelief on his face said it all. His eyes swept the passage floor taking in the grit and dirt on the carpet and the overlay of fine dust on the floor and on Anirudh's clothes.

'You've been up to something here, young man,' he said in a sharp voice. 'I don't know what it is, but you are going to tell me or I am going to call in my men to search you. Have you taken anything from here? What's inside that backpack?'

'Nothing!' ejaculated Anirudh. 'Just my books. I'm done with college for the day. My friend is with your attendant, Mr Singh. He is inquiring about rooms. I was simply waiting for him.'

'There you are, Anirudh!' exclaimed a voice.

Vikram!

'I was wondering where you'd got to. Come on. I'm done. It's getting late. There are other hotels we have to check.'

Anirudh turned.

Vikram and Mr Singh had climbed the stairs and were walking towards them.

'Do you know this boy?' asked the short man, addressing Mr Singh.

'They are friends,' replied Mr Singh, halting beside the short man. 'This young man here needs rooms.' Mr Singh pointed at Vikram. 'The requirement is for a marriage party. Twelve rooms for ten days next month.'

The short man's gaze switched to Vikram. His moustache was thin and the hair on his head was sparse. He wore his pants low, below a bulging stomach. His complexion was pale. The nametag on the lapel of his jacket identified him as Mr Palkhivala, the manager.

'The rooms are excellent,' said Vikram brightly. 'I shall tell my father.' He fished his wallet from his pocket and extracted a card and handed it to Mr Palkhivala. 'This is my father's card. He lives in Delhi. He will insist on a good price, of course. I would have liked to spend more time with you, but I am in a rush. There are two more hotels I have to see. You can talk directly to my father.'

Vikram shook hands with Mr Singh and a bemused Mr Palkhivala. Placing his hand on Anirudh's arm, he led him to the stairs. Descending quickly, they hurried through the lobby. Striding through the veranda they crossed the courtyard and stepped out on to the street.

COLABA

'It's unbelievable . . . UNBELIEVABLE!' exclaimed Anirudh. 'I had prayed to find proof . . . but this—' he clenched his fists and shut his eyes, 'This is beyond my wildest imagination.'

'Whoa!' laughed Vikram. 'Here we go again. You're like a talking parrot. That's probably the hundredth time you've squawked the word "unbelievable". It's getting a bit tiring. Why don't you try other adjectives? Words like—'

'Incredible, amazing, astounding,' blurted Anirudh.

'Yeah, and how about supernatural, otherworldly, miraculous—'

'Hey!' cried Anirudh. 'There's nothing supernatural or otherworldly about this. My dream might have seemed so. But that was only till we entered Seawind. Now it's flesh and blood, as you describe it. Rustom is the real thing. The paintings are documentary proof. They testify my dream; they are the ultimate stamp of authenticity.'

They were on Colaba Causeway, seated in a restaurant, a five-minute walk from Hotel Seawind. After bursting out of the hotel gate Anirudh had run blindly down the road, and when they had turned a corner, he had whooped and leapt in joy. Vikram had steered him away from curious bystanders who had stopped to stare. Anirudh had continued to prance and skip like a child, and Vikram had clung firmly to his arm and led him away from the hotel to the Causeway. Finding a restaurant amongst the mass of shops that lined the Causeway's cluttered pavement, he had settled him there.

The restaurant was brightly lit, yet Anirudh's eyes managed to overpower their brilliance. His face mirrored the elation of an archaeologist who had stumbled upon a fabled lost city.

'Face-to-face,' he babbled. 'Rustom . . . right before my eyes . . . on that canvas. The most exhilarating moment of my life. The spookiest also, I have to admit. The image I have of him is the one from my dream. That of Rustom in his prime—a youngster—a boyish Rustom. In that hotel, on that canvas, was this mature adult, aged fifty, or whatever. You can imagine what I felt like. It's like you see me as I am today and in twenty-four hours there is this apparition of me three times my age staring at you. It can blow you off your feet, seeing something like that, I swear to you. That's how I felt as I stared at the painting—a creepy something sucking at my insides. Yet the recognition was instantaneous. Believe me, Vikram—this is the real thing.'

'I don't need convincing,' assured Vikram. 'It isn't possible for anyone to walk into a hotel the first time in his life and set off a mechanism that hasn't been activated in years. What you pulled off there is a confirmatory test for

129

even the most sceptical person on earth. Yes, Rustom lived, and, echoing your pet adjective, unbelievably, not only have you stumbled on proof of his existence, but in addition, we now know he came back to Bombay.'

'Yes . . . he came back,' whispered Anirudh, eyes shining even brighter, a pair of incandescent bulbs now. 'He fulfilled his dream too, building the house he always wanted. His goal—one of the many he had—was to be rich and successful. He achieved his ambition for sure—on that front, at least.'

'If indeed it is Rustom who built Seawind, then he surely was a rich man,' said Vikram. 'Obviously, Wallace's treasure helped. He was the sole inheritor of all that wealth, after all.'

Anirudh's euphoria vanished suddenly, like sunlight in a cloud. He glowered, outraged. 'That's nonsense!' he cried.

'I see,' said Vikram evenly. 'I take it you didn't just establish Rustom's identity from the portrait, but in some mystical manner, the source of his wealth too.'

'You speak as if you were the one who experienced the dream, not me.' Anirudh glared indignantly at Vikram. 'If you had known Rustom, you wouldn't for a moment have doubted he was self-made. The Rustom I knew was ambitious, sincere, hard-working and a very capable young man. He might have dipped into the treasure on Koleshwar.' Anirudh shrugged. 'There's no saying whether he actually did or ever needed to. But the fact that after all these years there is still treasure on Koleshwar proves he didn't depend upon it. There isn't any evidence, sure, but knowing him as I do through my dream, I am certain he returned penniless from Koleshwar and made a success of his life through his own efforts.'

Vikram did not agree but, sensing deep-rooted truculence, kept his reservations to himself.

A white-shirted waiter placed two frosted glasses of iced tea on their table.

Anirudh's face had turned a deep red. He refused to look at Vikram as he sipped cold tea, preferring instead to stare at the backpack at his feet.

Ignoring the awkward pause, Vikram resumed their discussion. Steering safe from controversy, he chose a neutral topic. 'The concealed safe indicates Rustom had tied up with Mario and Ajit when he returned, doesn't it?' he queried.

'It does,' nodded Anirudh. He dragged his eyes from the backpack and met Vikram's gaze. 'The mechanism is identical to the one Mario had installed for Jehangirbhai. The safe is a sure pointer that Rustom renewed his acquaintance with them. Rustom valued companionship and friends above all else and, after Irfan, they were his closest friends. It's possible he met up with Forjett too. That depends on when he returned though . . . whether it was before Forjett left India.'

'He would be taking a risk, wouldn't he?' asked Vikram. 'Didn't you say Rustom and Irfan were fugitives and that Forjett had said he would be forced to arrest them if they came back?'

'The fugitive branding was only for Irfan,' clarified Anirudh. The wrathful red had faded from his cheeks and his eyes were aglow again. 'Rustom hadn't done anything wrong. Sure, Rustom must have kept a low profile after returning, but if Forjett was still around, he would certainly have met up with him. Don't forget, Forjett genuinely liked Rustom. He would have landed Rustom a job again if he requested.'

Anirudh's gaze returned to his backpack.

'You are itching to see what's inside, aren't you?' asked Vikram.

'Of course I am.' He compressed his lips, 'But this isn't the place.'

'It isn't,' acknowledged Vikram. 'I'm glad you agree. If it was Aditya, I'd have a fight on my hands holding him back.' He smiled fleetingly. 'What do you think is inside?'

Anirudh nudged the pack with his foot.

'It's heavy for sure. It doesn't rattle, which makes me believe that there's just one thing inside, not a collection of small things, but I could be wrong. Could be anything. I have no idea, no clue.'

'Think it might be gold?' asked Vikram. 'Or jewellery?'

'Nah . . . it isn't heavy enough for gold. Jewellery?' Anirudh shrugged. 'Could be . . . but it doesn't have that feel.'

'It's something Rustom thought important enough to hide away,' observed Vikram.

'How do you know it was Rustom?' challenged Anirudh. 'One of his descendants might have been aware of the existence of the vault. He might have placed something in it.'

'That's true. You're right. Could be anybody's stuff in there.' Vikram swigged a mouthful of tea. 'Who do you think owns Seawind?' he asked. 'Do you think it's run by Rustom's descendants?'

'Did you notice the name of the Parsee manager?' asked Anirudh.

Vikram nodded. 'That's what got me thinking actually. Rustom's brother-in-law was a Palkhivala, wasn't he?'

'Yes,' nodded Anirudh.

Vikram stared at the glass in his hand, thinking.

'No,' he said finally. 'Linking him to the Palkhivala of your dream isn't exactly rational. Too many years have passed.'

'That's how I read it too,' said Anirudh. 'But it's an interesting coincidence.' He raised his glass and drained it in a single gulp. 'My guess is that the hotel is Parsee-owned or, at the very least, Parsee-run. Parsees are noted for keeping their properties spic-and-span, and you saw the condition of Seawind.'

'Outstanding,' said Vikram. 'No peeling paint, no dust, no grime. Everything sparkled.'

'Yup, excellent maintenance, which builds a case for Parsee involvement. But that's speculation still, doesn't prove ownership. For me, the most significant outcome of our visit, besides establishing Rustom's existence that is, is that it was Rustom who built the building. That's something I'm dead certain about.'

'I'm with you there,' concurred Vikram.

'Though, I'm sure that Rustom did not construct Seawind as a hotel. He built it as his home, a large opulent home, yes, but not a hotel. Somewhere along the line, it was converted—for business reasons I would imagine.

It couldn't have been Rustom who turned it into a hotel. He wouldn't. His descendants must have made the decision to commercialize the place.'

'Property prices?' queried Vikram.

'Obviously! Think about it. Does anyone live in such big houses nowadays? No one; unless of course you are a crorepati many times over. The value of Seawind must have shot through the roof with the years. Getting back to your question of who is running the hotel, it is possible that Rustom's descendants still do; the Parsee touch seems to indicate so. But—' He made a face. '—like most conclusions we are leaping to, it's questionable too. The place could have been sold off. Who knows?'

'We can only guess,' agreed Vikram. He drained the remnants of his glass. 'I wonder,' he continued, turning the empty glass in his hand, 'whether Rustom's living descendants have any idea of their ancestor and his life. It is a wonderful story after all. Full of achievement, loyalty and valour, certainly something to be proud of if associated with one's lineage.' He set the glass on the table, frowning. 'Yet I kind of doubt it. Too many years have passed, haven't they? I myself have little idea of my great grandparents or great, great grandparents or ancestors before them. No one told me and I'm sure no records exist either.'

Anirudh pondered Vikram's remark. 'It's true,' he said. 'Memories of ancestors are forgotten with time. But Parsees, at least those that I know, are different. They maintain their genealogy through family trees. They consider it important. But why are you talking only of Rustom's story? There's Mario and Ajit's too.'

Vikram shook his head. 'Nah. I don't see Ajit and Mario's story surviving. One has to achieve something for their memoirs to be recorded and endure. Rustom's life was remarkable. Seawind is a testament to what he achieved. An ancestor like that is someone to be proud of. If Rustom was part of my family, we would recall him with great pride.'

'Yes . . . I agree. But we're still talking of a 150-year-old history.' Anirudh's tone was doubtful. 'It would be wonderful if Rustom's heirs remember him. I certainly hope they have enshrined his memory. But one has to be realistic.'

The waiter returned. Collecting their empty glasses, he asked whether they needed more refreshments. When Anirudh shook his head, he placed a bill on their table and withdrew.

Anirudh snatched the bill, refusing to let Vikram pay.

'I called you to Bombay, you are my guest,' he said, rummaging in his wallet for change.

'Thanks,' said Vikram, accepting graciously.

Anirudh placed money on the table and the waiter collected it.

'That Palkhivala,' said Vikram. 'He suspects something. You know that, right?'

'Yes, I do,' said Anirudh, reaching for his backpack.

'All that muck on the ground, dust everywhere, even on you.' Vikram pushed his chair back and rose to his feet.

Anirudh slung his backpack on his shoulder and rose. 'What does it matter? He'll never know what happened. There's no way he'll ever locate Mario's pin-sized knobs.

They are superbly crafted, almost flush with the wall. I found them only because I knew they were there. Anyway, who cares? The safe's contents are with me.' He grinned.

'What next?' asked Vikram, as they tramped towards the restaurant doors.

A roar of noise greeted them as they stepped on to the pavement outside. A large truck, commandeering a considerable width of the road, had halted nearby. Traffic on the Causeway was heavy and the offending vehicle had drawn the ire of the drivers of the cars jammed behind it.

Anirudh had to shout his reply. 'This, of course,' he said, pointing at his backpack. 'I'm going home.'

'You want to be alone?'

'Well—' Anirudh shuffled his feet.

A bus was adding to the commotion, its driver revving his engine aggressively and furiously pressing his horn.

'It's okay,' said Vikram, shouting to make himself heard. 'I understand. The stuff in your bag is personal . . . between you and Rustom.' Anirudh looked relieved. 'In any case, I have to leave soon,' he continued, looking at his watch. 'My aunt and uncle must have returned by now. I have to catch my bus from Churchgate Station. How long a walk is the station from here?'

'Hey, that's my bus,' said Anirudh, his attention drawn to the powerfully protesting vehicle. He turned to Vikram. 'The walk is twenty minutes. I have to go now. We'll talk. If we don't, show up at my place tomorrow morning, ten-ish or so. The car from Pune will have arrived by then. Thanks for everything. Ciao. See you later.'

Vikram watched as Anirudh dashed towards a bus stop further down the road. The erring truck driver, prompted no doubt by the fact that he was responsible for the commotion, started his vehicle and shifting it, freed the way. Immediately, as if a blocked pipe had been cleared, the cars sorted themselves out and traffic flowed again. The impatient bus driver sped forward and halted at the bus stop with a shrill squealing of brakes. Vikram watched as Anirudh boarded, clutching his precious backpack. He waved as the bus started forward and Anirudh waved back, smiling.

Vikram made to turn away and then halted.

A car was cruising down the road. The vehicle was a sparkling-white I-10. It wasn't the car that had arrested Vikram's attention; it was the man behind its wheel. The driver was short and bald, his head barely topping the steering wheel. Managing only a glimpse, Vikram thought the man was Mr Palkhivala of Seawind Hotel. The I-10 was instantly obscured behind a deluge of buses, taxis and cars, leaving Vikram no opportunity to confirm his fleeting impression.

Vikram went still. Could it be that Palkhivala was following Anirudh? It seemed unlikely. To begin with, he wasn't even sure if it was Palkhivala, and even conjecturing that it was him, the hotel manager could well be travelling on business that had nothing to do with them. But Vikram was a cautious boy by nature and he informed Anirudh, calling him on his cellphone.

'It's Palkhivala, all right,' confirmed Anirudh. 'I can see him from my bus window. The same bald head and glasses. Do you think he suspects something and is after me?'

'I honestly have no idea, Anirudh. I just thought I'd inform you.'

'Thanks. I'll keep an eye out for him. We're caught in a traffic jam right now. He doesn't seem interested in the bus. He's staring out of the window, at nothing in particular.'

'Keep a look out, especially when you hop off the bus. Call me if you see any funny behaviour.'

Anirudh laughed. 'You're like a mother hen, Vikram, suspicious about everything. I'll call if there's a problem. Ciao.'

MALABAR HILL

It was evening and Bombay's rush hour had begun in earnest. There was no call from Anirudh, so Mr Palkhivala and his car slipped from Vikram's thoughts as he hiked to Churchgate Station. The walk wasn't enjoyable, as for most of the distance he was hustled by a stream of humanity surging turbulently towards the station. It was as Vikram was crossing the Oval Maidan that his phone rang. Detaching himself from the crowd, he stepped off the paved track and answered the call.

It was Chitra.

'Hi!' he greeted, puzzled but glad to hear her voice. 'What's up?'

'Listen,' whispered Chitra. 'This is a quick call. I have to preserve my battery, as I can't charge it here.' She paused and then her voice turned sugary sweet. 'Do you know where I'm calling you from?'

'Yes!' recollected Vikram. 'You're out in the hills with Salim. You lucky so and so.'

Chitra's laugh pealed like tinkling bells through the airwaves. 'I'm up here on the very mountain that Anirudh passed out on, Koleshwar. And where exactly are you?' she queried.

'At the Oval in South Mumbai, if you must know. In the midst of tens of thousands of people, caught in a stampede to reach Churchgate Station.'

Chitra's voice turned sugary again; even sweeter this time. 'Let me describe where I am. It's evening and I'm at the edge of the mountain where the cliffs drop away. There's no one here. Just me and the clouds and the valley. It's cold; I'm wearing a sweater. The mists are swirling. I can see snatches of the valley and Dhom Lake far below. There are so many waterfalls that I can't count. It's green everywhere, the kind that glows. The view is intensely beautiful and wild—'

'Stop rubbing it in,' barked Vikram, interrupting Chitra's merry flow.

Standing at the edge of a crush of humanity, with the buzz of traffic snarling in his ears, Vikram found it impossible to imagine the serenity and wild beauty of the high Sahyadri.

Chitra snickered loudly. 'Serves you right for choosing Mumbai instead of hanging with me. Too bad Aditya isn't around either. He and his paragliding!' Chitra snorted.

'Is Salim with you?' inquired Vikram.

'He preferred to spend the night in the valley, at his home in the village.'

'What about those men?' asked Vikram. 'The ones who attacked us. Isn't he taking a chance returning to his village?'

'We checked at the police station. Salim had to report there, remember? So, we stopped by there first. There's been no progress in the case as you might have guessed. The only thing they've been doing is keeping an eye out for those men, but there has been no sign of them. So Salim mustered the courage to spend the night at his home. He even offered me space in his hut, but I chose to be up here. It's infinitely nicer on the mountain. There's a cute Dhangar village up here. It isn't far from that darwaza where Kiran and Aditya's stone-hurling battle took place. There are only four huts; simple ones, made from mud and thatch. The people who live here are called Dhangars. They are poor but decent and hospitable. They've let me spend the night with them. I have a hut all to myself—besides two buffaloes that is. They are a mother and calf pair, adorably cute, even though they are a bit smelly. The Dhangars are happy to have me. I'm paying for my stay and the women cook meals for me. Nothing fancy. Roti, dal, rice and lots of chillies. Fresh and wholesome food.'

'Mmm . . .' mouthed Vikram, imagining smoke from a wood fire and the mouthwatering smell of dal and rotis. 'What about snakes?' he asked. 'Did you find those shieldtails you were searching for?'

'Not yet. Most of our day was spent on travel and at the police station. We have the entire day tomorrow. Salim is upbeat, so I'm hopeful we'll find them. My plan is to visit the cave too, the one Anirudh fell in. The cobra that startled Anirudh might still be there. I want to find it and explore for more snakes.'

'On second thoughts, these crowds and the noisy traffic aren't so bad, you know,' said Vikram. 'All of a sudden I'm happy not being there with you.'

Chitra giggled. 'You guys are all the same . . . Wimps!' She paused, expecting Vikram to hotly contest her slur. But aware he was being baited, Vikram refused to respond. Laughing, she continued, 'I'll have to go now. Apologize to Anirudh on my behalf for not calling him. I have to go easy on my battery, and I still have to speak to my mom and dad.'

Exchanging goodbyes, Vikram resumed his journey. Forging a path through the station throng, Vikram located his bus stop and attached himself to a long queue of patient commuters. It was after two buses had arrived and carted off the front section of the queue that his phone rang again.

The call was from his father, and he was not in a good mood.

'What is this nonsense about me wanting rooms for a marriage party? Were you trying to be funny? If you were pulling someone's leg, your joke has backfired. I thought you knew better than to use my card for stupid pranks.'

Vikram clapped his hand to his head. Palkhivala! It had never been his intention to hand the hotel manager his father's card, but the immediate need for deflecting the man's attention had forced him to. Vikram had meant to tell his father to expect a call but had forgotten.

'I'm sorry, Dad,' he apologized. 'Terribly sorry. I meant to warn you, but it completely slipped my mind. What . . . what did the man say?'

'Nothing at all! He understood at once that you had pulled a prank on him. He muttered something and hung up. I'm deeply disappointed, Vikram. I had never expected something as incredibly stupid as this from you. I thought you were grown up and responsible. Obviously, I'm wrong.'

Vikram tried to defend himself, but his father refused to entertain his efforts and disconnected curtly.

The bus journey to Malabar Hill was painfully slow as the entire city of Bombay seemed embroiled in one endless traffic snarl. Although Vikram managed to land himself a window seat, the bus ride could hardly be termed enjoyable. He disembarked finally as the light started to fade and trudged along a wet, tree-lined road to his uncle's building.

Vikram's uncle Satish was the elder of two brothers of his late mother. Since his grandparents were also no more, his mother's brothers were Vikram's only surviving maternal family. Both lived in Bombay and Vikram was yet to come across a pair of brothers with such contrasting personalities. The younger brother, Mr Sunil Nair, was a flamboyant and hugely successful businessman whose sole passion in life was money and everything involved in the earning and accumulation of it. Satish, the elder brother, was a scientist, an astrophysicist, whose chief pleasures in life, besides his work, were travelling, reading, wildlife and music. Vikram had little in common with Sunil uncle and his family and consequently did not enjoy spending time with them. Satish uncle, however, was always a delight. He and his silver-haired wife, Geetha—a mathematician and scientist too—were fun-loving, uncomplicated people who genuinely loved him and took a deep interest in his upbringing and welfare.

Their home was a small flat on the thirteenth floor of a tall building on Malabar Hill with a wonderful view of the splendid necklace-like sweep of Bombay's famous Marine Drive. Satish was a balding, middle-aged man, thin except for noticeable padding about his stomach, which Vikram enjoyed teasing him about. Geetha was slim and graceful, and her lustrous white hair contrasted elegantly with her dark complexion. Having just returned from Alibag, they were relaxing on their balcony, drinking tea when Vikram arrived. He was greeted with enthusiastic warm hugs. His cheeks were pinched and his hair fondly ruffled.

'Looks just the same,' said Satish, inspecting Vikram closely, as if he were an exotic fruit he wished to purchase.

'Hair's a bit longer,' said Geetha, a touch of disapproval in her voice.

'You should be happy he hasn't coloured it and that he isn't sporting an earring.'

'Should I show you my tattoos?' asked Vikram with a straight face.

They both looked at him with horror.

Vikram guffawed, laughing heartily. 'That was a good one, even if I have to say so myself. You should have seen yourselves.'

Geetha made a face and smacked him lightly on the shoulder. She pulled up a chair for him and poured him a cup of tea.

'Why the hurry?' she asked, placing the cup before him. 'You were to join us at the end of the month.'

'My friend Anirudh wanted me to come down,' replied Vikram.

'The one who had that fall in the cave, right? You said he had recovered, I recollect.'

Vikram updated them about Anirudh, steering clear of the dream and their extraordinary afternoon investigation.

'He called me down, probably because he was lonely and needed company . . . I couldn't refuse,' he ended.

They chatted companionably, discussing whatever came to mind, except scientific pursuits, which his uncle and aunt never talked about, as they believed firmly that their work interested only fellow scientists. Vikram enjoyed himself immensely. He loved their company and also their balcony and its fabulous view.

Their cosy sit-out commanded a panoramic vista of the southern reaches of Mumbai, with the harbour and the distant hills of the mainland beyond added in as a bonus. It was dusk already and the harbour and the sea were in shadow. But the streets of Mumbai were radiantly lit, their brightness spilling into the sea and illuminating the sky too. On Marine Drive, the headlamps of the cars were a river of sharp brilliance, and in the harbour, ship lights twinkled like a knot of fireflies.

Vikram was aware that both his uncle and aunt possessed a deep knowledge of the city. He steered the conversation to the city's history, a topic he knew his uncle enjoyed.

'Tell me,' he said, during a lull, 'is it true that Bombay comprised of several islands once?'

'Seven, dear,' said Geetha. 'There were seven islands here.'

'See, that's the beauty of it,' said Satish. 'No one can tell. They did a brilliant job fusing them all. Now Bombay is just one big island.'

'It was mostly the British who bridged the islands,' said Geetha. 'Took them several hundred years. They worked on and off, whenever they had the funds that is.'

'During that period there was also a place called the Esplanade, wasn't there?' asked Vikram.

Satish sat upright in his chair. 'How on earth do you know about the Esplanade?'

'There's a plaque at Oval Maidan. It said the area used to be called the Esplanade.'

'That's observant of you,' said Satish, looking approvingly at Vikram. 'Yes, the Esplanade was a huge open area spread over all the maidans and then a lot more too. No trees or anything grew on it. It was just one big flat expanse fronting the sea. The history books say that it was a fine area where the sea winds blew.'

'The British had their reasons,' added Geetha. 'They hacked down any tree that dared to raise its leafy crown on the Esplanade; not a shrub, not a bush was allowed to grow. Their aim was to keep a clear view of the area. They were afraid of being attacked in those days. Trees would shelter their assailants. But an open ground would expose the enemy and give a clear view to their gunners in their Fort. Cannons bristled along the Fort ramparts, primed and ready to blow their imaginary enemies to bits. Yes, the Esplanade was a pretty place, but it had strategic value also.'

'Clever of them,' said Vikram. 'I would never have thought of it that way.' He smiled, clearly impressed. 'You know, I was walking there today and for the first time, I truly looked at the buildings: the University, the Court, Flora Fountain, the Clock Tower. I've been there so often before, but I never really noticed them. They are fine buildings.'

'That's a refreshing development dear, that you are actually using your eyes,' said Geetha. 'Most young people don't. Yes, the architecture there is magnificent. If you want to see something truly outstanding, visit the Chatrapati Shivaji Terminus. The railway station is one of the finest examples of Gothic architecture in the world.'

'The British built a great city here,' said Satish. 'But the odd thing is that they weren't the first European power to rule Bombay.'

'It was the Portuguese, wasn't it?' said Vikram.

'You are a knowledgeable boy,' said Satish. 'The Portuguese were here first. They won the islands from a local raja in those days.' Satish laughed. 'The Portuguese must have rued the day they presented the islands to the British. They handed them to the British back in the 1600s as a dowry when the then king of England, King Charles, that was his name I believe, married a Portuguese princess.'

Satish leaned forward, eyes gleaming, clearly enjoying himself.

'The Portuguese thought it a masterstroke in those days. They believed they were getting away cheap, gifting a set of marshy mosquito-ridden islands, worthless to man and beast. The king of England too was afflicted with the same shortsightedness. He didn't think much of his dowry either, because he then rented the islands to the British East India Company for the princely amount of ten pounds a year; so ridiculous a sum that it makes me laugh. It was the Company's men who saw the light. They were the intelligent ones. They understood the value of Bombay's splendid harbour and saw potential in its strategic location on India's west coast. It was the East India Company that transformed the islands into a major trading centre.

They laid the foundations of one of India's greatest cities. Understandably the British showed tremendous reluctance to leave when the time came. But our dear freedom fighters were a persistent lot and they made it impossible for them to hang about. Of course, we've made certain changes since they left . . .'

'Bloated the city to an unmanageable size for starters,' interjected Geetha.

'Yes, it has grown,' agreed Satish. 'But then so has our population. People lament over a lost Bombay. Your dad cries the loudest, Vikram.'

'I've heard the two of you argue,' said Vikram.

'Like little children,' said Geetha. She raised a finger at her husband who was turning red. 'Don't you get started again. You are like a child when it comes to defending your beloved city.' Changing the subject, she turned to Vikram. 'Tell me about your trek to that plateau opposite Mahabaleshwar. What did you call the place? Koleshwar . . . right? It sounds so interesting. I'd like to visit it one day.'

They chatted long into the night. Having no children themselves, Geetha and Satish treated Vikram like their son and were always curious about him and his activities. Vikram, in turn, enjoyed their company, not just because they doted on him but also because just being with them was a refreshing and enriching experience. Both were extremely well-read and Vikram acquired keen insights on an array of subjects ranging from the latest revelations of the Hubble Space Telescope to erudite discourses on the performance of the Indian cricket team.

Their conversation was interrupted when the phone rang. Geetha returned with the instrument. 'For you, Vikram.' She covered the mouthpiece with her hand and spoke in an undertone. 'It's Suresh. He had called earlier in the evening, he somehow got to know you were here.'

Vikram groaned inwardly. Suresh was the eldest son of his other uncle, Sunil Nair. Suresh was eight years older than Vikram, and as there was little in common between them, Vikram found his company tiresome. Vikram hadn't breathed a word of his visit to his cousin or members of his family, but the news had obviously leaked.

Suresh's voice was loud, like his manner.

'Saw you this evening, crossing the road at Churchgate. You should have told me, I would have given you a lift in my brand new Honda. I couldn't halt because the cops would have taken my number.'

Vikram experienced a surge of appreciation for Churchgate's chaotic traffic and the hapless policemen who conducted it. The bus ride home, despite all its discomforts, was infinitely preferable to being closeted with Suresh and listening to him gloat about his new car. He mumbled a false apology, indicating that his trip wasn't planned.

'Never mind,' responded Suresh, his voice effusive and loud. 'We can have breakfast together tomorrow. You are in luck. I have a meeting at the Taj at 9.30. Correction, we'll have to change the breakfast to coffee, if that's okay. Breakfasts take forever there, and I don't have the time. I'll treat you to coffee at the Sea Lounge Restaurant. You'll love it. Be down at 8.30 sharp. I'll pick you up.'

Vikram hesitated, his mind ticking furiously, seeking an excuse. But Geetha admonished him with a finger, and though the prospect of breakfast with his cousin was as rousing as an outing with a self-infatuated peacock, he obediently accepted.

Both Vikram and Satish glared accusingly at Geetha when the conversation ended, but she crushed their protests with a wave of her hand.

'Suresh is his cousin. He may be a conceited boy, but as he has taken the trouble to call, Vikram must go.'

There was no further mention of Suresh and his family. A mild gloom settled on Vikram, but only briefly, evaporating quickly when their discussion resumed. Time passed companionably. Dinner was served on the balcony. Later the moon broke through the clouds, showering its pearly radiance on them.

It was well past midnight when they finally retired. The window in Vikram's bedroom possessed an identical view to that of the balcony. Though he was tired, Vikram stood at the window for a long time. The lights of the city blazed undimmed despite the late hour. Although it was impossible to distinguish the Fort area, Vikram turned his gaze in its general direction. Visions of the Esplanade and the Fort swam before his eyes. Irfan, Rustom, Forjett and all the characters of Anirudh's dream flitted ghostlike in his thoughts. Recollecting finally that he had to wake early the next day he turned away, and the image he fell asleep with was of the sky and clouds and the moon shedding its silver light on the shadowed sea.

SEAWIND AGAIN

The morning commenced with a blur of activity: a quick shower, a kiss for Geetha and a hug for Satish, hurried goodbyes, and a promise to return at the end of the month. The elevator rushed Vikram to the parking lot where a fancy new Honda, dazzling red and shining all over, waited for him.

The drive to the Taj was worse than what Vikram had braced himself for. Predictably, Suresh started by gloating about his latest toy. The capabilities of his car were described in excruciating detail, along with the fancy gadgets he had installed. Suresh was particularly proud that his father had paid only half the cost of the vehicle, underscoring smugly that he had managed the rest from his own salary—a detail that impressed even a grudging Vikram. But Suresh instantly quashed Vikram's budding regard for him by boasting that the car was only temporary and that very soon he would have an even more expensive one. In the time it took to reach their destination—thankfully very quickly, as the roads were empty—Vikram learnt whatever there was to know about Suresh's job and how he had twice won awards, for the best new recruit and also the best employee.

By the time he stepped into the elegant corridors of the Taj, Vikram had resigned himself to a dismal morning. But on entering its much-acclaimed Sea Lounge Restaurant and being seated beside a large window overlooking the harbour, his mood underwent a remarkable reversal and he started to enjoy himself. The promenade he and Anirudh had walked on the previous day was immediately below. Pigeons fluttered in the still air outside, and morning walkers, enjoying the early freshness, marched stiffly, chests out and hands swinging. In addition, the window flaunted a splendid view of the harbour waters with its complement of bobbing ships. In the far distance, the hills of the mainland, like the ships, looked as if they were afloat too, marooned between water and a cloud-speckled sky.

The magnificence of the vista was entirely lost on Suresh as after a mere glance, he turned his eyes from the window. Suresh was a young man with a thick head of hair, swept back and combed carefully behind his ears. His jacket was draped on the chair behind him, and he wore a bright blue shirt with a red tie. His eyes were dark and piercing. The nervous energy Vikram had noticed in him on the last occasion they had met was visibly evident. It showed in the velocity of his speech, in the jerkiness of his gestures, and the quivering of his throat.

'You're losing direction, Vikram!' he exclaimed, as a smartly attired waiter poured coffee for them. 'All this nonsense about wildlife and environment won't get you anywhere. Life is all about making the right choices.'

Suresh had never thought highly of his cousin's ambition of a career in wildlife and conservation, and he never failed to voice his disapproval.

'I see nothing wrong with my choice,' said Vikram neutrally.

'It's not going to fetch you any money,' came the blunt rejoinder. Suresh was always swift to the point. Like a pugilist he glared at Vikram, challenging him to dispute his contention.

Vikram spoke calmly. 'Of course I'll make money,' he said. 'Wildlifers get paid for their work, if you must know.'

Suresh glared at Vikram. 'I'm talking of real moolah,' he snorted. 'Not about crumbs and handouts. There'll be no sexy cars for you. No great pad. You'll lead a down-market lifestyle. No breakfasts in places like this.' He waved a hand.

'This is a great place, Suresh, and thanks for bringing me here. But I can assure you I will have breakfasts in places infinitely better than this: like on a veranda on a mountainside with a view of the Himalayas; or on a beach overlooking a crystal-clear lagoon with a coral reef below. Could also be in a forest with trees and birds and wildlife all around me.'

Suresh snorted again, more forcibly this time. 'I know about your forests! You guys spin a myth around them, making them out to be so heavenly and beautiful. You never tell people of the insects, the snakes and those horrible mosquitoes that infest them. Even your coral reefs and lagoons are nothing but eyewash. It's hot and miserable on those beaches and there's no air-conditioning. Same thing about your mountains. There are no loos in those places, no hot water, not even proper beds. Come on . . . stop trying to have me on. Your kind of forests and mountains will never top this.'

Vikram stared at Suresh. They were cousins, they shared the same blood, but the gulf between them was enormous, an ocean in itself. He didn't even try to defend his beloved wilderness areas, so contemptuously dismissed by Suresh. He smiled and sipped his coffee instead.

Suresh launched into a monologue of the advantages of living in big cities, especially Bombay, the commercial and financial capital of the country. Vikram was thankful for the magnificent view from the window and also the first-rate coffee the restaurant served, as together they enabled him to endure Suresh's tiresome discourse. Vikram nodded, as if accepting whatever Suresh said, but he protested when the word 'environmentalist' cropped up and Suresh spat it out with undisguised contempt.

'It is becoming fashionable to deride people who stand up for the environment nowadays,' said Vikram, 'But you should know that they are the ones who protect the planet.'

'Protect the planet!' echoed Suresh, sarcasm dripping with every word. 'Protect the planet, my foot! Environmentalists are just a bunch of spoilsports. People without a vision, without a job, interested only in halting progress, simply because it pleases them, gives them something to do. My company has a mining division. We set it up because we need iron ore, a raw material for our products. But a bunch of idiots, masquerading as environmentalists, shut it down, saying that our mining was affecting a forest and troubling wildlife. I have never heard of a lamer reason, but can you believe it, they've taken us to court and our lawyers are telling us that they might even win.'

'There are very few forests left in our country, Suresh.' Vikram spoke dispassionately. 'About three per cent of our land area is reserved for forests. Don't you think we should preserve the precious little that remains?'

'What about progress?' cried Suresh. 'You can't halt progress for the sake of forests. Forget about mining; think about power. India desperately needs power, electricity to run the country, but environmentalists block power projects too, saying dams are bad because forests get submerged and people are displaced. What's all this about? We have to get our act together, progress with the rest of the world. A few forests gone, what does it matter? It's happening all over the world. Look at China . . .'

Vikram refrained from protesting any further. Arguing with Suresh was pointless, like banging his head against an unyielding wall. His efforts would only result in a splitting headache. He helped himself to several cups of excellent coffee instead. Their talk ended when a plump man, clutching a laptop and wearing a jacket similar to Suresh's hurried into the restaurant and halted at their table. The man spoke urgently to Suresh and withdrew, not sparing even a glance at Vikram.

'Have to go,' said Suresh, stuffing a bunch of notes into the fancy folder that contained their bill. 'My boss has insisted on certain changes in our presentation and it's got to be done before our clients arrive.'

Suresh surveyed Vikram with his dark eyes. 'Think about joining me one day,' he said earnestly. 'You are a sharp boy, Vikram. You have the brains to even go further than me. I know it.'

The flash of modesty from Suresh was entirely unexpected. Vikram's gaze softened. 'Wildlife and the outdoors are my life,' he said. 'They are my passion. Career choice should be guided by what one loves to do. Isn't that right?'

Suresh's gaze flickered with disapproval. 'You are young and idealistic.' He sighed as he rose from the table. 'One day you will realize that money is important too. We all need money, it gives us security. We need a lifestyle. You are my cousin; I don't want to see you making the wrong choices.'

There was genuine concern in Suresh's voice. His bluster and flamboyance notwithstanding, it was obvious to Vikram that Suresh cared for him.

Vikram was touched. He had always suspected that beneath his swagger and boastful ways there was a soft side to his cousin. Today he had stumbled upon it. As individuals, they were worlds apart. But their relationship had matured. It was possible now for them to agree to disagree and still be friends.

Though Suresh was in a hurry he accompanied Vikram to the hotel lobby.

'Get real,' he said in parting. 'The time has come for you. Make the right choices. Mail me when you change your mind.'

'You'll have to wait forever for that mail,' grinned Vikram, shaking hands.

Checking his watch as he stepped out of the hotel Vikram saw he had time on his hands, which suited him as a pleasant wind was blowing in from the harbour and the promenade looked bright and inviting.

Vikram fed pigeons. He smiled at tourists. He stared up at the gleaming walls of the Taj and identified the window where he had drunk coffee with Suresh. He gazed at the distant mainland, savouring the breeze. The harbour waters were far calmer today. The sea sloshed softly, breaking with barely a swell against the promenade wall. Deciding to stretch his legs he ambled along the walkway. Enjoying his stroll, he halted finally opposite the lion-crowned gates of Seawind Hotel.

Staring at its painted facade he was reminded of Anirudh and their exploits of the previous day. The mysterious box Anirudh had appropriated came to his mind. Unable to hold his curiosity in check he plucked his mobile from his pocket. But even before he could dial, his phone jangled, indicating an incoming call.

It was Smita Dongre, Anirudh's mother.

'Good morning, Vikram,' she greeted, her voice oddly breathless. 'Hope you are enjoying Mumbai.'

'I am,' replied Vikram, wondering what the call was about.

'Is Anirudh with you?' asked Smita. 'I'd like to speak with him.'

'Anirudh isn't with me,' said Vikram, his tone puzzled.

'But he is . . . he left a note on his bed saying so.'

'Note?' Vikram scratched his head. 'What note?'

'His grandmother found a note—' Smita broke off. 'Look this isn't a joke or something, is it? Because if it is, it isn't funny at all.'

'Joke? I assure you I'm not joking.'

'Then where is my son? I've been trying his number all morning, but he isn't answering his mobile. I got through finally to my mother when she woke up. She says he's not at home and that there's a slip of paper on his bed saying he has gone out with you.'

'But he isn't with me!' exclaimed Vikram. 'Give me a minute Smita aunty. This doesn't make sense. I'll call Aaji and get back to you.'

'Immediately!' Smita Dongre's nervousness surged across the airwaves.

'The minute I finish speaking with her,' assured Vikram.

He disconnected and called Aaji's Colaba landline.

The phone rang for nearly a minute before it was answered.

Aaji's voice turned furious when Vikram inquired about Anirudh. 'What is this, a joke or something?' she demanded. 'Isn't he with you?'

'No aunty,' said Vikram. 'I promise you he isn't with me.'

'Then why is there a note on his bed saying he has gone out with you? And why is his room such a shambles? This is my house, not his. I've never seen such a messed up room before.' She paused a moment, then Vikram heard an intake of breath. 'You boys are making a fool of me, are you? Anirudh is hiding with you and has left a note just to trick me. You boys want to laugh at me. Think you're smart, do you? Think you can joke with me because I'm old. Here, that's what I think of you!' There was a crashing sound and the line went dead.

Vikram stared at his phone, the old lady's anger ringing in his ear. A note saying Anirudh had gone with him? Why on earth would Anirudh write such a note?

As he stood there mystified, the polished gate of Seawind Hotel was pulled back and the short, portly figure of Palkhivala stepped out. For a moment Vikram considered slinking away, because, if he chanced to look across the road, Palkhivala would identify him as the boy who had hoodwinked him. But Palkhivala's attention was focused on the gate and he was pointing out something to a turbaned doorman.

Vikram's thoughts reverted to Anirudh. He was not the sort of boy who lied. Neither was he a prankster. Even on the remote chance he decided to be untruthful, he would never have misled his grandmother. There was no reason to lie to her. And why was his room a mess? Anirudh did not strike him as a messy sort, certainly not to the extent of antagonizing his grandmother. Where was Anirudh and what was going on? Disturbing thoughts swarmed Vikram's head. Uneasiness prickled his veins.

Across the road, Palkhivala had seen him.

The doorman had returned to the hotel. Palkhivala stood alone, like a fat well-groomed cat. Vikram steeled himself for a show of anger: a raised fist, or furious words at being made a fool of. But strangely, it was anxiety that he saw instead, followed by what could only be a flicker of fear on the man's face. Vikram was taken aback, but only for a moment as suspicion suddenly seized him. The memory of Palkhivala and his car following the bus flashed in his head. Anirudh had stolen something from the man's hotel. Palkhivala had followed. Anirudh was missing.

Driven by impulse, Vikram dashed suddenly across the road, and a car cruising past at that precise moment swerved to one side, missing him by inches.

Vikram sprinted grimly across the road, not sparing a glance at the vehicle and its angry driver.

Palkhivala had turned pale. He was slow to react, and by the time he started to back away, Vikram was by his side.

'Where is my friend?' asked Vikram, in an angry but controlled voice.

'How . . . how should I know?'

The tone of the man's voice betrayed him. Vikram was certain he was lying.

'You followed him yesterday in your car. I saw you.' Palkhivala's face crumbled. 'He is missing. Where is he? I will have the police on you.'

Sweat broke on Palkhivala's bald head. He was rattled and it showed. He flashed a worried glance at the hotel. 'Not here,' he said. 'Come this way.'

Palkhivala set off at a fast trot. His gait lessened at the next building and Vikram caught up with him.

The pause had enabled Palkhivala to regain some of his poise.

'Your friend stole from my hotel,' he blustered.

'That's what you say.'

'We have remote cameras,' shot back Palkhivala. 'He is a thief. We saw him tuck something into his pack. That's why I followed him.'

'He will return whatever he took. Anirudh is not a thief. But that's not the point. Why is he missing?'

The troubled expression returned to Palkhivala's face. 'I don't know,' he said lamely.

'You know! Tell me or you are in deep trouble.'

Palkhivala's head turned wet again. 'Your friend is okay, believe me.' But Palkhivala did not look convinced.

Vikram pressed on relentlessly. 'Is it the hotel owners? Don't shield them.'

There was the sound of a car pulling up behind them. 'No. You don't understand. The owners are decent people, they live in London. It's . . .'

'WHO?' boomed Vikram, shouting.

Palkhivala looked miserable, as if he were about to cry. 'They promised they would be nice to him. This is terrible—'

There was the sound of hurried footsteps. Palkhivala glanced behind. His face froze. 'Run . . .' he whispered. His voice was so low that Vikram barely heard him. 'Run!' he hissed again. 'You must go or they will catch you too.'

Vikram whipped around. There were three men behind him. Close . . . just a step behind. Their faces were intent, eyes fixed on him. A car drew up beside them.

Vikram instantly knew he was in trouble. He turned to flee. Two sets of hands clutched him with furious intensity. Though he struggled, he felt himself being lifted off the ground. The car door opened and he was jostled into the vehicle. He struggled, but something coarse was dumped over his head and he couldn't see. His shouts were muffled, useless. Doors slammed. The car jerked forward, wheels screeching and spinning. Hands pushed Vikram to the floor. The car was speeding. Vikram struggled. Something crashed against his head and he knew no more.

ON KOLESHWAR

It was afternoon and Chitra's snake count was disappointing—just two. A highly unsatisfactory number, especially as it was the windswept wilderness of Koleshwar that she was scouring. Worse still, the snakes were common rat snakes. There was not a trace of the stub-tailed shieldtails that Salim had promised to find her.

On any other day, her indifferent success would have prompted frustration, perhaps even anger, as Chitra was an impatient girl. But on the rolling expanses of Koleshwar—deflected from her goal by a beguiling spectacle of wind, light and cloud—she had experienced barely a trace of disappointment. Like the disbanding cloud everywhere about her, her resolve had begun to recede and in a rare turnabout—wilderness, beauty and landscape—temptations Vikram was notorious for succumbing to, overcame her. The majesty of Koleshwar seduced her and though acutely aware she was wavering from her purpose, she yielded to distraction, and a telling consequence of her digression was her below-par snake count.

The Dhangar tribals had been good to her. Four simple huts, an acre of barely cultivable land, and a handful of cattle were all they possessed. In spite of their penurious circumstances that left little to share, they had looked after her every need. Her father, who had spent the majority of his life in the remote, impoverished parts of India, often said that the poorest of the poor are far more willing to share than the moneyed and the rich. Chitra's brief stay with the Dhangars backed his observation—the first part at least.

The women had warmly received her, opening their simple mud and stone homes to her. The elder ladies had fed and mothered her. The younger ones, those her age or even less, had watched, suckling babies to their breasts. Their only income was the money from the sale of a few litres of milk they extracted from their cattle each day, they said. Farming wasn't possible during the monsoons as the intensity of rain was such that it drowned their plateau. Their men had no choice but to migrate to Bombay where they worked as labourers. Their settlement was remote with no electricity, no running water, no school, no hospital, no amenities whatsoever, but to them, it was the only home they knew.

They inquired after her, about her home, her family, her friends, her life; and as Chitra talked and the women gazed at her with big round eyes, she understood the inequalities and the unbridgeable gulf separating their lives. It was true that she and the villagers belonged to the same country. In flesh and blood, the women were no different from her, but their existence was as far removed from hers as Earth was from Mars. In their smoke-filled huts, with rain pattering on their simple thatched roofs, she was humbled as never before. She felt small and undeserving, and she wished hopelessly for the world to be more just and accommodating. Later, she had spread her sleeping bag, and with only the rain and the buffaloes for company, had fallen asleep.

She was roused at first light when the cattle departed, shepherded by the lone adult male at the settlement. The women fed her chapattis and a green vegetable she could not identify. When she was done they had packed more of the same for her as her lunch.

Salim had arrived promptly at 7.00 with a mild heaviness of breath to show for the steep climb from his home in the valley. Chitra chose only her small daypack for their excursion. She had packed it in advance, placing inside her camera, her torch, her cell phone, emergency medicines, a pen and a pad for notes—taking care to wrap each item individually in a plastic bag for protection from the rain. The women stowed her remaining gear away, promising to safeguard it for her. Then bidding them goodbye, she had set off.

As a rule, Chitra always carried her own pack, but Salim insisted on taking it, and sensing she would offend him, she gracefully handed it to him.

The initial section of the walk, through thick forest and heavy cloud, was dark and gloomy. They had emerged at last on to a vast cloud-bundled plain. They tramped through fields of bushes with white flowers that had winked at them in the gloom. Then, after a long, dreary march

165

the wind had begun to blow. The cloud mass, solid and unyielding till then, started to waver. The wind punched holes in it and then shredded it into fine wisps. When a gap materialized beside her, Chitra saw with a start that their path skirted only a few feet from a dizzying fall. Sheer cliffs plummeted to a mist-laden valley far below.

The fog began to clear rapidly and after a while, Salim halted and pointed at a tall mountain on the far side of the valley. Girth-wise, it was the most enormous mountain Chitra had ever seen. Equally impressive was its summit, an astoundingly flat top, stretching endlessly forward, like the deck of an oil tanker.

'Raireshwar,' announced Salim. 'It was on the great plateau of Raireshwar that Shivaji Maharaj took his oath of swaraj. And look, you can see the peaks now. There is Torna, the fort we had climbed last month.'

Like a mouthful of gigantic teeth, an assemblage of peaks was poking through a sea of cloud. Chitra instantly identified the distinctive crown of Torna. Even though the distance was immense, its turreted walls were visible. Sinaghad, the lion-fort of Pune, was lost in cloud, but Rajgadh, Torna's sister fort, rearing its ship-contoured head, sailed serenely in the sea of vapour. Pivoting an arc of mountains Salim identified other visible forts for Chitra: the shapeless Pandavgadh and the hulking mass of Kinjalgadh with its tabletop crest.

The panorama was stunning. It was as if they were adrift in an ocean of cloud pierced by upheavals of rock. Below, when the surging clouds permitted, they spied deep green valleys, wooded slopes, flashing spirals of water and dark rock. The wind, blowing like a tempest now, buffeted them, clutching at their clothes and howling in their ears.

Salim proclaimed that it was these mountains that were once the lair of Shivaji, the great warrior king. Pratapgadh, the fort where Shivaji had outwitted the hapless Shaista Khan, and the majestic fort of Raigadh where the great king breathed his last, were in the vicinity too but masked by mountain and cloud, he said.

Chitra followed Salim wordlessly as he led her westward along the precipitous edge of Koleshwar. Tramping huge distances they travelled alternately through forest and undulating expanses teeming with ferns and bushes. In some areas, the ground was ablaze with tiny, yellow pansy-like flowers. Sometimes the flowers were blue and sometimes purple. Often, they were accompanied by dragonflies, entire squadrons of them, that hovered like tiny aircraft and sallied forward every now and then with eye-popping bursts of velocity.

Finally, they came to a place where not just the mountain but also the world seemed to end in an immense void of cloud and space. Chitra instantly sensed that she had arrived at a transition point, a geographical limit. It wasn't only the plateau of Koleshwar that terminated here, but obeying the dictates of an invisible boundary, the plateaus on either side—that of Mahabaleshwar and Raireshwar—also discontinued at this westward terminus.

'The Konkan,' said Salim, sweeping his hand across the cloud-draped infinitude below.

At the snake park, Chitra had pored over books on the Sahyadris of Maharashtra and they all spoke of a well-defined cut-off, the westward edge where the Sahyadris abruptly ceased and gave way to the rolling lowlands of the Konkan.

Immense walls of black rock undulated serpent-like to the distant plains below. The scale of the fall was dizzying and alarming in the extreme. Enormous cliffs and steep gorges hung before their eyes, so precipitous that even a mountain goat would have baulked at them.

They wandered the plateau leisurely thereafter, traversing from its northern limit to its southern Mahabaleshwar-facing edge. Along the way they found a stream and tracked it, inspecting the abundant holes along its banks, which Chitra believed had been excavated by rats. About a kilometre upstream she spotted their first snake of the day. The reptile had been slithering at the edge of a thicket of grass and a flicker on the ground had betrayed its presence. Startled, the creature froze, presenting Chitra the opportunity to observe its long, coiled body and banded colours. Even as the creature swayed a scaly head at them, she identified it as a common rat snake. The serpent's tongue flashed, as it was thrust repeatedly from its mouth. Chitra and Salim stood absolutely still, displaying no threat whatsoever, yet the snake backed away and was lost in a matter of seconds in the grass.

They came across the second snake late in the afternoon while they were traversing a belt of karvi, the tall, thin plant, common in the Sahyadris, which according to Chitra was neither a bush nor a tree but somewhere in-between. Though they caught only a glimpse of the slithering creature as it sped away from them, Chitra was certain it was a rat snake again.

Later, after a prolonged break for refreshments, Salim led Chitra to a stretch of sloping grassland pockmarked with rocks. This, he said, was the area he had often seen the snake with the stubbed tail. Chitra immediately started upturning rocks, a method commonly used for finding snakes. Though rock-turning was fun, Chitra was always cautious, as it was impossible to tell what lurked underneath. The displaced rocks, which she took care to replace exactly as she found them, yielded tiny scorpions, a variety of beetles, geckos and centipedes. Then she finally found the shieldtails.

Chitra gasped, experiencing a dizzying rush of joy.

There were two together beneath the same rock. The snakes had gone still the moment their shelter was yanked aside. They were small and thin and barely a foot long. They were iridescent black with a yellow stripe on each side of their body, and their tails were distinctively stubbed with a rounded, shieldlike tip.

The shieldtails ignored Chitra and Salim's presence. They posed uncomplainingly as Chitra clicked away excitedly with her camera. When she gently lifted one to inspect closely, it curled around her finger, exhibiting no haste or desire to slip away.

Burrowing like worms in the soil, shieldtails spend the majority of their lives underground. When monsoon rains flood their burrows they are forced to the surface and it is mainly in this season that observations are possible. The snakes are found only in India and Sri Lanka. In India, they are localized to the Western Ghats and certain species, like the Mahabaleshwar shieldtail, are restricted to Mahabaleshwar and possibly one or two surrounding plateaus, thus elevating their status to special, a must-see for avid snake lovers.

Salim, like most villagers, despised snakes, and consequently wasn't enamoured by Chitra's discovery. He sat patiently as she made observations, scribbled notes, took endless photographs and swooned delightedly over the uncomplaining reptiles. With great reluctance, Chitra finally replaced the stones and helped the snakes crawl back under.

When she rose to her feet, her face was flushed and her eyes shone like Diwali lanterns. She turned even more upbeat when Salim said this wasn't the only area where he had seen the snakes; there was another rock field nearby, just around the fold in the mountain.

Instead of satisfying Chitra's appetite, the shieldtail find had stoked it, and all she wished was to ferret out as many more as possible. But the evening was nearly upon them. To speed the search, she decided to split their efforts. She requested Salim to turn rocks on the next slope. She would remain where she was as it was a lucky area for her. Salim was reluctant to leave her, but accepted as the search areas were only a few hundred metres apart. They agreed to allocate a half-hour for the search. If Salim found shieldtails he would call her, else they would meet when the work was done.

Lightheaded and happy, like a child in a candy store, Chitra knuckled down to her toil and her delight knew no bounds when she found another shieldtail. After photographing the creature and allowing it to slither free, she flipped more stones and almost immediately stumbled upon another. It was while she was observing her fourth shieldtail that a sound disturbed her, and resting her camera on the ground, she turned.

DISTURBING DEVELOPMENTS

Commander Vikas Dongre had left work early, returning home shortly after noon. His wife, Smita, and his best friend, Ishwar, were already there. Anirudh's absence in the morning had troubled Smita, yet she had left for work as usual, more irked than actually worried. But she had grown restless when Vikram mysteriously stopped answering his phone. After an hour of continuous calling without any response, her anxiety had steadily mounted till she could take it no more and she had finally driven back to NDA.

Ishwar had rushed to the Dongre residence on hearing about the worrisome absence of the boys.

On arrival, Vikas Dongre strode into his living room, attired in a spotless white naval uniform.

'I am leaving for Mumbai,' he announced, flinging his cap on a chair. Not breaking step, he marched down a corridor to his bedroom door, which he flung open.

Smita stumbled after him, wringing her hands. 'You can't. You might be needed here. The police—'

'That's why I'm leaving,' snapped Vikas Dongre. He yanked the shutters of his cupboard open. 'Don't you understand . . . the police will need me. One of us has to be in Mumbai to answer their questions. There's going to be an inquiry, an investigation. My sitting here isn't going to help them, or us.'

Ishwar had followed the Dongre's to their bedroom. Smita turned appealingly to him.

'You might want to reconsider, Vikas,' said Ishwar. 'It's early hours yet. The boys could still show up.'

Vikas Dongre tossed a pile of clothes on the bed. 'You think so? Come on, Ishwar . . . do you really think so?'

'Vikram is a responsible boy,' said Ishwar.

'That's just it!' cried Vikas Dongre. 'All of us know he is a responsible boy. Anirudh might pull a prank, but Vikram's not the sort who will do anything so worrisome. He was speechless, dumbstruck when Smita called him, right?'

'Yes,' replied Smita, 'but—'

'Vikram had no idea Anirudh had left home to meet him,' went on Vikas Dongre. 'He said he would call you back immediately, which he never did . . . and he still hasn't.' Vikas Dongre looked like a bear, an angry one, as he glowered at Ishwar and his wife. 'What is it that you want me to do? Twiddle my thumbs and keep waiting for a call that might never come . . . or do something?'

'The boys might still show up,' repeated Ishwar.

'If they do I'll turn back. But I know Vikram—' He gestured with his hands. '—we all know him. Something has gone wrong. I can feel it in my gut and it's worrying me terribly. I have to go to Mumbai. If the boys have indeed disappeared and there is an investigation, I don't intend leaving it to the police this time. I'm going to be part of this inquiry. I'm going to get my son back.'

Vikas Dongre turned away. Dragging a suitcase from under his bed he started filling it.

Smita wrung her hands again. 'How are you going to go there?' she asked. 'The car is already in Bombay.'

'He can take mine,' offered Ishwar.

'But—' protested Smita Dongre. She turned furiously on Ishwar, appalled at his capitulation.

Ishwar defended himself. 'What option do we have, Smita? You know your husband. He's the sort who has to be in the thick of things. He'll drive us mad if he sits here waiting for a call that might never come. Go ahead and take my car, Vikas. I'll hold the fort here.'

Vikas Dongre looked up from his packing. 'Thanks, mate,' he said. 'Use my scooter till I return. Stay here if you can. It will be a load off my mind if you give Smita company. Don't leave her alone.'

'Sure,' said Ishwar. 'Today's skydiving is cancelled in any case. The wind is too strong. So don't worry yourself. I won't leave Smita's side.'

Smita stared at both the men. Her face was pale and her eyes glistened with unshed tears. Uttering a sound halfway between a snort and a whimper she strode out of the room.

Vikas Dongre paused from his packing. Ishwar gestured pacifyingly and followed after Smita.

'He's crazy,' sputtered Smita, when Ishwar caught up with her in the living room. 'The boys could be fine. There's no need to rush insanely to Bombay.'

Ishwar placed a hand on Smita's arm. 'Something is the matter,' he said. 'We'll be kidding ourselves if we don't admit it. Your mother is hopping mad at the state of Anirudh's room and you know that your Anirudh is not a messy boy. Do you think he would have trashed his own room?'

'But—'

'And don't forget Vikram. He has vanished. Disappeared like smoke. There's more to this than meets the eye, Smita. Vikas believes he'll be wanted down there. He's only making sure that no time will be wasted.'

A tear trickled down Smita's cheek.

'This isn't the time for weakness,' said Ishwar. 'You are a strong lady, Smita, we both know it. We'll face this together.'

Smita stared at Ishwar. Then she threw her shoulders back. 'Vikas hasn't had lunch,' she said, her voice brisk. 'You better hold him back if you call yourself his friend. I'm not going to let him travel on an empty stomach.'

Vikas Dongre swallowed his meal in five minutes flat. His orderly collected his bag and stowed it in Ishwar's car. He hugged his wife. When she made to speak he placed a hand on her lips.

'Shush, darling,' he whispered. 'No speculating now. It's pointless. Just wish me luck. I'll get our son back for you.'

Smita embraced her husband and kissed his furry cheek. Wiping her eyes, she bid him goodbye.

Ishwar shook hands with his friend, wishing him luck.

Thanking him, the officer marched to Ishwar's car, a sturdy Scorpio Jeep. Reversing it out of the compound he waved and drove away.

Aditya learnt of his friends' predicament only late in the afternoon, upon returning from a wildly satisfying session of windsurfing on Khadakvasla Lake. He was unaware of the drama of the morning as his hosts had left for work before he had woken. Ishwar's call informing him of the possible abortion of the afternoon skydiving session on account of fierce winds had excited him instead of disappointing him, as the stormy weather had roused the prospect of a fabulous windsurfing session.

If Aditya had to grade the day on a scale of 1 to 10 from a surfing point of view, he would have scored it a perfect 10, as the blustery weather had created conditions surfers would have willingly parted with an arm and a leg for. Sailing out from Peacock Bay, he had sped up and down the lake, delighting in the wind and water. If his body had permitted him, he would have sailed on till darkness, but windsurfing, especially in stormy conditions, is a physically demanding sport. Dropping finally from exhaustion, he had quit late in the afternoon.

His buoyant mood evaporated the moment he was informed of Vikram and Anirudh's disappearance. The atmosphere in the Dongre household was grim, like a hospital waiting room, as any hope that the boys were pulling a prank had long been crushed. It was nearing evening and it was no longer possible to deny that something was the matter.

Smita maintained a vigil beside the telephone in the living room. Her wrists and palms were red from constant wringing. Seated nearby, Ishwar leafed aimlessly through an aeronautical magazine. Unable to sit still, Aditya paced the veranda.

Nothing of what Aditya had heard made sense. Why would anyone kidnap Vikram, or even Anirudh for that matter? Neither of them had enemies. If anyone, it was Salim who could have been at risk. The speculation of a prank was absurd. Vikram was far too responsible to even consider a joke of this nature. A clear pointer at trouble was Vikram's assertion on the phone that he would return today. Vikram never reneged on his commitments. The fact that he hadn't come back confirmed that something was the matter.

Could an accident explain his absence, wondered Aditya? He shuddered at the thought and although he tried to expel the notion from his head, it refused to leave him. A knot started to tighten in his chest. It stiffened quickly into a cramp, forcing a halt to his pacing.

Extracting his phone from his pocket, he dialled Vikram's mobile. A female voice informed him that the mobile he was calling was switched off. In despair, he tried again, but the result was the same. He thought of Chitra. It was she who had spoken to Vikram last. Could he have mentioned anything to her? Maybe she could shed some light on his absence. Highlighting her name on his instrument, he called her number.

Salim paused from his work. A blanket of mist had fallen upon the mountain. He was fed up of turning stones, and although quitting was on his mind, it wasn't weariness that prompted the break. An outburst of sound had caught his attention. He heard voices, several voices. The most strident was Chitra's, and she was indignant and angry.

Rising, Salim hurried back along the way he had come.

Chitra was speaking unnaturally loudly. She spoke Hindi and her words were comprehensible in part: 'Leave me alone . . . come any closer and I will hit you . . .'

Salim broke into a sprint, but after a few strides, he slowed his gait. Whoever was troubling her wasn't aware of his presence. Any noise he made would give him away, warn her assailants.

Chitra's voice floated through the mists. 'I have a knife. I will use it . . .'

Salim dodged stones as he ran. The fold in the mountain separating their work areas was coming up. Salim dropped to the ground. On hands and knees, he stole forward and sneaking behind a large rock balanced on a sloping mound, he edged his head around it.

Salim went numb all over.

Chitra wasn't far from him and she had a knife clutched in her hands.

Three men stood around her, their attitude unmistakably hostile. They watched her knife warily, not sure how to handle her.

'Hold on!' bellowed a voice in Hindi.

Chitra's assailants paused, gazing up an incline. Salim looked up and his heart missed a beat.

Shadows were visible through the mists, high up on the crest of the slope. There were four of them: two men and two boys. The boys were walking awkwardly, shoulders stiff, their hands immobile behind their backs.

'Chitra!' shouted one of the boys.

'VIKRAM . . . ANIRUDH!' Chitra's voice was incredulous.

Salim was equally astounded.

The taller of the two men, a man with long, unkempt hair and spectacles, clamped an arm around Anirudh's chest and held him tightly. His other arm wrapped itself about Anirudh's shoulder. The hand held a large knife and its blade was pressed against Anirudh's neck.

A terrifying chill spread through Salim. So unnerved was he that his legs started to tremble. The tall man . . . he knew him. He was the sadist. . . the man who had almost killed Salim when he had stumbled upon the treasure that fateful summer afternoon.

The tall man yelled at Chitra. 'Drop your knife or I will hurt your friend. Drop it! Drop it this instant!'

The men surrounding Chitra smirked at her.

Salim's jaw started to shake. These were the men who had attacked him on Torna, and here on Koleshwar too.

'It's pointless, Chitra,' Vikram shouted from above. 'They mean business. They'll hurt you and Anirudh too.'

Anirudh yelled suddenly. The man holding him laughed throatily.

Chitra dropped her knife. The men around her made snickering sounds. They stepped closer. Chitra raised her hands and bunched her fists. The men halted, eyeing her.

Anirudh was pushed forward. The two men and Vikram followed. The second man, the one accompanying the tall bespectacled man, was short and corpulent. He wiped sweat from his brow as he stumbled down the slope and he spat, revealing red, stained teeth.

They grouped at the bottom of the slope, beside Chitra and her assailants.

'What are you doing here?' snapped the short man in Hindi.

'Finding snakes and minding my business. It is I who should be asking what—'

'Are you alone?' barked the man.

Chitra regarded him coolly. 'Does it look like there is anyone here? I can take care of myself.'

'Where is your gear?'

Salim clutched the strap of the bag on his back. The question was shrewd. Gear was essential on a remote plateau like Koleshwar.

'At the Dhangar settlement,' replied Chitra, not missing a beat. 'I spent the night with them.'

The short man stared at Chitra. 'I don't believe you,' he said. 'Your villager friend returned last night.' He wiped sweat from his shining head. 'My men saw him and they know he climbed here this morning. He is here with you.'

Chitra shrugged. 'Think what you want. It's a free country.'

The man looked at the men surrounding Chitra. 'Tie her hands,' he ordered. 'Quick. Then search the area. Get me that villager. He's skulking around here somewhere, I'm sure.'

The plump man turned to his tall companion. 'It's bad luck that she's here, but she won't be any further trouble. We'll find that villager and take care of the Dhangars. No one will know.'

The men held Chitra roughly, wrapping rope around her hands. 'You both okay?' she asked, looking at her friends.

'We're fine,' grinned Vikram. 'Sorry about all this. Didn't mean to barge in and disturb you.'

Chitra sniggered. 'Jealous,' she joked, a smile flickering on her face. 'Had to come and spoil the party, didn't you? Couldn't bear that I was here on my own.' Then her face hardened. 'Seriously, Vikram. What's going on? They obviously haven't brought you along to enjoy the scenery.'

The tall man turned irritably. 'Stop your chit-chat!' he boomed.

The short fat man turned to Anirudh. 'You there,' he snarled. 'It's best you understand that we have no time to waste, because if you don't, your parents are going to grieve. You are either going to find me the treasure or you and your friends are all going to die.'

Chitra goggled at the man.

Behind the rock, Salim swallowed.

The fat man looked at his companion. 'Show them we mean business, Peter.'

The tall man stepped casually towards Vikram and without warning struck him a mighty blow across his face, sending him tumbling to the ground. Chitra yelled in protest and then grunted and collapsed beside Vikram as Peter turned his hand on her with equal force.

Salim half-rose as fury welled inside him. But common sense prevailed and he subsided, trembling with anger and fear.

Vikram and Chitra lay on the ground. The men beside them made no move to help them back to their feet.

The short man looked at Anirudh. 'They will die,' he said in a cold voice, deadly with intent. 'There are two hours till sunset. If you haven't found the treasure by then, we will finish off the girl. And by morning if the situation hasn't changed the boy will die. Don't whine about not knowing what I'm talking about because Peter will thrash your friends again.'

Peter made a sound that was both a snarl and a laugh. 'Chaggan and I have been denied our inheritance too long. Twenty-five years, we have waited for this moment. Today we will gain what is rightfully ours. But if we don't, there will be consequences to pay. All of you will die . . . you last, master Anirudh.'

Chaggan took over from his friend. 'You somehow knew where to find the safe in the hotel and you found the Parsee's manuscript too. You know the story of this mountain and what lies here. If you cooperate, we will be kind. Else you will die, all of you, and your fate, young Anirudh, will be the worst, yours will be a slow and lingering death.'

An uneasy silence settled upon the slope.

'That villager,' said Chaggan, remembering.

Salim jumped as if struck by a bolt of lightning. A jarring sound, loud in the stillness of the mountain slope, buzzed from the bag strapped to his back.

Chitra's phone! It was ringing.

With shaking hands Salim unstrapped Chitra's pack. He darted a nervous glance at the men. They were standing in a huddle, talking. The phone hadn't alerted them. Unzipping the bag Salim reached inside. His palm encircled the instrument, muffling its sound. His finger located the 'talk' button and he pressed.

Aditya was on the point of disconnecting when his call was finally answered.

'Chitra . . .' he said.

There was no reply.

'Chitra . . . is that you?' he queried.

Aditya heard heavy breathing. Then a voice: 'Saab, it is me!'

Salim! Aditya immediately identified his voice. Why was he whispering?

'Saab, help us. Those men are here . . . they have captured Chitra.'

'What men?' Aditya spoke sharply. 'What are you talking about, Salim?'

'Those men who chased us on the mountain. They are here, on Koleshwar. They are going to kill us.'

'KILL YOU?' Aditya was shouting now. 'What are you talking about?'

The floor shook with the rush of running feet. Smita and Ishwar arrived breathlessly at Aditya's side.

On the mountain, Salim ducked his head and peered around the boulder.

'Oh no!' he groaned into the phone. 'They are searching for me.'

The men who had roped Chitra were fanning out across the slope. Two were headed in his direction.

'They will find me,' babbled Salim. 'Rescue us, Aditya saab. They will kill Chitra first . . . by sundown . . . then Vikram.'

Aditya's voice erupted in Salim's ear. 'VIKRAM. Is he with you?'

'Yes, saab. They have tied his hands. Even the others.'

Salim chanced another glance at the men. He had barely half a minute. They would see him once they crossed the boulder.

'Saab . . . what do I do? They are coming.'

'Salim!'

A stern voice spoke his name. It was Ishwar.

'Listen to me, Salim. How much time do you have?'

'A few seconds, Ishwar saab.'

'Then hide the phone. Hide it now. Don't let them see you. Don't let on you have spoken to us. They will kill you. We are coming there. I'm switching off.'

'Saab . . . save us!'

'Hide the phone!'

The instrument went dead in Salim's hand.

Salim looked frantically about him. The stones he had been upturning were strewn everywhere about him. Reaching for the nearest one, he lifted it. He slipped Chitra's phone under it and replaced the rock carefully. Zipping Chitra's bag, he strapped it to his back. Crouching, he edged around the boulder.

Immediately there was a shout.

Salim sprang to his feet and ran.

'Halt!' roared a voice.

Salim kept running.

'Halt, or I will shoot!'

There was a deafening explosion and something whistled past Salim's ear.

'STOP!' screamed Anirudh. 'Stop, or they will kill you.'

Salim halted. Raising his hands, he stood still.

Ishwar handed Aditya his phone.

The knot in Aditya's chest was suffocating him now. 'They are on Koleshwar,' he breathed. 'The plateau we were attacked on.'

Ishwar stared. 'And Vikram and Anirudh are with him?'

Aditya nodded dully. 'Yes . . . Vikram is there.'

'No,' cried Smita. 'It isn't possible. You have heard wrong. Vikram is in Bombay.'

Aditya shook his head. 'Salim wouldn't lie. He confirmed Vikram's presence when I asked.'

'Who are the men with them?' asked Ishwar.

'The same men who pursued us on Torna—that's what I understood. He said they would kill Vikram and Chitra. They are on Koleshwar, the plateau near Mahabaleshwar.' A hunted look came into his eyes. 'How do we save them?'

Smita grabbed Aditya's arm. 'What about Anirudh?' she demanded. 'Did he say anything about Anirudh?'

'No,' replied Aditya. 'But Anirudh is on the plateau. If Vikram is there, he is there too. He has to be . . . they disappeared together.'

'Bombay to Mahabaleshwar is five hours,' said Ishwar. He looked at his watch. 'It is possible. If they were abducted in the morning, they could be up there on the plateau now.'

185

'We have to get there fast,' said Aditya. 'Immediately, if we are to save them.' Horror blanched his face. 'He said Chitra would die by sundown.'

Ishwar stared. 'Was Salim certain they were going to be killed?'

'Why would Salim lie?' said Aditya. 'I could feel his terror. He was sure they were doomed. We must leave this instant.' But despair overcame him. His voice dropped to a whisper. 'It's three hours to the mountain.'

'And another hour to climb,' muttered Ishwar. 'It might be too late.' He dropped his head, thinking. Then he looked up again. 'The Cessna!' he exclaimed. 'It could get us there in minutes.'

A light shone in Aditya's eyes.

Ishwar quickly punched a number into his phone.

'Prabhakaran,' he said when the call was answered. 'I have an emergency. Don't ask questions now. Is the Cessna ready to fly . . . good . . . could you come down to the NDA airfield now? I'll brief you later. Great, I'll see you in five minutes.'

Ishwar turned to Aditya and Smita. 'There is no time. Tell Vikas that I have gone. Inform the NDA Commandant and the police. I must leave now.'

WINGS OVER KOLESHWAR

Ishwar stopped by Vikas Dongre's bedroom on his way out. With Smita's help, he located and borrowed a warm jacket. In addition, she dug out her husband's private revolver from a safe inside her cupboard and handed it to Ishwar along with several extra clips of ammunition.

Vikas Dongre's scooter was parked in the garage and Smita handed Ishwar a helmet and the keys. Aditya grabbed a helmet too and when querying brows were turned on him, he requested permission to accompany Ishwar to the airstrip.

'Just to say goodbye,' said Aditya.

Ishwar's eyes twinkled. He gave Aditya a knowing smile as he kick-started the scooter.

Smita stared at Aditya, unsure.

Aditya shuffled his feet. 'I won't be long, aunty. I'll bring the scooter back too,' he added brightly.

'All right,' sighed Smita. 'No hanging about and come back soon.' She placed a hand on Ishwar's arm. 'Be careful.

It's just another mission for you . . . but it's my son and his friends involved this time.'

Ishwar looked deep into Smita's watery eyes. 'Anirudh is like a nephew to me. You know that. I'll get him back for you, I promise.'

Smita Dongre attempted to smile, but sniffled a sob instead.

Ishwar revved the scooter. 'There are a couple of things I need you to do for me,' he said. 'First, ask Vikas to call the air force training team and authorize my flight. The official at the airstrip must have instructions to let us take off. Next, tell Vikas to contact the Satara Police. Mobilizing the policemen there will take time. Several hours, while I'll be there in minutes. Yet, we'll need all the help we can get. Request them to despatch as many policemen as they can spare to Koleshwar.'

'I will tell Vikas,' assured Smita. She hugged Ishwar and waved as the scooter, with Aditya seated behind, was driven away.

The NDA airstrip was a short length of asphalt runway in a large grassy field with a control tower and a couple of hangars to one side. A wind was worrying the grass and the sky was swamped with cloud. Prabhakaran, Ishwar's business partner and owner of the Cessna, pulled up in his jeep as Ishwar halted the scooter beside the hangars.

Prabhakaran was short, dark-skinned and slim. He wore olive trousers and a black T-shirt with a jacket draped across his shoulders. His eyes were red and he stifled a yawn as he trotted in an effort to keep up with Ishwar who was striding towards the hangars.

'No courtesy nowadays,' grumbled Prabhakaran. 'Robbing people of their precious sleep. What's the hurry?'

'I need a para-drop,' said Ishwar. 'Speed is crucial. Could be tragic consequences otherwise. I'll explain in the aircraft. I'll take a minute strapping my equipment on. You start the pre-flight routines meanwhile. We need to get airborne as soon as possible. And yes . . . we are travelling south, to Mahabaleshwar.'

'Mahabaleshwar?' Prabhakaran scratched his head. 'There's no landing strip there.'

'That's why the drop,' said Ishwar.

'Have you seen the weather?' Prabhakaran breathed heavily as he kept up with Ishwar. 'We cancelled the skydiving session because of it, remember?'

Ishwar halted. 'Are you saying you won't fly?'

'I didn't say that. Just pointing out it's not going to be a picnic up there.'

'I wouldn't be asking this of you without good reason, Prabhakaran. I have an emergency. I need a favour.'

Prabhakaran gazed long and hard at Ishwar. 'Okay,' he said finally. 'But you owe me one . . . remember that. Get yourself ready. I'll be waiting in the aircraft.' He strode away, shaking his head.

Aditya followed Ishwar to a small building to one side of the hangars. A young officer dressed in blue overalls saluted smartly when Ishwar entered.

'Did you get a call?' asked Ishwar.

'Yes, sir,' said the officer. 'I have instructions to lend you whatever assistance you need.'

Deepak Dalal

'Good,' nodded Ishwar. 'I'm collecting my gear stored here and we'll be off.'

'Yes, sir. Go ahead, sir.'

Ishwar's skydiving equipment was stored in a rack-cluttered room. Entering, he strode to a rack that stood by itself to one side.

Reaching for what looked like an oversized backpack, Ishwar dragged it from the shelves. Aditya held it while Ishwar shook loose a jumble of straps and sorted them out. There were two leg straps that Ishwar first stepped into. Then he passed his hands through the shoulder straps. Working quickly, he adjusted the rig harness so that it fitted snugly about him.

Aditya cleared his throat. 'Can I strap a rig on too?' he asked.

Ishwar turned, grinning. 'You think I didn't know that was coming?' he asked.

Aditya shuffled his feet, not looking Ishwar in the eye.

Ishwar's gaze turned soft. 'I see a lot of me in you, Aditya. I was no different from you when I was your age. It's amazing how similar our temperaments are: the same readiness to take up a challenge, the absence of fear, and . . .' he paused, winking, 'a willingness to bend rules when necessary.'

Ishwar sighed. 'I want to encourage this spirit of yours, I truly do. That's why I've been giving thought to the possibility of your coming along. But even if I were to overlook what your dad and the Dongres would have to say, I still have problems. You heard what Prabhakaran said, that it's not going to be a picnic upstairs.'

'You've seen me jump, Uncle Ishwar,' said Aditya. 'I land on target every time. I have good control. I'm experienced. I've jumped often, you know that.'

Ishwar nodded. 'Yes, I do,' he said. 'But this is different. Conditions are rough. You could get blown away, probably miss the plateau altogether and land in the Krishna Valley below.'

Sensing resistance, Aditya adopted another strategy. 'I've been to Koleshwar before, uncle. I know its terrain. It's a massive mountain, bigger than you can imagine, and easy to get lost upon. We only have till sundown; I can help save precious time. And besides . . . it's my friends who are out there,' he added finally.

Ishwar nodded. 'Yes, they are your friends.' He stared at Aditya, assessing him. 'Your knowledge of the mountain could be useful. I could do with a guide.' He broke off as Aditya's face shone like the moon swimming free of cloud. 'Don't let your glee get ahead of you, young man. I'm willing to let you board the aircraft, but there are conditions.'

'I promise!' exclaimed Aditya. 'I promise I'll follow whatever you say.'

'My demand is total obedience.' Ishwar's tone was stern, headmaster-like. 'On board the aircraft, you will listen to whatever I say. You will be the soldier and I your commanding officer. You must obey me . . . even if I tell you not to jump. If the conditions are too tricky, I won't let you jump. Is that understood?'

'Yes, uncle.' Aditya spoke breathlessly. 'I won't jump if you tell me not to. I will listen to you.'

'And if you do indeed jump, you will not engage the enemy. Your role will be limited strictly to backup and guide.'

Aditya nodded, feeling light on his feet.

Ishwar was all business the moment he made up his mind. Selecting a rig, he unwrapped it and helped Aditya strap it on. When Aditya was bundled up, he turned him round and ran a swift check on him.

Ishwar was satisfied with what he saw. 'Right,' he said. 'I haven't tightened your leg straps. You can do that inside the aircraft. Let's go.'

The Cessna was a tiny aircraft with room for the pilot and two, maybe three passengers at a squeeze. Prabhakaran was already seated and strapped when they clambered inside. The door was controlled by a single lever and Ishwar shut it by pulling on it.

Prabhakaran started the engines and ran a final check. Satisfied, he rolled the aircraft to one end of the runway. He turned, revving the engine noisily. Then he opened the throttle wide, speeding down the runway. When he yanked the joystick the Cessna lifted into the sky.

After a short shuddering climb, the aircraft banked and Aditya saw the leaden expanse of the Khadakvasla Lake below. Sinhagad Fort reared towards the aircraft like a blunted spear from the ground. Its summit was shrouded in cloud, but the tips of its transmission towers were visible, bristling like artillery guns at the sky. At ground level, the cloud cover had seemed impenetrable, but up in the sky, Aditya could see spaces in-between. The Cessna struggled as it climbed through the voids between the clumps of dark fleece, and then they were through with the sun shining on them and the clouds bright and far below.

A luminous vista of cloud, mountain and valley unfolded below. Immense masses of cotton wool drifted everywhere. The thicker ones exhibited a distinct preference for the peaks, wrapping themselves like scarves about them. The valleys were gashes of shadow and light, blurred and indistinct.

The panorama absorbed Aditya. He thought of Vikram, as he always did when caught up in scenic splendour, and the tightness in his chest, forgotten till then, returned. Though they were travelling to Koleshwar faster than he could ever have dreamt of, he wished fervently for more speed.

Very quickly, the summits of Torna and Rajgadh appeared below. There was cloud on Torna, but sections of its fortifications were visible, and Aditya spotted the temple with the tiny courtyard where they had spent the night.

The aircraft droned onward. Prabhakaran navigated visually, following Ishwar's instructions. Aditya leaned forward, peering over their shoulders. Rock, cloud and valley stretched endlessly below, smothered in shades of grey beneath a crystalline blue sky.

'Mahabaleshwar dead-ahead,' said Ishwar presently. 'Coming up in a few minutes. There's a tower poking through the mess of cloud at 12 o'clock. That's Wilson Point and the Panchgani Table Land is at 10 o'clock. There's no cloud there, it's clearly visible.'

Aditya looked. To the east, Panchgani and its famed Table Land Plateau basked in sunlight, but to the west, there was only cloud. Beneath the Panchgani Plateau stretched a blue expanse, broken here and there by cloud.

Aditya found his bearings instantly. The band of blue was the River Krishna, its flow constricted at its very source. Aditya's gaze travelled along the mass of water to where it was split by a huge mountain with an enormous plateau, reaching far to the west, its distant edge lost in mist.

Koleshwar!

Aditya's heart leapt. They had arrived. It was amazing. He had spoken to Salim less than an hour ago. Now they were here, just a para-jump away. There was hope. His friends could be saved.

Prabhakaran tilted the Cessna's nose downward as the plateau drew near. Koleshwar was a monstrous mass of mountain, shaped like a finger: A long stubby finger that stretched for kilometres on end, widening and thickening into broad knuckles at its western edge.

The Cessna swooped low, Prabhakaran aligning its flight path with the plateau.

'West,' said Aditya, shouting to make himself heard. 'The cave where Anirudh fell is to the west, where the plateau broadens.'

They were barely a thousand feet above the mountain. In the areas where there was no cloud, every fold, every wrinkle, every slope was visible. Although most of the plateau was forested, there were scars to the east where fields had been gouged from the land. On the western side, there was no human habitation, only forests and grasslands. A sizeable area was free of cloud, yet significant stretches near Koleshwar's western and southern reaches were lost beneath folds of mist that were smoothed like a one-sided wig on the mountain.

The Cessna droned over the plateau. Its passengers peered at the ground, searching. On the eastern side, in the area free of cloud, there were huts beside the fields. But except for a lone herdsman tending buffaloes near the mid-section of the plateau, the area stretching to the west was lifeless and empty, a massive wilderness of trees and grassland.

'We'll look again,' said Prabhakaran as he turned the Cessna, banking over the cloud-swathed slopes of Mahabaleshwar.

The hum of the aircraft was audible beneath the misted forest canopy. Chaggan, the short fat man, hadn't given the sound any thought the first time the plane flew by. On its second pass, he looked up, disconcerted, but the forest and enveloping mist annoyingly put paid to any possibility of spotting the machine.

'Vikram!' hissed Anirudh tremulously, hope flashing in his eyes.

Vikram pushed his spade into the damp earth, thrusting hard so that it stood upright. Wiping mud and sweat from his face he stared upwards.

A vile snarl flared on Peter's face. The tall man crossed to where Vikram stood and struck him a vicious blow that sent him reeling to the ground. Yanking Vikram's spade from the mud he stood over him, brandishing the implement like a weapon.

'You don't seem to be getting the point, do you?' he spat. 'There's less than an hour till sunset. Your girlfriend dies if you don't find the treasure for us by then. Next time you take a break it's not my hand I will use, I will thrash you with this.' He thrust the spade down till it was an inch from Vikram's bruised cheeks. Then flinging it aside, he stalked away.

Mouthing curses, Peter strode to where his comrade Chaggan stood. On the way, he lashed his foot at a crumpled body on the ground. The body twitched but made no sound.

'Leave him alone!' shrieked a high-pitched voice. 'You filthy swine . . . you dirty coward. You've beaten him almost to death already.'

Chitra's chest heaved as she screamed at Peter. Such was her anger that if she could have, she would have struck Peter with her fists or whatever she could have laid her hands upon. But Chitra couldn't move. Though she stood on her feet, her hands were stretched behind her, wrapped around the trunk of a tree and roped tightly together. There was mud and blood on her face and one of her eyes was swollen.

Chitra's tirade provoked an animal expression on Peter's face. Eyes blazing, he strode to the tree Chitra was bound to, his hand raised.

'Stop it, Peter!' Chaggan spoke sharply. 'You've thrashed her enough. Come here. I need to talk to you. That plane is bothering me.'

Peter halted. If looks could kill, the glare he directed at Chitra would have knifed her heart. He spewed a stream of saliva that splattered Chitra's jeans. Then he turned, and passing the inert body, kicked brutishly once more as he crossed to where Chaggan stood.

'That aeroplane,' said Chaggan. 'It has passed twice over us. There is no airstrip here. Why is it circling the mountain?'

The roar of the aircraft engine had receded, but it was still audible.

'There's cloud up there,' said Peter. 'Could be some stupid pilot who is lost. Serves the idiot right if he crashes.'

Chaggan turned silent. He fidgeted as he stared at the shadows bent double, excavating a patch of forest that the boy from Colaba had selected. Except for him and Peter, the rest of his men were working, sweating alongside the boys, digging for the treasure he knew was buried on this mountain.

Chaggan was irritated at Peter. The man was overzealous when it came to beating up people. It was a trait of his that had landed him in trouble several times with the police. Often, the thrashings had been so bad that Chaggan had had to draw on the political influence he wielded to prevent Peter from being arrested. This time Peter had beaten the hapless villager till he had fallen and even then had continued to assault him. That Peter was upset with the villager was understandable. The man had eluded Peter for weeks on end. The escalation of his anger when the villager had pleaded he had no knowledge as to the location of the treasure was justifiable too. But there had been no need to trounce the man till he had fallen comatose to the ground. Peter's exhibition of brutality was unnecessary, stupid in Chaggan's opinion, as they had lost an extra hand for the digging. Even the girl. Peter had thrashed her when she had tried to escape. It was only his intervention that had prevented her from suffering the

197

same fate the villager had. Chaggan could not bear to see women being beaten up. He had saved her from further distress by convincing Peter that the boys wouldn't dare attempt to escape with her bound to the tree and helpless.

Chaggan stared at the boy from Colaba, the one named Anirudh. With the villager out of the equation, their hopes of finding the treasure rested upon him. When Peter had struck the boy, Chaggan had exchanged sharp words with him, warning Peter not to lay his hands on him again. Chaggan was convinced that if anyone could find the treasure it was Anirudh.

It certainly wasn't by chance that Anirudh had located the hidden safe at Seawind Hotel. How he had known of its existence inside the wall was inexplicable. The rubbish he had spouted about a dream didn't make any sense. It was hogwash and the boy had been stupid enough to think he could hoodwink them with his nonsense. The contents of the safe—what they had recovered when they raided the boy's house—had turned out to be a manuscript dealing with the biography of Homi, the man who had built Seawind. The manuscript had established, beyond doubt, what he and Peter had known all along—that there was treasure buried on the mountain. Even though the boy had denied it, both Peter and he had been certain that a map for the treasure must also have been hidden alongside the manuscript inside the safe. They had ransacked the boy's room, but hadn't found any trace of the map. With limited options to choose from, they had settled on the most practical strategy. They had abducted the boy and his friend and brought them here to Koleshwar.

Chaggan was not a murderer. Though during the course of his giddily fluctuating political career he had never hesitated at pulling down his opponents—mostly by unfair means—he was proud of the fact that he had never physically harmed anyone. But in the case of the treasure, he was willing to abandon his scruples. He was ready to shed blood if necessary. The treasure, after all, rightfully belonged to Peter and him—even the manuscript said so. No one was going to stand between them and the treasure. Peter, through his savage beatings, had demonstrated they meant business. By now it was clear to the boy, Anirudh, that if he refused to put to good use the knowledge he possessed he would not see the next sunrise. If a killing was necessary, so be it. He would not raise a finger to prevent it. The deed was justifiable given the magnitude of the gain that could result from it.

After decades of fruitless search for the treasure, things finally seemed to be going their way. Chaggan had never felt as confident of finding it as he felt now. It was Anirudh who had selected the excavation area. Anirudh had said he was searching for a banyan tree beside a path that led to the Krishna Valley below. The boy had taken the names of Homi and his companion Irfan. He had even shown them the page on the manuscript where it was written that the treasure chests had been buried near a banyan tree, beside a path that led to the valley below. Displaying uncanny knowledge of the mountain, the boy had led them into the misted forest and had found the path that wound down to the valley.

Chaggan's heart had leapt with joy when not far from the path he spotted a banyan tree. More than anything else it was the enormous size of the tree that confirmed they were on the right track. Its hanging roots suspended like pillars had long since thickened into trunks, expanding the tree's canopy till it was the size of a circus tent. Even Chaggan, who was city-bred, knew that the size of a banyan tree was an indicator of its age, and going by the girth of the tree's canopy, its age spanned many centuries. The tree had certainly been around during Homi's time. If the manuscript was to be believed, the treasure was buried somewhere here.

The roar of the aeroplane disrupted Chaggan's thoughts once more. When it swept over the forest again, icy pinpricks punctured the bubbles of anticipation fizzing in Chaggan's stomach. He could not ignore the aircraft any more. There had to be a purpose to its circling; this was the fifth sortie it had made.

'Riaz, Chintu,' shouted Chaggan. 'Stop your digging. Come here.'

Peter turned on Chaggan angrily. 'Whatever for?' he demanded, hands on his hips. 'Are you mad? We've never been so close to finding the bloody treasure and you want them to stop!'

'The plane!' snarled Chaggan. His voice matched Peter's coarseness. 'You must be deaf if you can't hear it, and stupid if you still think it's lost. It's circling and that's worrying me. I'm sending these two to investigate. The digging can go slow for a while. The treasure's not going to disappear because of the delay. The plane's presence has to be sorted out.'

Peter was taken aback at the ferocity in Chaggan's voice. He kept silent as the men trooped across and halted before Chaggan.

Chintu was tall and lanky. Riaz was bearded. He was fleshier and shorter than Chintu, though not by much.

Chaggan quickly briefed them.

'The forest edge isn't far from here,' he said in conclusion. 'Go till where the mist ends and check what the plane is up to. You have your mobiles. Call me from there.'

The men handed their implements to Peter and hurried off into the murky forest.

The mood in the aircraft stopped short of gloom, but only just so. Flying in parallel grid lines, they had scoured the western section of the plateau, but had found only cloud and emptiness below. From their vantage point in the aircraft, the magnitude of their task was starkly apparent. The plateau was immense, with wide, empty reaches and equally large forested sections. The empty reaches could be discarded. That left the forests. But they would take forever to search, while there was just an hour till sundown.

Ishwar grew restless. The light would also soon start fading, and that would make the task even harder. He couldn't delay his jump any further. While criss-crossing the plateau, he had settled on the shepherd as his best bet. The shepherd must have seen something. Visitors were rare here and if any had turned up, he would have noticed them. If he drew a blank, the forests were only a short distance away and he could quickly cut across to them.

But before he jumped, he had to break the bad news to Aditya.

He turned in his cramped seat so that he faced Aditya. 'I'm afraid you cannot accompany me, young man,' he said. He paused as disappointment flooded Aditya's face. 'The wind is far too strong. I've discussed the conditions with Prabhakaran and he agrees with me. Sorry, I can't take the risk. I know you are upset. But there is a line I cannot cross.' Ishwar cut Aditya's protests off. 'No arguing. That was your promise, remember? I don't have time. I must jump now.'

Ishwar spoke quickly to Prabhakaran. The conversation was inaudible to Aditya. Not that it mattered to him as he was dealing with shock and crushing disappointment.

The plane was at the misted edge of the plateau. Prabhakaran turned the machine so that its nose pointed east.

Ishwar rose to his knees and turned to Aditya. 'I'm opening the hatch,' he shouted. 'Shut it after I'm gone.'

Ishwar reached above him and yanked the door lever. A cloud-spattered rectangle of blue appeared in the space the door had occupied.

'DROP ZONE COMING UP,' shouted Prabhakaran.

Ishwar smiled and raised a thumbed fist at Aditya who sulkily returned the gesture.

'ALMOST THERE,' cried Prabhakaran. 'Jai Sri Krishna! May God be with you! JUMP!'

Ishwar reached across and squeezed Aditya's shoulder. Then he slid sideways and was gone, his body shrinking with startling speed, hurtling to the ground like a meteorite. Then an orange canopy flowered behind him.

Aditya watched Ishwar fall through the cloud till Prabhakaran shouted at him to close the door. After the door was fastened, Prabhakaran banked the aircraft in a long turn and by the time Ishwar came into view again, he was halfway down to the plateau. The Cessna completed one more circuit before Ishwar touched down beside the shepherd. Surprisingly, the man's cattle did not back away as Ishwar floated into their midst, his orange canopy first flaring, and then collapsing behind him. From up in the aircraft Aditya saw Ishwar quickly reel in his canopy and fold it into a bundle.

Prabhakaran had turned the aircraft round and was retracing their flight path, winging westwards.

'Look there!' shouted Prabhakaran suddenly.

Aditya drew a sharp breath. Two men had emerged from the mists. They were running and it was obvious Ishwar was their quarry. But Ishwar hadn't seen them. He was walking towards the shepherd who hadn't moved since Ishwar had dropped alien-like into his world.

'Those men aren't villagers,' said Prabhakaran.

'It is them!' hissed Aditya. 'Ishwar is in danger and he doesn't know.'

'Hold tight!' cried Prabhakaran. 'I'm turning.'

The fuselage tilted beneath Aditya's feet, and he clung to his seat as Prabhakaran banked in a stomach-twisting turn.

The whine accompanying the aircraft's abrupt swerve must have alerted Ishwar because by the time Prabhakaran had levelled the machine and they could gaze down upon the plateau again, Ishwar had turned away from the shepherd and was staring at the approaching men, his gun in his hand.

203

A stretch of boulders and grass separated Ishwar and the men, who were sprinting now.

Prabhakaran abandoned his earlier flight plan, circling instead. By the time the aircraft completed two circuits, the running men had cut the intervening distance by half. A clump of vegetation was visible to one side of Ishwar. Ishwar must have sensed that the men were hostile, because after a brief consultation with the shepherd, he crossed towards the vegetation.

Aditya was watching when Ishwar suddenly dove into the bushes. He switched his gaze to the men and gasped when he saw that their hands were extended forward. From up in the sky, it wasn't possible to discern what they held in their hands, and even though the blast of gunshots did not pierce their envelope of engine clamour, it was apparent that the men were shooting at Ishwar.

Ishwar was defending himself. He lay flat on the ground his hand extended. There was pandemonium in the area. The shepherd's cattle were galloping in all directions. The shepherd was fleeing too.

Aditya wished with all his heart he was down there beside Ishwar. It didn't matter that he had no weapon and could not have been of any use to Ishwar. This was his fight. It was his friends who were down there and he was up in the aircraft—helpless, a mere onlooker. But there was nothing Aditya could do, except watch.

ADITYA

It was Vikram who chanced upon the first chest. When his spade stabbed upon something that felt different from the heaps of mud and stone he had been unearthing, his heart stood still. He prayed fervently that it was a treasure chest he had stumbled upon. There was a terrible dread inside him—a dread that had pervaded his being since Chitra had been roped to the tree. Time was running out for her. In the mist and gloom, it wasn't possible to tell whether the sun had set or not. Peter had sworn he would kill her, and Vikram was certain that the tall brute's threat wasn't a bluff. If indeed he had struck upon a buried chest, there was hope for Chitra . . . and for all of them.

Dropping his spade, Vikram bent low, sifting mud with shaking hands. There were stones everywhere in the pit. His breath quickened as he swept mud and rocks aside. He brushed trembling fingers along the cleared area. The surface beneath was bumpy and rounded. It wasn't particularly smooth, but he inhaled sharply when his fingers detected a bow-like arch. The curvature wasn't natural; certainly not a shape an ordinary rock could acquire.

'I've found something!' he shouted in a hoarse voice.

Peter arrived at Vikram's side in two bounding leaps. He pushed Vikram roughly, sending him stumbling. By the time Vikram recovered, Chaggan, the fat man, had hurried across too. Both men knelt excitedly in the pit.

'There's something hard and rounded down there,' said Vikram. 'Between those two large stones. You can feel it with your hands.'

Vikram's spade lay at his feet. Anirudh held his in his hand. For a moment, as Peter and Chaggan crouched in the upturned mud, Vikram toyed with the idea of attacking them. Then remembering the presence of the man working beside them, Vikram turned. The man's gaze was fixed on Vikram, and he smirked when their eyes met. The spade he held in his hands put an end to the ideas buzzing in Vikram's head.

'Nothing but bloody stones!' snorted Peter.

'Wait!' hissed Chaggan. 'There's something here.' He swept the area with his hands for a while. 'Yes . . . it is rounded,' he breathed.

Snatching the spade at Vikram's feet, he cleared mud and stones. Then he reached into his pocket and pulled out his mobile phone. Pressing a button, he shed a beam of light on the mud. He bent closer, staring.

'Yes!' he exclaimed finally. 'Yes . . . there's something down there.'

Peter stood still for a moment. Then with a mighty exertion, he launched himself sideways. The man who had been eyeing Vikram stepped backwards as Peter landed at his feet.

'Chinkya!' barked Peter. 'Give me your spade!'

Chinkya handed the implement over.

Peter strode enthusiastically to the pit and began to dig.

Chaggan waved a hand at the boys, indicating they get back to work. Then he began to stride up and down.

Although the find had elated Chaggan, a sense of foreboding was spreading acid-like inside him. Chintu, the tall man, had called a short while earlier, breaking news of the parachutist. It was clear now that the presence of the circling plane was not an event of chance but a genuine threat. Somehow, and Chaggan had no idea how, he and his men had been tracked to Koleshwar.

The most sensible course of action—the one Chaggan would have chosen under normal circumstances—would have been retreat. Full and unequivocal retreat. At this point, he could still extricate himself from damning involvement, as except for the villager, no one had been seriously hurt.

But the irresistible lure of the treasure had swayed Chaggan's decision. After all these years, the myth of the treasure, which he had firmly believed was just that—a myth and nothing more—was now relaying powerful signals that it was in truth, reality. The manuscript had destroyed the myth. It authenticated hearsay and rumour. He couldn't possibly turn away. Not now. Not when it was clear that if he did so, others would claim the treasure and it would be lost to Peter and him forever. Despite his every instinct urging him not to, Chaggan had ordered his men to attack the parachutist. Later, just a minute before the boy had discovered the chest, there had been further bad news. Riaz had been wounded. A bullet had pierced his shoulder. Apparently, the parachutist was an expert shooter.

The backup men, Chintu, Riaz and Chinkya, were Peter's associates. Chaggan's acquaintance with them was through Peter, and though he had little contact with them, he knew they were members of Mumbai's seamy underworld. So it was no surprise that when Chaggan requested that they keep fighting, the men readily agreed. But the possibility of their being out-gunned by the parachutist plagued Chaggan. The prospect of being thwarted at this crucial time was unbearable.

Chaggan ceased his pacing. His eyes fell on Chinkya who was standing to one side, watching the boys and Peter. Chinkya would be useful in the fight with the parachutist. He was doing nothing in any case. He could serve as a backup for Chintu.

'Chinkya!' cried Chaggan. 'Come here.'

Chaggan quickly explained the situation to him. 'Go!' he commanded. 'Run! Run as fast as you can and join Chintu and Riaz. Back them up. Under no circumstances is that parachutist to enter the forest.'

There were no objections from Peter. So immersed was he in his task that he barely noticed Chinkya's departure.

When Vikram stared after Chinkya, Chaggan drew a revolver from his pocket.

'I don't want anybody getting ideas,' he said in a loud voice.

Vikram and Anirudh looked up.

Chaggan smiled, displaying his revolver. 'No funny play,' he said. 'I'm warning you. No tricks . . . it's the girl I will shoot first.'

It was when Aditya saw a third man emerge from the mists that something snapped in his head. All along he had been watching with frustration from above as a gun battle played out on the plateau below. Only once had Prabhakaran swooped in low in an effort to intimidate the gunmen, but they had fired at the Cessna and there had been a metallic 'ping' as a bullet grazed the fuselage. Since then, they had been circling high above the plateau, well out of gunshot range, too high, in Aditya's opinion.

On the ground, Ishwar was effectively pinned down by the sharpshooters. With the passage of the Cessna's circuits, it became steadily clear that Ishwar's goal of entering the forests was doomed to fail. As time passed Aditya's anxiety mounted exponentially, as from his lofty station above the clouds he could see the red orb of the sun dip towards the horizon. Time was running out for his friends. The most terrible thought, the one that haunted his every moment in the aircraft, was the possibility of the threat to his friends being carried out while he sat in the sky twiddling his thumbs. At every circuit, he begged Prabhakaran to be allowed to jump. It was not to lend Ishwar a hand, he explained. As he did not have a gun there was little he could do to help the embattled ex-soldier. His intention was to fulfil Ishwar's thwarted goal and head for the forests to rescue his friends before time ran out for them. But his appeals were curtly refused. When his pleas reached fever pitch, Prabhakaran erupted in anger, yelling at him to shut up so that he could concentrate on the job at hand.

Then the third man appeared, sprinting out of the cloud that shrouded the forests. His arrival sealed the odds in favour of the gunmen. When Aditya realized that the possibility of Ishwar making it to the forest was now virtually nil, reason and sense completely deserted him.

Reaching for his goggles he strapped them on. Prabhakaran failed to register Aditya's intention as his attention was focused on the newcomer below. It was only when Aditya buckled his helmet and rose that Prabhakaran turned. Horror sprang to his face as Aditya yanked the lever above his head, springing the aircraft door open.

'NO!' yelled Prabhakaran, but by then it was too late.

Squatting in a crouch, Aditya thrust hard with his legs and tumbled out of the machine.

On falling, Aditya slipped unconsciously into the routine drilled into him by his instructors. Splaying his hands and feet about him, he arched his body till it took on a curved, bow-shaped contour, the classic pose of all free-falling skydivers. The plunging free-fall was what Aditya enjoyed most, when he felt as one with the sky. Though he was hurtling like a meteor to the ground, the sensation that came to him, like it did to all skydivers, was that of extreme freedom, as if the wide-open spaces of the sky belonged to him. But on this occasion, it wasn't the liberating freedom of a bird that Aditya sought. Aditya did not need reminding that this wasn't a pleasure jump. Even if there had been no death threat to his friends, the sub-5000 foot reading on Prabhakaran's altimeter would, in any case, have warned him so. Unlike pleasure jumps, where the start altitude was usually 12,000 feet, he had little time, just minutes in the air.

After a few seconds of stabilized free-fall, Aditya reached behind him. When his fingers fastened about the ball-like knob of the chute deployer, he yanked hard. Almost instantly his harness tightened, and as the pilot chute dragged out the main canopy, there was a sensation of being lifted as the ballooning fabric above him arrested his fall.

Cords suddenly sprouted from his rig, taut and strong, like steel. There were four of them, the front risers and the back risers. Reaching up along the back risers, his hands grasped the toggles attached to them and with a heave, he detached them so that the steering lines were in his hands.

In control now, Aditya looked about him and when he saw nothing but a sea of cloud beneath he was seized by a wave of panic. There was not a sign of the plateau. Every trace of its wide expanse had been obliterated.

It was then that the folly of his brainless reaction to impulse hit him. In a manner that was typical of him, he had responded to a rush of blood, and in doing so, overlooking something as elemental as noting his position to the ground before hurling himself into space. Now, as he sank earthwards, the flight path of the Cessna flashed a red light in his brain. There were moments during its circuit when it winged over the southern extremity of the plateau. Had his blind impulse driven him to dive at the moment when the aircraft was hovering above the valley instead of the plateau? His stomach turned as it struck him that it could well be the case. The endless bank of cloud indicated so. His dive then was fruitless as instead of the plateau he would end up in the valley.

But all was not lost yet.

He was in the air. As long as he stayed up, there was hope. He could steer himself to the plateau while still in the sky. Time, or lack of it, would be decisive. Success could depend on how fast he reacted.

First, he had to get a fix on his bearings.

Aditya tightened his hold on his left toggle and yanked. Instantly, the sea of cloud below began to drift to one side. But the drift was only an illusion; it was he who was turning. He yanked the same toggle again. The sea of cloud moved further away and he spied a massive stripe of blue beneath.

The river Krishna! He looked up, and in the distance, he saw the flat tabletop that capped the plateau of Panchgani. Aditya stifled a whoop of exhilaration. He had established his bearings.

Aditya yanked again and the looming hulk of Koleshwar spun into view beneath. There were streaks of cloud beneath him again. In spite of their shrouding presence, he spotted Ishwar and the two gunmen. Far above them sailed the Cessna, its tail facing him. Next, Aditya tilted his head, spearing his gaze downwards, past his dangling feet.

The craggy boundary of the plateau unfurled in a squiggly childlike scrawl beneath him. Past the plunging cliffs lay the forested valley floor. To his horror, he saw that his feet hovered not far from the plateau edge. And to make matters worse, a wind, the same tearing wind that had convinced Ishwar to call off his jump, was driving him to the valley.

As always, in difficult conditions, Aditya's mind slipped into crisis control. His reactions turned razor sharp. Instantly, he released the toggles. His hands grasped the front risers and he pulled down on them with all his strength. Aditya was aware of the consequence of the manoeuvre. The pressure from his hands was tilting the canopy forward in a manner that aided it to penetrate the wind. Fending the wind was his only hope. If he managed well, there was every chance he could land upon the plateau. His theory classes had taught him the operation, and he had employed it before for precision landings under windy conditions.

Though the wind plucked and tore at him, Aditya didn't feel it. The risers twitched and shuddered in his hands. The ground was rushing up at him. The trees were getting larger and the cliffs were taking form, their silhouettes dark and wet and seemingly smooth.

A cloud coalesced suddenly beneath him and the plateau and its terrifying edge vanished. Aditya held his nerve. He was falling through a sea of cotton that tumbled and swirled in waves. Then the cotton turned wispy and the wind snatched its strands away. There was grass and stones beneath him. His feet were hanging above the plateau, but only just. The ground rocketed upwards at him. Aditya pulled the risers down with all his strength.

Yes! The manoeuvre had worked. He would be deposited on the plateau. The valley chasm was dropping from view behind the rim of the plateau. It wasn't possible to pull the brakes as he couldn't release the riders. But there

213

was no need to as his descent was controlled. His feet hit the grass as lightly as if he had stepped down upon it.

Yet, in spite of the perfect touchdown, Aditya experienced no elation. A terrible fear, far worse than any during the descent, seized him instead.

The canopy . . .

The web of cloth that had deposited him like a feather on the plateau could prove to be his undoing. His landing had crumpled it, but that was only temporary. The wind was bound to flare it, and when it did so, he would be dragged over the edge. He had to get rid of it. There was a cut-away handle, which when pulled, detached the canopy. Aditya's hand darted to his shoulders where he knew it was located.

But even as he did so the rampaging wind flared the canopy and Aditya was yanked off his feet. The power of the tow took his breath away. Though he scrabbled desperately it was clear that his efforts would be in vain. The canopy was hauling him to the edge.

A backward glance warned him he had only seconds. A few metres of smooth, black rock was all that lay between him and the clouded void. There was nothing on the ground that could save him. No handholds to cling to, no barriers to halt his propulsion to the valley below. His only hope was the cut-away handle. Once more, in the face of certain disaster, Aditya displayed nerves of steel. There was no grabbing, no clutching, no snatching. His fingers knew exactly where the handle was. The canopy tugged. The edge came closer as he was whipped along hard, black rock. Aditya's hand wrapped around the handle. He was barely a body-length from the abyss when he pulled.

The release was instantaneous, but his momentum dragged him forward. Skin tore from his hands as he clutched at the ground. A fingernail broke, but he didn't notice. As cloud and nothingness loomed before Aditya, it struck him that he would perish if he went over. There was no canopy now to arrest his fall. At the very edge, his scrabbling hands found a bump in the rock. He jammed his hands against it, and when at last he came to a halt, overshooting the rim, his head hung suspended above the valley.

Chasm and cloud spun like a giant wheel in Aditya's head. His bloodied hands, shaking now, clutched the cliff edge. He screwed his eyes shut, blanking out the spinning emptiness. Then he thrust himself backwards, retracting his head, till the whirling void was replaced by solid rock. Immediately, he felt the start of a shuddering spasm. There was a giddiness inside him, the sort that came to him when he was near throwing up. He wanted nothing more but to lie where he was, but the crackle of gunfire, penetrating the helmet wrapped about his head, volleyed on his fatigued consciousness.

Drawing on all his willpower, Aditya pushed himself to a sitting position. His head started to spin again and he retched. An explosive sound, flat and loud, echoed about him. Something smashed into the mound of rock that had saved his life. Aditya rolled instinctively, retching again as he did so. Somehow, he lurched to his feet. Staggering, he looked about him.

A man was running towards him. There was a gun in his hand and he was shouting. But the wind and the helmet stilled the man's words. The sprinting figure was undoubtedly the third man, the newcomer. On seeing him fall from the sky, the man had chosen to come after him.

Aditya ran. He stumbled, almost falling to the ground. His strength had deserted him. The terror of his brush with death had taken its toll.

The man's gun boomed again.

Aditya weaved as he ran. There was a wall of mist ahead. Aditya dashed blindly towards it. The earth-level perspective of the plateau was different from what he had grown accustomed to from the sky. But endless aerial circuits had embedded a snapshot of Koleshwar in his brain and Aditya knew he was running westwards, towards the forests.

The gun cracked again, but Aditya kept running. With each lunging stride, Aditya experienced a welcome return of energy. The unspeakable terror of being blown over the edge was receding and though his life was still in danger, the threat of a bullet thudding into him seemed far less terrifying than the ordeal he had survived. But the near-death experience had drained Aditya, and the harness, still strapped around him, was impeding his running.

A runner gaining on him was unthinkable as Aditya was an excellent sprinter. But as the mists drew nearer each backward glance confirmed he would soon be overtaken. Even the gunman seemed to think so as he was no longer wasting bullets on him.

The parachute harness . . . he would have to jettison it. But Aditya couldn't, as his pursuer would cut the distance to half during the time he took to shed it.

The rippling mists drew closer. Then he was in them. At first, the cloud was thin and gauzy, then it thickened souplike about him, blotting out the sky.

The ground was uneven and strewn with boulders and bushes. Ahead was the forest, dark and deep. Maybe he could lose his pursuer inside the depths of the forest. His pursuer was struck possibly by the same thought because the man shouted, commanding Aditya to halt. A gunshot exploded when it became obvious that Aditya had no intention of doing so. The bullet smashed into a bush barely a metre from Aditya.

Aditya kept running. A line of trees appeared and when he entered them darkness engulfed him. The gloom cheered Aditya. Marksmanship would turn twice as difficult in the forest.

Aditya's feet sensed the softness of leaves. The leaves were wet and they dampened his footfalls. In spite of the suppression of sound, it was impossible to run silently. It wasn't long before he heard the sound of leaves being pounded behind him. His pursuer had entered the forest. The man shouted again, ordering him to halt. There was another explosion of sound. The bullet was way off its mark, crashing into trees far from Aditya.

Then, a fresh sound rang from deep in the forest.

A call . . . a human voice.

Though the cry was distant, it unsettled Aditya. Convinced he was running into the arms of his enemies,

Deepak Dalal

he panicked and veered from his bearing mid-stride. But his tired legs—hindered as they were by the harness he wore—were unprepared for the sudden swerve. They tangled in mid-air, tripping Aditya, sending him crashing to the ground.

THE TREASURE

The first gunfight—the one that had tied Ishwar down—had been inaudible to Chaggan. But the second one, involving Aditya, had been near enough for the sharp retorts of Chinkya's gun to penetrate the trees and cloud to him. Rattled by the blasts, Chaggan had dialled Chinkya's phone repeatedly, but the man had not responded. Then he had called Riaz and Chintu—the men who had pinned Ishwar down—and had learnt of the second parachutist, and that Chinkya was chasing him. When the battle had finally entered the forests, Chaggan, frustrated at Chinkya's refusal to answer his phone, had begun to shout, and it was his calling that had so panicked Aditya that he had fallen.

After several lusty yells, the phone in Chaggan's hand began to jangle.

It was Chinkya and Chaggan exploded violently. 'Why can't you pick up your phone?' he howled.

'I was running, saab,' replied Chinkya, breathlessly. 'The badmash would have got away from me if I had stopped to reply. But he has fallen, I heard him. I have him now, so I have called.'

'STOP HIM!' bawled Chaggan. 'STOP HIM! I don't want him here. Hold him off.'

'Saab, don't worry,' calmed Chinkya. 'He has no gun and he is just a baccha. I've tracked down many like him before. They never get away from me.'

'Make sure he doesn't,' snapped Chaggan. 'And when you are done, go back and help Chintu and Riaz. I don't want anyone getting through here.'

Chaggan disconnected and returned to his pacing. His throat was dry and his heart was hammering painfully in his chest.

It was certain now that the treasure had been found. There wasn't just one chest. Peter's frenzied digging had revealed that there were other similar chests in the earth. Chaggan was feeling distinctly heady. The treasure had cast its spell on him. Under its sway, common sense, reason and restraint—traits that personified Chaggan—had deserted him altogether. Now that he was so close, he wasn't going to let the treasure slip from his hands. He was prepared to do anything to ensure it did not . . . anything!

Chaggan stared impatiently at the excavation site. Peter and the boys were toiling side-by-side, their bodies slick and glistening with sweat. The presence of innumerable boulders was hampering their efforts. And on account of their weight, the chests too were contributing to the delay.

Only a few minutes, thought Chaggan. After a lifetime of story, fable, incredulity, hope and myth, now it was down to a matter of minutes.

Aditya had fallen hard, his shoulders and hips smashing to the ground with bone-crunching force. He lay on the leaves, winded. By the time he pushed himself to his knees he knew it was too late. His pursuer had dramatically cut the distance between them.

The absence of footfalls warned him that the man had halted. Then the man suddenly started to speak. Several heart-stopping seconds passed before Aditya established that the man was speaking into a phone.

Aditya rose silently. He flicked his eyes about him. A deep gloom lay upon the forest. Taking heart from the misty murk he extended a foot, but the crunching sound when he transferred his weight prompted him to hurriedly withdraw it. Movement would betray his position, something Aditya could ill-afford.

It was clear to Aditya that resuming his flight would be a folly. His pursuer was a top-flight sprinter, and the distance separating them wasn't enough to sustain a chase. Aditya had run out of options. The absence of light was the only factor in his favour. The man, at best, had a vague idea where he had fallen. Aditya decided to wait and lie in ambush. A tree with a thick trunk was rooted nearby and he stole silently towards it.

The man's conversation was short and Aditya caught his closing line, '. . . just a baccha. I've tracked down many like him before. They never get away from me.'

Disparaging remarks roused Aditya's deepest feelings, inspiring him to prove otherwise. He grimaced in the dark. He would show the man. Teach him that he was no pushover, no baccha.

Chinkya stepped carelessly forward, making no effort to silence his movements. There was no need to. It was he who possessed the weapon. The confrontation was no contest, in any case, so he believed. It was a youngster he was pitted against. He had honed his skills on far more worthy opponents.

Aditya waited, not moving. The silence was absolute. Even the crickets had stopped singing.

Chinkya had a fairly good idea of the area in which Aditya had fallen, and when he neared, his footfalls turned soft. Aditya tensed when Chinkya's tread ceased. It was as he strained his ears that Aditya realized that his helmet was still clamped to his head. The run and the chase had occupied him the moment he landed, leaving no time to think of it. His hands reached to remove it but halted. The helmet's fit was tight. If he made even the slightest noise while releasing it, he would betray his position. Aditya dropped his hands. He was going to have to keep it on.

Aditya heard footsteps again. The man was nearby, just metres away. He was moving fast and treading lightly. A shadow materialized on Aditya's left. It halted. The breath froze in Aditya's chest. The shadow's head turned. The man was staring at Aditya. Gambling on the shadows and the dark, Aditya stared back, not batting an eyelid. He was standing under a tree, his body pressed against its trunk. The light was such that Aditya was confident he could deceive the man. Chinkya's gaze lingered on the tree for a long, heart-stopping moment and then travelled on, searching another section of the forest.

This was it, thought Aditya. The moment to attack was now, while the man was looking away. But Aditya hesitated. A widening length of leaf-littered floor stretched in-between. The man would surely hear him before he reached his side . . . and he had a gun.

At that precise moment, a shrill sound shattered the quiet. It took all Aditya's self-control to prevent himself from leaping rabbit-like in fright. His recovery from shock was remarkably swift, far quicker than his adversary's. The jangling noise disoriented Chinkya, possibly because it originated just inches from his ear, from his shirt pocket. Before he could identify his phone as the source of the jangling, Chinkya's finger involuntarily squeezed the trigger of the gun in his hand. The ensuing blast stunned him, driving him backwards, and he stumbled.

Aditya leapt forward, the gunshot ringing in his ears. The force of his offensive sent Chinkya reeling. Chinkya's gun hand shot forward as he attempted to break his fall. Like a striking cat, Aditya twirled and leapt on him again. The gun exploded once more as Chinkya hit the ground. The combined force of the weapon discharging and his hand hitting the ground dislodged it from his fingers.

Though Chinkya was smaller than Aditya, he was no slouch when it came to a fistfight. He turned around snarling, spitting and raining punches. Aditya realized the worth of his helmet when one of Chinkya's blows smashed into it with knuckle-crunching solidity, and the discomfort of it was no more than a jolt. The effect on Chinkya couldn't have been more contrasting. The man pulled back, jerking his hand, yowling with pain. The opening was exactly what Aditya needed. Bending, Aditya plunged forward, ramming his helmeted head into his opponent's stomach. Chinkya reeled. While he tottered, Aditya bunched his neck muscles and speared his head upwards with all the energy he could muster. Aditya's helmet ploughed sickeningly into Chinkya's jaw. The force was such that Chinkya was lifted off his feet before crumbling to the ground, unconscious.

'Just a baccha, huh?' gasped Aditya, gazing at Chinkya's sprawled body.

The fallen gun lay at Aditya's feet. As he scooped it from the mud, Chinkya's phone rang again. Aditya turned Chinkya around and plucked the phone from his pocket. He waited for the instrument to stop ringing. Then he switched it to silent mode and transferred it to his pocket. Bending, he ran his hands through Chinkya's pockets. He found a wallet, a diary and a folded knife. He pocketed them and examined Chinkya once more. The man was out cold. There was little chance of him causing any further trouble. Aditya rose. Then he remembered his helmet. Grinning, Aditya peeled it from his head and dropped it at Chinkya's feet. Turning, he set off into the forest.

Beneath the banyan tree, Peter laughed maniacally. Vikram, who toiled beside him, felt as if a deranged hyena was cackling in his ear. The man's fit had begun when the rounded lids of two chests had emerged from the earth. And with each passing minute, his crowing grew louder as the pit around the chests grew wider and deeper.

The gunshots from the forest had had no effect on Peter. Ignoring the distant reverberations, the man had continued to dig, jabbering ceaselessly. Vikram and Anirudh had paused at each burst of sound to exchange looks. Vikram had glanced at Chitra after the second bout of blasts and she had nodded energetically at him, smiling.

Though Peter ignored the explosions, they deeply perturbed his comrade, Chaggan. Vikram heard him curse and saw him punch numbers on his phone continuously. Then frustrated, he abandoned his post beside Chitra and crossed to the pit.

The mud-encrusted chests were still partially buried, but now their locking mechanisms had been freed from the soil. Ordering the boys to step aside Chaggan focused the beam from his phone on the chests. The glow fell on rusted locks of antique design. Each chest was secured by two locks.

'Those locks,' said Chaggan, speaking to the boys. 'Break them with your spades.'

'HALT!' roared Peter. 'Don't touch the chests. They are mine, only I will open them.'

'The treasure isn't yours alone, Peter.' Chaggan glared at his friend. 'How many times do I have to repeat that it is ours? And if you are going to open the chests, then start now! In case you've forgotten, there's a plane circling above. Men have parachuted to the ground. We're holding them off, but we're running out of time.'

'Men . . . parachuted?' Peter gazed incredulously at Chaggan.

This was the first Peter had heard of the developments of the past half-hour. The revelation was news also to Vikram and Anirudh, the best they had heard the entire day.

Peter sprang from the pit, spade in hand, his face convulsed with rage.

'Damn the bloody plane!' he screamed, brandishing his spade. 'This treasure is ours.' He stared savagely at the boys and Chitra. Then he gazed at the forest. 'Just anybody try to steal it from us!' he yelled. 'Anyone! I'll kill anybody who tries!'

He then strode back to the pit. 'Out!' he roared. 'Out of my way. The locks are mine to smash.'

Vikram and Anirudh hurriedly backed away.

Grasping the handle like he would a hammer, Peter raised his spade and bore down on the nearest chest.

Vikram's heart raced as he watched Peter pummel the chest. Men had parachuted to the plateau. The gunshots made sense now. There was a battle on to save them. Salvation was at hand.

But Vikram's euphoria was destined to be short-lived.

Anirudh spoke in Vikram's ear. 'There's going to be trouble,' he whispered.

Vikram glanced at Peter, flinching involuntarily. The man had thrashed him every time he had spoken. But Peter was immersed in his task, oblivious to the world.

'The chests,' continued Anirudh. 'There's no treasure in them . . . only stones and boulders.'

Vikram stared.

'He'll kill us,' said Anirudh, his voice shaking. 'The man is mad. He's capable of anything. Watch out . . . prepare for trouble.'

Though old and rusted, neither the locks nor their latches yielded easily. Peter was forced to pause from his assault twice to regain his breath before the first of the locks gave way. The second stubbornly refused to buckle. Mouthing a string of abuses, Peter finally lost his temper and pulling a gun from his trouser pockets he fired twice at the latch.

The crash of the gun was followed by a roar of triumph from Peter.

'It's broken,' he cackled, leaping around the pit like a child. 'The bloody chest is finally open. The treasure . . . Chaggan . . . it's ours.'

Aditya had been making his way through the forests, guided by Peter's shouting. His advance had been deliberate, taking care to suppress the sound of his passage. That was till he heard the blasts from Peter's gun. Fearing the worst, Aditya threw caution to the winds, charging forward recklessly.

Gibbering incoherently, Peter knelt beside the chest, struggling with the lid. Metal grated against metal and the lid swung open, parting with the chest.

Peter's gibbering ceased.

Chaggan stared.

Anirudh stood riveted to the ground, equally entranced, but Vikram broke into motion.

A deep chill had iced Vikram's heart. He trusted Anirudh implicitly on all matters concerning Koleshwar. Anirudh's prophecy of the chest and its contents had horrified him. The shock of finding ordinary stones instead of precious ones would understandably upset anyone, but in Peter's case, it could result in temporary insanity. His fury could drive him to anything, even murder. Chitra had goaded Peter recklessly earlier, and if anyone it was she he would target. The possibility was too terrifying to ignore, and he stole to the tree Chitra was bound to the moment the chest transfixed attention on itself.

Vikram had almost reached Chitra's side when a blood-curling roar erupted from Peter.

'STONES!' he screamed. 'Nothing but bloody STONES!' His voice broke, as if the blow was too much to bear. 'Stolen,' he wailed. 'They've stolen my treasure.'

Peter started to shake.

First, it was heartbreak that consumed him. Then quickly, the pain was replaced by anger—the wild, uncontrollable fury Vikram had feared. Staring at the worthless contents of the chest he rose to his feet, his body shaking. Then he turned with controlled deliberation to Anirudh.

'YOU . . . you rotten, scheming devil, you've been leading us on! You are going to pay the price.'

'NO!' shouted Anirudh, as Peter reached for his gun. 'Wait!' he begged. 'There are other chests down there. This one had stones, but that won't be the case with the rest. The treasure is there. The manuscript says so!'

Vikram's heart ground to a standstill when Peter unsheathed his gun. He had made it to Chitra's side, but his efforts were wasted, as it wasn't Chitra but Anirudh who was being targeted. He watched in horror as Peter squared his gun on Anirudh's chest.

'NO!' shouted Chitra and Vikram in unison.

Vikram prayed that Chaggan would stop Peter. But Chaggan was in no state to do so, recovering as he was from the anguish of unearthing stones instead of gold.

Time stood still as Peter, drawing great shuddering breaths, held his gun on Anirudh.

Then Peter swivelled violently and his gun roared again. He pumped four bullets at the unopened chest. His gun still smoking, he reached down and yanked at the lid.

Anirudh watched in horror as the lid was flung back. Peter and Chaggan both seemed to freeze as they stared at the chest's contents. A hushed silence descended on the clearing. Then, as Chaggan slumped, Peter slowly straightened himself. His chest was shuddering again, only more violently this time. When he spun, tiger-like, on Anirudh, there was a replay of the earlier drama.

Peter's gun-hand rose, rage contorting his face. The gun's barrel halted when it centred on Anirudh's chest.

Chitra and Vikram both cried out again.

The inevitable finally happened.

A gunshot boomed.

Anirudh stood, a hand half-raised, his mouth frozen in a soundless scream. Vikram felt the wind exit his lungs. A terrible hopelessness overcame him. He waited for Anirudh to slump . . . but for some inexplicable reason, Anirudh did not.

It was when Vikram spied a figure rushing into the clearing that he realized that the gunshot had erupted from elsewhere, not from Peter's weapon.

ADITYA!

Vikram couldn't believe his eyes. Chitra too was stunned into silence.

'Squeeze that trigger and you are a dead man,' bellowed Aditya, the gun in his hand pointing at Peter.

The contortion on Peter's face changed to an animal snarl. In one swift movement, he turned his gun hand around and fired at Aditya.

Aditya dived to the ground, rolling, and when he rose, he squeezed his trigger. But there was no response except for a harmless click.

'GOT YOU!' screamed Peter triumphantly.

With the deliberation of a hunter whose quarry is trapped with no hope of escape, he took aim at Aditya and fired. But in a macabre repeat of Aditya's failed discharge, his gun too plunked a harmless click.

'FREEZE, EVERYBODY!' shouted Chaggan.

The short man was on his feet, his gun in his hand. He squeezed the trigger, expelling a bullet that thudded into the dirt at Aditya's feet.

'My gun is loaded. Anyone who moves is dead.'

Peter flung his empty gun away. Stooping, he grabbed a spade. 'Tried to kill me, huh?' He strode towards Aditya, the mad light flaring in his eyes. 'You are dead, you dog . . . dead.'

With that Peter broke into a run, charging at Aditya. When he passed what seemed like a lifeless body on the ground, the body raised a leg. Salim's foot tripped Peter in full run, sending him sprawling to the ground.

Chaggan knew it was all over the moment Peter crashed to the leaf-strewn earth. The worthless chests had returned

Chaggan to his senses, extinguishing the temporary Peter-like madness that had raged inside him. Chaggan had never killed anyone in his life, and now that there was no treasure to fight for, nothing, not even the compulsion of self-defence could convince him to endanger another life.

Self-defence was imperative at that moment because the boys were rushing forward, ignoring Chaggan's weapon. It was a three-pronged attack. From behind, the boy from Colaba was coming for him; his friend Vikram was running at him too. The youngster who had just arrived was making for Peter.

Chaggan turned and ran. 'Peter!' he cried. 'Run! Save yourself!'

On seeing Chaggan flee, Vikram skidded to a halt.

On the ground, Peter managed to rise before Aditya reached his side.

Sensing a bloody battle, Vikram turned on Aditya. 'Let him go!' he yelled. 'Stop it! Leave him be!'

Aditya pulled up, but only after scooping Peter's fallen spade from the ground.

Confronted by Aditya, Peter shot a backward glance, searching for Chaggan. The mad light faded from his eyes when he saw the back of his fleeing companion. He swung around, his eyes darting first to Vikram and then to Anirudh, who had also collected a spade. Then he looked back at Aditya, who was slowly twirling his spade in his hand. There was another yell from Chaggan, urging him to run.

Peter backed away.

'Let him go,' repeated Vikram, when both Aditya and Anirudh stepped forward.

Peter continued to back away, watched by the boys and Chitra. Then, with a last wretched stare at the chests, he turned and followed his comrade.

The vanquishing of Chaggan and Peter did not induce a spark or even glimmer of celebration. All Vikram felt was an overwhelming sense of release. Anirudh rushed to Salim's side. Refusing Aditya's offer of first aid for her swollen and bloodied face, Chitra too hurried and knelt beside the villager the moment she was released.

While his friends attended to the Salim, Aditya called Ishwar's mobile, using Chinkya's phone. Sidestepping a tongue-lashing for jumping from the aircraft, Aditya quickly explained that Chitra and the boys were safe and that the battle was over.

Even though he was furious with Aditya, Ishwar was left with little choice but to congratulate him on his achievement. When Aditya learnt that the men who had pinned down Ishwar had not fired a bullet for some time, he told Ishwar it was probably because their boss, the fat man, had called and told them to flee. A minute later Ishwar confirmed that they had indeed fled.

Vikram then spoke to Ishwar, conveying that they would need medical help and a stretcher for taking Salim down. No, the villager's life was not in danger, but he required medical attention, and his condition was such that it wasn't possible for him to walk, let alone descend a mountain.

Three hours later, with the aid of the local police who had finally arrived, Vikram and his friends descended from Koleshwar with Salim strapped to a stretcher. When they reached the road-head near Salim's village, Anirudh was swept off his feet by his parents who had driven down in a naval ambulance. A doctor examined Salim, and only when he certified that the villager hadn't suffered any permanent damage and would soon recover, did the sombre mood afflicting everybody finally lift. Yet, there were hardly any celebrations, and it was a physically and mentally exhausted party that finally returned to NDA.

RUSTOM'S STORY

So stark is the contrast between the Sahyadri panorama of the wet season and the ensuing cold one that the observer can be forgiven for wondering whether he is gazing at the same mountain range. While the monsoon garb of the Sahyadri is a dazzling green, its winter apparel is a lustreless, faded brown.

The spiralling waterfalls that gild the mountainsides during the rains are conspicuous by their absence in the dry season. So also the pollen-like veneer of moss that breathes greenery and life everywhere in the dampness. The frogs, the crabs, the mists, and the haunting piping of the Malabar whistling thrush wither into memories with the departure of the rains.

Across the Sahyadris and much of the Deccan Plateau a new order emerges, enabled by the altered equation in the skies. No longer constrained by cloud, the luminescent disc of the sun takes charge of the heavens, stripping colour and life from the mountains. The glorious blooms of monsoon grass are the first to succumb to its desiccating onslaught. In its vengeful return to ascendancy, the sun hunts down the offending traces of monsoon, relentlessly extinguishing its eye-catching brilliance, till all that remains are faded pockets of green where forests cling to the mountainsides.

But monsoon or winter, it matters not. For the discerning beholder, an unconquerable beauty shines through. And so it was with Vikram when he returned a few months later. Regardless of the transformation the changing seasons had wrought upon the mountains, he perceived in them their indomitable wild beauty.

It was dawn in the Sahyadris. A frigid, bone-numbing winter dawn. Vikram had trudged up the slopes of Koleshwar in complete darkness, and now as he rested on the black rock of a cliff edge, the first signs of day were prickling the heavens. Flat, table-topped mountains took form around him, bright and sharp. The only cloud present was a mild fog that rested in feathery streamers on the valley floor far below.

Vikram was not alone. A young boy, short and thin, with a bitter-chocolate complexion, sat beside him. Unlike Vikram, who was smothered beneath layers of warm clothing, all the boy had to show for the cold was a shawl wrapped loosely around him. The boy was Salim's nephew, and his name was Altaf. It was Altaf who had escorted Vikram to the lonely plateau of Koleshwar. On Salim's instructions, Altaf had come to Mahabaleshwar in the early hours of the morning, to the hotel where Vikram was staying, and in pitch darkness had guided Vikram down into the Krishna Valley and up the slopes of Koleshwar.

Seated on Koleshwar's knife-edged drop-off, with the Krishna Valley and the plateau of Mahabaleshwar outlined in map-like detail before him, Vikram understood why it had taken three hours of a gruelling march to reach their destination. For a bird, the distance between the plateaus was no more than a few undulations of wing. But as Altaf and he were not blessed with avian appendages they had been forced to descend plunging slopes to the valley, and then, after crossing it, ascend to an equal elevation on Koleshwar—a strenuous task by any standard.

Daylight brightened the valley below now, but they had traversed its breadth in complete darkness. They had crossed not far from a village, and Vikram had been struck by the silence that prevailed there: there had been no movement, not a sound, not even a dog had barked. Possibly because of the cold, Vikram had speculated.

There were stirrings in the village. Peering through his binoculars, Vikram saw shepherds leading their cattle to graze, and children threading their way to a dilapidated structure in an open field that he presumed was a school.

Far above the children, casting a monstrous shadow, towered the plateau of Mahabaleshwar. Vikram had been in a foul mood when he had set off from there. The unearthly start of 4 a.m. had irked him. There had been no need to set off at that bitterly cold hour of morning. But Anirudh had insisted and Vikram, despite vociferous protests, had been forced to give in. Now, however, with a crisp winter dawn illuminating the sky, and a growing conviction that there could be few better places to enjoy the grandeur of daybreak from, Vikram's mood was brightening faster than the spreading glow about him, so much so that he had half-forgiven Anirudh's inconsideration.

This was Vikram's first visit to Koleshwar since that fateful evening when he and his friends had come perilously close to losing their lives. It had always been his desire to return. Not alone, but with Anirudh, as there had been so many unanswered questions when he had left Pune and returned to school. But Anirudh had set conditions for a rendezvous on Koleshwar. First, that he climb the mountain in darkness so that no one would see him ascend. Second, that he should be alone; accompanied by no one—not even Aditya. And finally, that Anirudh himself would not accompany him, but meet him directly there.

Anirudh's bizarre demands hadn't surprised Vikram, as he believed that their near-death experience on Koleshwar had profoundly affected his friend. Never a particularly sociable boy, Anirudh had turned even more reticent since that bloody evening on Koleshwar. Secrecy had become an obsession with him. Vikram was supposedly Anirudh's best friend. Yet, in spite of his best-friend status, Anirudh had consistently refused to answer his emails, and even when Vikram called him, he would respond only in monosyllables. So, although Vikram had been annoyed at Anirudh's strange stipulations for their meeting, they weren't entirely unexpected as they fitted in with his current fetish for secrecy.

As the pink brushstrokes of dawn yielded to the blue canvas of daylight, Vikram was distracted by a flock of small birds that buzzed dizzyingly in the sky. Vikram instantly identified them as swifts. It struck him that he hadn't seen the bat-like birds in the Sahyadris during the monsoons. They had obviously returned here for the cold season from wherever they had migrated to during the rains.

While Vikram admired the birds, Altaf, the village boy, sprang to his feet. The cliff edge they were seated upon was bordered by a thick forest. Altaf had turned to the tangle of trees, his ears cocked. The boy shouted something in Marathi that Vikram did not understand. Immediately, there was an answering shout and Altaf turned to Vikram, smiling and nodding.

Vikram experienced a flutter of excitement. The voice was Salim's. Anirudh was holding to his promise of meeting him at sunrise.

Salim materialized first from the forest. He wore a long kurta-like shirt and grey trousers and there was a rucksack strapped to his back. Vikram inspected his dark features for signs of the thrashing he had endured and was heartened to see that not a trace remained. He greeted Vikram with a namaste and a bow, which Vikram promptly returned. Anirudh emerged behind Salim, his face split by a smile as wide as the sky. He embraced Vikram in a bear hug.

'I knew you'd make it,' said Anirudh, stepping back. 'And on-time as usual.'

'You better have a good reason for all this subterfuge.' The magic of the Sahyadri dawn had dispelled most of Vikram's rancour, yet he spoke in a peeved voice. 'Walk in the dark.' He mimicked Anirudh here. 'No one should see you. As if there's something to hide and the villagers here have nothing better to do than spy on us.'

Anirudh ignored Vikram's pique, continuing to smile brightly. 'I knew I'd have to make it up with you. So, I brought along hot chai as a peace offering. There's a flask in Salim's rucksack.'

It turned out that Salim was carrying far more than just chai. His pack was stuffed additionally with biscuits, wafers and a dabba with aloo parathas.

Like the steam that fizzed from Salim's flask, Vikram's animosity dissipated completely when his frozen fingers wrapped around the warm mug handed to him. The treat was unexpected, and given the splendour of the setting, it tasted better than all chais he had enjoyed before.

Sunlight slowly penetrated the valley, vaporizing the sunken fog as it did so. Riding a gust of warm air, a black-winged kite soared out of the valley and hovered to a standstill over a shelf of yellowed grass.

'You have no idea how hard it was for me to get away from the others,' said Vikram, sipping chai and watching the kite.

'Couldn't have been a big deal,' said Anirudh. 'All you had to do was spin a story to Aditya.'

'Spin a story!' Vikram snorted. 'It wasn't just Aditya. There was Kiran too.'

'Kiran?' Anirudh frowned. 'Oh yes! The NDA parade . . . did he graduate?'

'He didn't just graduate. You make his passing out sound ordinary. It was anything but that. Kiran led his squadron during the parade. His mom and dad and several relatives had come to watch too.'

'They must have been happy for him,' said Anirudh, reaching for a paratha.

'Happy' was the understatement of the year, thought Vikram. Kiran's relatives had been exultant, his family joyous. Passing out of the National Defence Academy is no easy accomplishment. It marks the culmination of three years of arduous effort and hard work. The armed forces acknowledge the stellar achievement of their cadets and celebrate their graduation as officers with a grand parade. Everyone turns out to watch the parade; top politicians are flown in as chief guests, and a military band livens the proceedings. Dressed in a sparkling white uniform, Kiran had marched at the head of his squadron, sword in hand. There had been a cheer as he and his mates swept past the podium, and the crowd had risen to their feet, applauding. The best had been reserved for the very last, when as the young officers slow-marched to the haunting strains of Auld Lang Syne, a squadron of aircraft had swept over the parade ground, bestowing upon them the most magnificent salute imaginable. From the onset, it had been clear to Vikram that he had been witnessing a memorable moment, for through its grand adieu, the Academy was bequeathing not just a military rank on Kiran and his course mates, but manhood too.

Anirudh hadn't been present at NDA for the parade. He had never been a great fan of Kiran's, but it wasn't because of his dislike of him that he had missed the parade. Barely a month earlier, transfer orders had come through for his father, intimating him that his tenure at the Academy was drawing to a close, and that his next posting was to the

Naval Headquarters at Mumbai. So, though his father had stayed back to attend to his duties at the parade, Anirudh and his mother had travelled to Mumbai to set up home there and enrol Anirudh in a school.

A prickle of Vikram's earlier irritation surfaced, sparked by Anirudh's refusal to acknowledge his efforts to slip away from the others. 'For your information, Anirudh, Chitra is arriving in Pune today, and I'm putting it mildly when I say she is upset that I won't be there with Aditya to greet her.'

'Hey!' exclaimed Anirudh. 'You make it sound as if only you had difficulty getting away. Mom had to spin a yarn to Dad for me so that I could come here to meet you. Let's not get carried away. It hasn't been easy for either of us.'

Vikram experienced another surge of irritation. He hated lying, and he had been forced to concoct a story for his friends, spinning a yarn about a 'Western Ghat Bird Seminar' at Mahabaleshwar, which actually was true, but he had fibbed when he had said that his father had insisted he attend the seminar.

'It wasn't easy organizing our meeting, if you must know,' went on Anirudh. 'We didn't want anyone to know of our presence on Koleshwar and so, Salim and I had to get here in the middle of the night. We also had to arrange for Altaf to collect you. For your information, Altaf left at midnight from his village to get to Mahabaleshwar. You might think that the secrecy is odd, but you have no clue what's been happening the last few months. There are reasons.'

'Sure,' said Vikram. 'Like the reasons you have for not replying to my emails and also refusing to come on the phone. You have excuses for all that too, don't you?'

'No excuses,' said Anirudh. 'Justifications, yes. Stuff that I can explain, now that we are here, face-to-face—'

'Finally!'

'Yes, finally. Now, if you have cooled down we can be civil to each other again—friends too, if you like.'

The black-winged kite had located to another area. It was above the plateau now and was hovering again. Salim and Altaf had moved to an area of tall grass near the cliff edge. They wielded sickles and were squatting on their haunches, cutting the grass.

'For their cattle in the village,' said Anirudh, noticing Vikram's gaze on the villagers. 'They have cows that are yielding milk and they treat them specially. The cows are made to stay at home, so as to not stress them. The yield is better that way, so they collect grass and take it to the milk cows.'

'You've learnt a bit about village life,' observed Vikram.

Anirudh grinned. 'Yes, I have. Here, have another paratha.'

They ate their breakfast watching the sun strip away the valley fog. When they were done, Anirudh poured more chai. 'So . . . you want to know what's been happening these past months,' he said, handing Vikram a mug.

'No,' replied Vikram, his face expressionless. 'I walked up this mountain in the dark and the cold because this is what I do each day. I enjoy spinning yarns for my friends and ditching them when it counts. All this is routine for me, don't you know?'

Anirudh burst out laughing. 'You're upset!'

'What do you expect?' Vikram glowered at Anirudh. 'You called me to Bombay when you said you needed a friend. Then when your period of need passed, you quickly forgot about your friend.'

'Hey!' Anirudh protested. 'Not fair. Absolutely untrue! Give me an hour and I'll justify my silence.'

Vikram crossed his arms. 'I'm waiting,' he said.

Anirudh stared at Vikram. Then shaking his head, as if clearing it, he began: 'Vikram . . . you are my friend . . . my best friend . . . just about the only person I trust besides my mother. Keep that in mind, Vikram. I mean those words; I mean them from the deepest places in my heart. I'm going to tell you everything today. Not hold back anything, I give you my word. You were offended by my silence these last months. You believe all this secrecy and slinking up the mountain is a waste of time. From your point of view, it might seem so. But it's not what you think it is. You will understand as I explain.'

Vikram kept silent, his gaze refusing to soften.

Anirudh stared at the kite, which was still stationary in the sky. 'If you are worrying that this talk will be as long as the one describing my dream, don't.' Anirudh smiled. 'It will be short, I promise. But first . . . before I begin, I need to be updated on what you and Chitra and Aditya know.' Anirudh gestured with his hands. 'What have you learnt and who's been telling you?'

'It should please you that it isn't much we know.' Vikram's voice dripped with sarcasm. Anirudh's pledge to come clean clearly hadn't impressed him. 'We were told that Peter is in jail. We also know that the fat guy, Chaggan, was not arrested, not even for a single day. Your dad has been speaking to Aditya's dad. That's the source of our information. We also know that your dad is mad as hell that Chaggan has got away.'

'It's true,' said Anirudh. 'Dad is furious at him and at all politicians in general.' He sighed. 'Nobody can touch Chaggan.'

'It doesn't make sense,' said Vikram. 'The evidence was incriminating, by any standard. There was Salim, beaten to a pulp; and what about the thrashing we endured? How about the gun battle between Ishwar and those men? Isn't that enough evidence to book even the biggest hotshot in the country?'

'It should be, but that's not the way justice works. At least not in the case of politicians, my dad says.' Anirudh shrugged. 'But if, for argument's sake, you ignore Chaggan's political clout, forget that he is a politician, and consider him and Peter as equals—then there is some kind of rationality to the fact that of the two, it is Peter who is imprisoned. Peter is a genuine hoodlum. He is a gangster, a hardened thug.'

Vikram stared at Anirudh like he would at an insect floating in his soup bowl. 'I don't get it,' he said. 'Are you trying to absolve Chaggan?'

'Chaggan didn't lay a hand on us, did he?' countered Anirudh.

'No, he didn't. But that was because Peter did his dirty work for him. What's with you? Didn't you hear Chaggan when he said he would kill us? Do you think it was for a joke that he waved his gun at us?'

'You will have to hear me out,' sighed Anirudh. He paused for a while contemplating, then spoke. 'Do you remember that Chaggan kept claiming that the treasure rightfully belonged to him?'

Vikram nodded. 'To him and to Peter.'

'Yes, to him and to Peter,' affirmed Anirudh. 'Now, I know you're not going to accept this, but there was some truth in what they said. The treasure we were seeking, in a sense, does belong to them.'

Vikram wrinkled his brow in disbelief.

'It's true. And there's a story to back their claim. A story that I came upon when I took home that dirty box from the wall in Seawind Hotel. I told you that I found a manuscript inside the box.'

'Yes, you did, and that was several months ago, when I was in Pune last.' The peeved tone was back in Vikram's voice. 'You promised me then that you would fill me in on the manuscript. But despite all my emails, you didn't tell me.'

Anirudh spoke sharply. 'Listen, Vikram. You keep thinking that I deliberately kept information from you. Get it into your head that there were revelations inside the manuscript that I simply couldn't convey on either email or the phone. You might not be aware, but there's a buzz everywhere that there is treasure on this mountain.'

Anirudh glared at Vikram. 'Those empty treasure chests Peter and Chaggan forced us to unearth started it. The villagers in the valley below have seen them and they haven't stopped talking since. Treasure, or even the whiff of one, makes everyone sit up and talk. Peter made it worse when he was arrested by telling all who could hear that there was a treasure on the mountain. Only the fact that he is half-crazy and that they have certified him as mental has kept the hordes from swarming over Koleshwar. That manuscript was dynamite. It confirms the existence of the treasure. I would be nuts to broadcast its contents. You think that asking you to come up here in the dark was just a whim on my part? There are villagers in the valley below who are constantly on the lookout for visitors to the plateau. I have been followed up here so often that it's like I'm a pied piper. Salim and I drove in last night directly from Bombay and sneaked up in the dark. We spent the night on the mountain and only after confirming that nobody had seen us did we come here. So stop going on about my secrecy. There are reasons for it.'

Anirudh's face had turned red. He inhaled sharply before continuing. 'I don't have the manuscript now; I don't even know if it exists any more. Chaggan and Peter stole it from me when they broke into my grandmother's place. Chaggan probably has it or has destroyed it. Whatever the case, I am sure I will never see it again. But it doesn't matter as I must have read it at least ten times before I fell asleep that night. How do you think I knew where to find the chests? How did I know that the chests were filled with stones? It wasn't by prescience. It was the manuscript.'

Vikram kept silent. His grudge against Anirudh was deep and had festered for several months. Yet, against his will, in a manner not different from the evaporating fog below, Anirudh's narration was dissipating his rancour.

Anirudh continued. 'You are probably thinking that the manuscript was written by Rustom. So did I when I opened it. But there was a surprise in store for me. It wasn't Rustom, but his son, a gentleman by the name of Faradh, who had authored it. I can't tell you how thrilled I was when the manuscript turned out to be what I prayed for it to be—a biography, the story of his father's life. It is probably the only record of Rustom's life, and I am indebted to Faradh for writing it. It was written after Rustom passed away as Rustom was extremely secretive about his life, his past in particular, for which no one can blame him. It was something you would expect after the mayhem that occurred here on Koleshwar, especially the death of several white men—Wallace and his henchmen— an unpardonable offence in those days. The events that occurred here on Koleshwar were never made public. There were only a handful of people Rustom confided in, and one of them was his son, Faradh.

'Faradh, not surprisingly, had boundless admiration for his father, and it was to preserve the memory of such an incredible life that he wrote the manuscript. The interesting thing is that Faradh also kept the manuscript a secret, stowing it away in a vault whose existence only he knew of. And equally interesting, a fact I am certain about because the manuscript was still wrapped in Rustom's seal, is that no one had read it before I did. I don't think I am too far off in guessing that Chaggan and I are the only persons who have read the manuscript. I also doubt whether Chaggan would have had the patience to read the entire manuscript as the majority of its pages would not have interested him—they being a record of Rustom's life. For me, it was different. The manuscript itself was a treasure. It gave me all I wanted. I truly couldn't have hoped for anything better.'

Anirudh grinned at Vikram. 'Remember, we had a dispute about the treasure? You were arrogant and cocksure that Rustom had used the treasure for himself. It's been a while, yet even today your words still hurt. For your information, Rustom didn't use even a single paisa of that treasure. He never needed to because he made a fortune for himself as he had always said he would. During his lifetime, the treasure lay undisturbed here on Koleshwar, except for a period during which he and his son Faradh unearthed and then re-buried it. When Rustom passed on he willed the treasure to his heirs through his son Faradh, whom he appointed as his custodian. The will, as his heirs were to discover, was no ordinary one. Rustom set conditions for the inheritance of Wallace's booty; conditions so strict that they disrupted everything. Only if his heirs met certain standards, standards that were important to him, would they get the treasure.' Anirudh broke off. 'I think you know what I'm going to say now—'

'—that Chaggan and Peter are Rustom's heirs,' guessed Vikram.

'You are a sharp guy, Vikram,' grinned Anirudh. 'Yup, both are his heirs.'

'And also a pair of rogues who could never have met Rustom's standards.'

'Right again,' said Anirudh. 'But they aren't the only heirs. There are also other living individuals who qualify as his heirs. None are like Chaggan or Peter. Many of them are excellent human beings. Yet, whether good or bad, collectively they never fulfilled Rustom's requirements. That's why the treasure still lies here. All of Wallace's booty, except for tidbits like what Salim stumbled upon, is buried here on Koleshwar.'

There was a silence as Vikram digested what he had heard. Then his brow furrowed. 'I don't get it,' he said. 'Rustom was a Parsee. How could Chaggan, a Hindu, and Peter, a Christian, be his heirs? It doesn't make sense.'

'To explain that I will have to tell you Rustom's story,' said Anirudh. He poured two cups of chai. 'Have some more tea. The story will take a while.'

At the edge of the cliff, where the grass grew in tall clumps, Salim and his nephew worked with their sickles, singing as they did so. In the sky, the kite folded its wings and dived missile-like to the ground, but Vikram hardly noticed. This was the story he had been waiting to hear. He stared at Anirudh, engrossed.

'It wasn't a snakebite that killed Irfan,' began Anirudh. 'On that windswept evening in September 1857, if you remember, a leopard chased them to that cave. There, in the dark, Irfan stumbled upon a snake. Terrified at its touch, he stepped backwards. I'm guessing here, but I believe that he fell into the same chasm I toppled into. The difference between our accidents was that his head collided with the rocky floor of the cave more solidly than mine. The manuscript says that the back of Irfan's head was bashed terribly and that was why he died.' Anirudh shook his head sorrowfully. 'Poor Irfan. It was a sad end for someone who loved life so much. But it was even worse for Rustom. You can imagine Rustom's state then. It was the most devastating moment ever in his life. In that cave, the bottom of Rustom's already shattered world fell out. The loss would have destroyed most people, but Rustom proved, as he had often done before, that he was iron-willed and made of the real stuff.

'After the tragedy, Dagdu, the village boy from the valley below, became Rustom's companion. Rustom was pretty much inconsolable, and Dagdu devoted all his free time to him. Thankfully, Rustom's period of mourning on Koleshwar did not last long. The rains had lifted by the time October came along, and one sunny morning Dagdu delivered disturbing news. Men from Bombay had come to investigate Wallace's death. The bodies of Wallace and his mates had been discovered not long after their actual deaths, but since the rains had been in full force there had been no investigation then. Now white men had come and they were asking questions about Irfan and Rustom. The men had gone on to Mahabaleshwar, as that was where they believed the boys to be hiding, but not before offering a reward to anyone with information as to their whereabouts.

'The time had come for Rustom to leave Koleshwar. But he had to be careful because he was a fugitive now. The nearby cities of Wai and Satara were the easiest to flee to, but they were dangerous as the search would certainly be extended to those areas. Bombay too was out of the question. So, he chose Poona.

'Rustom left Koleshwar with mixed feelings. He was glad to get away from the place that had heaped so much sorrow on him, yet at the same time, he felt as if he were leaving a part of himself behind. Entombed beneath stone, in the cave he had died in, lay the remains of the person who had been the nearest and dearest to him. And there was another consideration too. Nothing as deeply personal, yet important all the same. He was leaving behind Wallace's entire loot.

'Only Dagdu and he were aware of the treasure's location, buried near the banyan tree, at the same spot where we found those empty chests. Dagdu being of simple mind had no use for the treasure, and Rustom did not doubt him when he said he would guard it for him. Rustom too had no need for Wallace's riches as he had his savings from Bombay, which were enough to look after his needs for a lengthy period of time.

'So Rustom, with a heavy heart, departed Koleshwar. Dagdu, who was upset to see him leave, volunteered to accompany him to Poona. But uncertain of his own future, Rustom would have none of it. He promised Dagdu that when his troubles were behind him, he would return. Which, by the way, is exactly what Rustom did. Friendship and loyalty were very dear to Rustom, coming first before all else. Not only did Rustom return a year later, but he took Dagdu back with him. Dagdu was to remain a constant companion for the rest of his life, serving Rustom till the day he died.'

Anirudh paused. He unzipped his jacket and loosened his collar. The plateau was warming and Vikram too peeled off one of the many sweaters he wore. Salim and Altaf were still cutting grass. The black-winged kite was nowhere to be seen.

'Salim's showing no signs of injury,' observed Vikram. 'He's recovered well.'

'These villagers are tough,' said Anirudh. 'You wouldn't believe it of him when you saw his state after Peter's thrashing, but he was back at work in a couple of weeks, and almost as good as new in a month.'

Vikram shuddered. 'The thrashing was brutal. It's so bloody unfair! Chaggan supervised his beating. He should never have got away.'

'We'll return to that later,' said Anirudh. 'We were talking about Rustom and his flight to Poona. His arrival in Poona was significant for Rustom. Not only was he returning to city life, but importantly, he underwent personal changeovers that would remain with him for the rest of his life. In Poona, his personality turned even more inward. From the dream you would know that he was a quiet boy by nature. Yet, on reaching Poona he adopted an even lower profile, and this trait became permanent. This, of course, was because of the deaths of Wallace and his mates. He lived in terror of being arrested. So strong was Rustom's fear that he even changed his name. From then on he referred to himself as Homi. He changed his surname too, taking on the name Poonawalla.'

'Wow!' whistled Vikram.

'It was a smart decision. The idea was that a name like Poonawalla would associate him with the city of Poona, rather than Bombay. The dropping of Rustom was complete and final. It was Homi Poonawalla all the way from then on. The biography too describes him as Homi, the Parsee from Poona. So, Homi—'

'Not Homi,' protested Vikram. 'Stick with Rustom.'

Anirudh laughed. 'I prefer Rustom too. For Irfan and me, he will always be Rustom. So Rustom it is. The first job Rustom applied for in Poona was at a stable. Irfan had taught him a lot about horses and he easily slipped into work as a stable hand. But Rustom was no ordinary stable hand. Before his first year was out, he dipped into his savings and started purchasing horses himself. He bought the animals that went cheap, the ones no one wanted. He picked fidgety animals that bucked and behaved badly. They were considered unsuitable for domestication, and he bought them at throwaway prices. He took on a partner, an extremely good rider, but importantly a kindly man of gentle disposition. They would choose the animals together and Rustom would pay for them. Then his partner, Ashok, would break them in. The trick, as Irfan had often pointed out to Rustom, was to treat the animals gently. This was a task Ashok was skilled at. Not all the animals would respond to Ashok's efforts, but several did, and Rustom would sell those at market prices for a fat profit.

'In two years, Rustom and Ashok had made enough money to start their own stables. Their business boomed and soon Rustom had more money than he had ever had before. It was during this period that Dagdu joined Rustom in Poona.

'The years passed quickly and with their passage, Rustom found it increasingly difficult to hold back his longing for Bombay. He missed the harbour, the sea and Bombay's docks. He still dreamt of owning boats that would do business across the seven seas. It was only the danger of being recognized on Bombay's streets that held him back. Finally, it was the news of Forjett's retirement and his imminent departure for England that gave him courage. Like Irfan, Rustom idolized Forjett. Something would forever be missing inside him if he let Forjett leave without bidding him farewell.

'So, in 1863, six years after fleeing the city, Rustom returned to Bombay. His homecoming was quiet, a non-event. He avoided all his former acquaintances, meeting only his sister, who was overjoyed at seeing him safe and sound. He swore her to silence, forbidding her to speak to anyone, especially her husband. She was not to breathe a word to his friends Mario and Ajit. Not even to Mr Ghadiali. His homecoming was confidential, a private affair.

'Rustom sought out only Forjett, who was delighted to see him. The news of Irfan's death saddened Forjett and he shed tears on hearing Rustom's story. He was upset at Rustom's plight, and for him to have to change his name and keep a low profile. Forjett was unable to set things right for Rustom. He was retired now and there was little he could do. He confirmed that Rustom would be arrested on the spot if he revealed his true identity. Colvin, the man who had taken over Seawind, had kicked up a fuss when news of Wallace's death reached Bombay. It was Colvin who had pushed the governor to send police to investigate his death. The men who had come to Mahabaleshwar had indeed been searching for Irfan and him. After they had returned empty-handed, both Rustom and Irfan had been charged as abettors in the murder of Wallace and his comrades. There was nothing anyone could do for Rustom. If he wanted to stay on in Bombay, it would have to be undercover.

'Although unable to help Rustom clear his name, Forjett was ready to assist him in any other manner. Never one to make personal demands, Rustom requested only two favours of him, both to do with Irfan. As Forjett was headed to England, he asked that he seek out Irfan's English friends, Ralph and Peter, and apprise them of his story and death. The twins were like brothers to Irfan, and it was only right that they be told of the fate of their friend. He asked Forjett also to find and buy him Irfan's horse, Mohini. The animal was special to Irfan, and Rustom wanted to lavish upon it the love his friend would have. Forjett located and purchased Mohini in a matter of days, and he gave Rustom his word that he would search for Ralph and Peter in England. In addition, despite Rustom's protests, he secured him a job. Rustom's ambitions and abilities were still fresh in Forjett's mind, and the Englishman was determined to set his career back on track. An Indian friend of Forjett's owned a fleet of passenger ferry boats and his glowing recommendation landed Rustom a placement at managerial level. And so Rustom, in a matter of weeks, was back at the job he loved.

'Shortly afterwards, as history has it, Forjett departed Indian shores forever. Rustom quickly lifted the fortunes of the passenger boat company and when the owner, an old man, retired, Rustom purchased the business. In the years that followed, Rustom rode from success to success. In a sense, life had turned full circle for him. He was back in Bombay excelling at what he loved doing. The only difference this time round was the matter of his identity. It pained him that he couldn't use his real name, but with time the hurt faded and he grew accustomed to being Homi Poonawalla. There was one more regret though; one that refused to leave him. It was to do with his friends Mario and Ajit and his inability to unite with them.'

Vikram interrupted here. 'You're saying that he never met them again?' he queried.

'I didn't say that. Things changed eventually, but that was years later when they were old men. In those early years, Rustom couldn't take the risk, but that didn't stop him from keeping track of their lives. On the occasion of the birth of Ajit's first child, a present of gold bangles arrived from a mysterious well-wisher. Mario received an even more expensive gift on his wedding day. You have to remember that Rustom valued friendship and loyalty. There was no way he was ever going to give up on his friends.'

'What about Rustom himself?' asked Vikram. 'Didn't he marry too?'

'Yes, but not then. In those early years, he was wedded to nothing but his work. The ambition and ability he had exhibited glimpses of as a youngster flourished and bloomed then. The years slipped by, filled with success and fulfilment. The most significant incident in that period was the arrival of Ralph, Irfan's childhood friend. Forjett, true to his word, had located the twins and related Irfan's story to them. Of the two brothers, only Ralph returned to India. Peter, who preferred life in England, never bothered. In stark contrast to his brother, Ralph had never forgotten the city of his childhood, and returning to Bombay was a homecoming for him. Since they both loved Irfan dearly it was inevitable that Ralph and Rustom became friends. Their shared history ensured that the friendship they struck wasn't an ordinary one. They carried their alliance to great heights, extending it to a business partnership and their families and beyond. In Ralph, Rustom finally found a worthy successor to his beloved Irfan, and a great peace and contentment fell upon him.

'With Ralph as his partner, Rustom found the courage to take his business forward and purchased vessels that could sail to overseas destinations. The two friends worked hard, and a combination of luck and outstanding business talent held them in good stead. Slowly and steadily Rustom achieved his dream, and in a matter of years, their shipping company rivalled the best operating out of Bombay.

'The years passed, heaping happiness and inevitable moments of sadness. Ralph married an English lady, and Rustom found himself a fine Parsee wife. Both families were blessed with two children, a boy and a girl each. Remember the portraits in Seawind Hotel? They were of Ralph and Rustom's families. As the portraits showed, the families were like a single unit, the bond between them as solid as steel. The sadness arose from the passing of Rustom's sister. Never a strong lady, she had grown frail with the years, and one day her heart gave up. Irfan's horse,

Mohini, passed away too, dying of old age, after a life filled with love and affection.

'I'm skipping the years here now, to the twentieth century, when both Ralph and Rustom turned senior citizens. They were extremely wealthy men by then. At this point in time, Rustom finally revealed his identity to Mario and Ajit. Rustom had never forgotten his childhood mates. Not a single year had passed without a mysterious well-wisher showering them with expensive gifts on Diwali and Christmas. Rustom had also kept track of the plummeting fortunes of the construction company they had started together. There was never a doubt that Mario and Ajit were excellent workmen, Mario possibly the most talented in the city, but both were poor businessmen and Lady Luck had refused to smile upon them. Their company had steadily notched losses, and Rustom finally bailed them out by buying their bankrupt business. So the friends were united again, this time not just as old mates, but also as business partners.' Anirudh paused here. 'That should answer your question, Vikram. You have the explanation now. You can guess why Chaggan, a Hindu, and Peter, a Christian, are heirs to the treasure on Koleshwar.'

'You mean . . .'

'Yes, even though Mario and Ajit were broke and hadn't contributed anything to his business, Rustom took them on as partners. Remember always that Rustom valued friendship above all else. Mario and Ajit—after Irfan and Ralph—were Rustom's dearest friends, and Rustom was generous to a fault with friends. It wasn't just their fortunes that Rustom looked after, he extended his generosity to their offspring as well. They were included in Rustom's will, on an equal footing with his and Ralph's heirs.'

Vikram tossed a pebble over the cliff edge. 'It's making sense now,' he said. 'So Chaggan is Ajit's descendant and crazy Peter is Mario's. You spoke of other heirs; people who you say are decent human beings. They have to be saints if they aren't interested in the spoils.'

Anirudh laughed. 'I don't know about them being saintly as I haven't met most of them. One of the heirs—we've both met him—is certainly a decent human being. I'm talking about Palkhivala, the manager of Seawind Hotel.'

Vikram's mouth popped open in astonishment.

'Yup. Seemed like too much of a coincidence then, didn't it? But it's true. Rustom's sister had children and they were inducted into the business about the same time as Mario and Ajit's were. Naheed's children were the only true family Rustom had, and he wasn't about to forget them.'

Vikram's face had turned red. 'Palkhivala!' he exclaimed. 'Have you lost your mind? Him . . . a decent human being?'

'Take it easy,' laughed Anirudh. 'Even you can be wrong sometimes. Palkhivala is a good man. But I'll get to that later. I want to talk about the other heirs first, Rustom and Ralph's families.

'Neither of the families live here any more. They migrated to England long back. For Ralph's family, it was expected. Ralph himself might have loved India, but his children preferred England and they went back after Ralph's passing. In the case of Rustom's family, it was different. Faradh, Rustom's son, was a copy of his father. He was hardworking, good at business and he loved India.

There was no way he was going to leave the country. Faradh had studied in England and when his children came of age, he sent them there to study. The children came back when they completed their studies, but by then squabbling had begun in the business. Then Faradh died around that time. The squabbling grew so intense thereafter that Mario and Ajit's descendants never allowed Rustom's grandchildren to settle. Matters reached a head when they engineered their expulsion from their own family home. I'm talking about Seawind, the luxurious mansion that Rustom had built. Angry, hurt and disgusted, Faradh's children left India after that. They returned to England where they settled, and the generations after have remained there.

'The thing is that Rustom had seen this coming. He had foreseen the breaking up of his business and the squabbling. Way before all the bickering and anger began, Rustom had devised a plan that he hoped would keep the families together. You've probably lost count of the times I said family and friendship was dearer to Rustom than anything else. This plan that Rustom came up with had its roots in his absolute commitment to friendship. The treasure on Koleshwar was the focal point of the plan. The treasure wasn't needed in Rustom's lifetime as his shipping enterprise looked after the requirements of all five families. But he knew that the business would not last forever and that there would come a time when the descendants would need the riches that lay in waiting on the mountain. The goal of Rustom's plan was simple. If the five families came together in their hour of need, the treasure on Koleshwar would be theirs. However, if there was disunity and infighting, they would never be able to access it. To set the plan in motion, Rustom, Faradh and Dagdu unearthed the treasure and carefully reburied it in thirty different locations on Koleshwar's expanses. Each location was carefully mapped. Then the mapped information was put on five sheets of paper. These sheets were sliced into a jigsaw puzzle of several components. When pieced together, the components detailed the exact locations of the reburied treasure, but if read separately, the information was incomplete. Rustom then separated these jigsaw components into five sets, one for each of the five families he hoped to keep together. Are you getting what the plan was? The five families would have to gather and piece together their different components if they ever wanted to locate the treasure. Unless the families—every one of them—united, the treasure would elude them.

'Rustom's will passed the jigsaw sets to Faradh. His instructions to Faradh were to pass them on to the descendants of the various families. There was to be no hurry, he set no date. Faradh could decide, based on when the anticipated squabbling actually began. Rustom's hope was that the lure of the riches of the treasure would unite the families again. In case they did not unite, then so be it. It was their loss. They would have proved themselves unworthy of what he had willed to them.'

Anirudh sighed. 'As I said earlier, the squabbling started round the time Faradh's children returned from England. And it was shortly afterwards that Faradh himself died. As per his father's instructions he left behind a will. The will did not speak directly about the treasure. Instead, it spoke about the unity of the families and a great wealth that lay in store for them if they stayed together. It went on to say that five parcels had been put together for them, one for each family. The parcels would be held in custody for ten years. After the stipulated time, the parcels would be distributed and if the families were still united, the wealth the will spoke of would be theirs. Ten years later, the parcels were distributed. Two were sent to England, to Ralph and Faradh's descendants. One each handed to Palkhivala, Ajit and Mario's families. The treasure still lies here on Koleshwar because, sadly for Rustom, the coming together that he had hoped for has never taken place. And there you have it. That's the story.'

KOLESHWAR'S SECRET

Anirudh rose to his feet. 'I've inconvenienced you, haven't I? Pulled you up this mountain in the dark and the cold. I hope it's been worth it.'

'But you haven't finished!' exclaimed Vikram.

Anirudh's lips creased in a smile.

'What about the treasure?' demanded Vikram. 'You just confirmed that there is a treasure up here. So where is it?'

Anirudh's smile grew wider. 'Come along,' he said. 'We've been sitting here too long. Follow me.'

Vikram rose hurriedly. 'Are you taking me to the treasure?' he asked.

Anirudh stooped and collected the mugs and empty flask. 'How would I know where it is?' he asked.

'The manuscript, of course,' said Vikram.

'Oh! Come on, Vikram.' Anirudh placed the mugs and flask in his backpack. 'You disappoint me. If the manuscript had the information, then Chaggan would know where it was. I told you at the start that there was nothing concerning the treasure in the manuscript. That's why the manuscript was of no use to Chaggan.'

'Well, if you are so smart then tell me how you know about Faradh's family migrating to England. The manuscript couldn't possibly have given you that information as they left India after their father died. So then how did you come to know about them?'

'Ah, ha!' laughed Anirudh. 'Now you are talking. That's the Vikram I know. Yes, the manuscript ended with Faradh's passing. You're absolutely right. I didn't get the information about his family from there.'

Anirudh flicked his eyes, searching the area for litter. 'See,' he said. 'I've learnt from you about not littering these places.'

'Glad you've learnt,' said Vikram, scooping up a wrapper. 'Footprints are all we should leave behind in areas like this.' He straightened. 'Where are Salim and Altaf? I don't see them.'

'They've moved on,' said Anirudh, hitching his pack to his shoulders. 'Salim's gone to check whether any villagers are about. They spy on us if they get to know we are here. Not to worry, Salim knows where we are going. He'll be waiting there for us.'

Anirudh strode forward, away from the cliffs and the valley. 'Come on,' he called over his shoulder.

Vikram fell in step beside him. 'So, you're taking me to the treasure.'

'I didn't say that,' said Anirudh.

'Then where are we going?'

'You'll know soon. It's some distance from here, so let's get a move on.'

The forest bordering the cliff was thick and overgrown. Shafts of sunlight streamed through a tangle of gnarled and twisted trees. On the ground, knotted roots corkscrewed everywhere, thrusting through a carpet of red and brown leaves.

'Oh, yes,' said Anirudh, remembering. 'You were wondering how I know about stuff that happened post the manuscript. My source is Palkhivala.' Anirudh winked. 'Yes, Percy Palkhivala from Seawind Hotel. We are good friends now. We've met often in Bombay, and before I forget, Percy wants me to convey his apologies about Peter and his men and their attack on you. He was trying to warn you when their car drove up, but they were too fast.'

Vikram turned wrathful. 'The miserable coward could have tried to save me! He didn't lift even a hand to help. Assault and kidnap . . . before his very eyes. The very least he could have done was go to the police.'

Anirudh shook his head. 'I'm disappointed in you, Vikram. 'Again you pass judgements without knowing the facts. You wouldn't know that Peter had threatened Percy that he would cut off his ears and nose if he breathed a word.'

'That's nonsense,' said Vikram, ducking as he passed a low-hanging branch. 'Why would he be afraid of a stranger on the street?'

'You're wrong there,' said Anirudh. 'Peter has terrorized Percy all his life. They've known each other since they were kids. In the past, they used to run Seawind Hotel together, a period of his life that Percy says he would like to forget. Percy didn't choose Peter as a partner. The hotel was handed to them when their parents died. It was a wonderful hotel till then, according to Percy. But once Peter took over as managing partner he ruined it. He went berserk, slapped the employees and even roughed up the guests. He stripped the hotel bare, and within five years he accumulated such heavy losses that they were forced to sell the hotel. Poor Percy was devastated. The hotel was a family heirloom.

'Remember I had said that Rustom's family had been ejected from Seawind? After they moved to England, the place came to be owned by Chaggan, Peter and Percy's families. It was still a home then, and not a hotel. Then at some point, Chaggan's ancestors sold their share to the others and moved on. Many years later, the remaining owners—Peter and Percy's families—decided to run it as a hotel. It was a great hotel till about fifteen years back. But then the elder generation passed on and it came into Percy and Peter's hands, which is when it fell into ruin.'

'Hold on,' said Vikram. 'Are we talking of the same hotel or am I mistaken? The Seawind I know is a top-class hotel.'

'Right you are. It is a great hotel. And that's because the first thing the new owners did was to eject Peter. The man is forbidden from entering its premises. You see Percy did something extremely sensible during the time Peter wrecked the hotel. He wrote to Rustom's descendants in England, telling them of Seawind's condition and appealing to them to save it. Rustom's family in England is wealthy. Percy knew that. He also knew that Seawind was as much a family heirloom for them as it is for him. Rustom's family funded the purchase of the hotel. They have full faith in Percy, and he runs it for them. Percy is a decent man, a fine soul.'

Unlike Anirudh, Vikram was in no mood to forgive the diminutive manager of Seawind. 'You are a great fan of Percy's, aren't you? So much so that you seem to have forgotten that it was because of him that we almost lost our lives. Wasn't it Percy who told Chaggan and Peter about us?'

'It was a mistake, Vikram. Percy is ashamed of himself. You have to see it from his point of view. Seawind was his family home once. A home that he had shared with Chaggan and Peter's families. He couldn't help calling Chaggan when he saw me opening the secret vault on the hotel security cameras. What would you do in his place? The vault, when it emerged from the wall, was like magic for him. Wouldn't you share something like that with your childhood friends who had once lived in the house? How could he anticipate what would follow?'

Vikram halted. He turned to Anirudh, hands on his hips. 'Are you blind or—' he began, but broke off, disturbed by a sudden noise.

Anirudh reacted too, turning swiftly.

There was a burst of sound not far from them. Leaves flew and the underbrush shook. The boys caught a flash of brown and the creature was gone in a flurry of hooves.

'Deer,' muttered Vikram, staring in the direction of the receding sound. 'Either a chital or a barking deer . . . I didn't get a proper sighting.'

'There are spotted deer here,' confirmed Anirudh. 'I've seen them often.' His face turned rueful. 'What you see now is a fraction of the wildlife during the time of my dream. You can't compare. Koleshwar would have been a Noah's Ark for you, Vikram.'

Vikram smiled. 'Yeah, sure,' he said. 'Must have been a wildlife paradise then.'

They resumed walking, Vikram paying attention to their surroundings now. But all he heard was birds and his thoughts reverted to Anirudh's baseless vindication of Palkhivala. 'It seems to me, Anirudh, that you are in a mood to forgive everyone involved in the attacks on us,' he said. 'I can understand what's going on in your head. These people are descended from the families that Rustom held dear. But it's wrong to let their ancestry colour your judgement. Generations have passed now. You cannot brush away the fact that this current bunch of descendants instigated this attack on us.'

'That's not true,' said Anirudh hotly. 'Where have I absolved Peter? Have I once defended him? He's the bad egg, the man responsible for everything that happened to us.'

'Okay,' said Vikram. 'You haven't defended Peter. But what about Chaggan? You've been harping only nice things about him. You've conveniently forgotten his intentions to knock us off. His threats of murder were made in fun and jest, were they?'

Resignation replaced Anirudh's anger. 'I'm never going to be able to convince you about Chaggan. I know that. All I can say is that I have met Chaggan in Bombay.

He admitted to me that the treasure had driven him to temporary madness. He apologized for what he had done, and he promised he would never behave so unthinkingly in his life again.'

Vikram threw his head back and laughed. 'And you believed him? Come on, Anirudh. Are you so daft that you forget he is a politician? That he is the kind of person who can glibly convince you the world is flat, not round. You fell for his line. You are not stupid, I know. But on this subject, you are truly gullible. Gullible because you want to believe only the best of everyone associated with Irfan and Rustom. Don't you see?'

Anirudh sighed loudly. 'Have it your way,' he said. 'I said I wouldn't be able to convince you, and I'm not going to try any more. All I can tell you is this. Of Rustom's five chosen families, Chaggan's was the first to lose belief in the treasure. As a youngster, he would visit Koleshwar, but that was more because of the house, the Parsee Ghar that he had inherited, rather than the treasure. His grandparents, and even his parents, never believed in the story of the treasure. They even threw away the jigsaw pieces of the will that they had inherited. In the recent past, it is only Peter who has been keen on the treasure. It is him and his cronies who have been hanging round Koleshwar. It was Peter who beat up Salim when he stumbled upon the cache he found, and it was his hoodlum buddies who chased us. Chaggan was nowhere in the picture nor was Percy Palkhivala. It was the phone call from Percy of my finding the manuscript that injected the madness in Chaggan. For that one day, he went nuts. Yes, he behaved like a beast and was willing to kill us that day. But the truth is that we can thank our stars that Chaggan was there on that day. If it had been only Peter, we would have been dead by now. Chaggan was the calming influence, our saviour that evening. It was when he saw those empty boxes that he came to his senses. What he saw convinced him that the treasure didn't exist, and he's back to his normal self now.'

'Sure,' scoffed Vikram. 'Back to his wily political self. He put his skills to use brilliantly, wriggling out of a jail sentence for assault and kidnap.'

Anirudh allowed himself a smile. 'True,' he said. 'He had a cast-iron alibi created for himself. He got all kinds of people to swear that he was with them on the night of the assault. The police couldn't do anything because he left no trace of his presence on the plateau, and the heavy downpour that struck afterwards wiped away whatever evidence there might have been. Peter too, might have gotten away. He also tried to cook up an alibi. We have Chinkya, the man who Aditya knocked down, to thank for his arrest. Chinkya managed to get away, but it was his diary, which Aditya pocketed, that led to Peter's downfall. Chinkya was a hitman, a hired assassin, one of many unseemly characters Peter has been associated with. Peter has always lived on the fringe of civilized society. He never had money and could never hold a job. When the new management of Seawind Hotel threw him out he descended into Bombay's underworld. Chinkya's diary contained details of several murders that Peter had commissioned him for. That was sufficient to throw Peter into the locker where he belongs. He will be locked away from society for keeps, I hope. The latest on him is that he has gone mad—'

'He was half-mad in any case,' Vikram cut in.

'True,' grinned Anirudh. 'Chaggan and Percy Palkhivala agree with you there. They think that the shock of seeing those empty chests finally tipped him over. You see, Peter believed in that treasure. To Chaggan and Percy, it was little more than a family story. But for Peter, finding it was the goal of his life. It makes sense then that the trauma of the empty chests must have been too much for him to bear. He's gone cuckoo according to his jailers. He spends his entire day talking to himself about the treasure. Chaggan says he has bailed Peter out several times in the past. He's going to try to help him again, but this time the charges are murder and the evidence is stacked against him. Chaggan feels there isn't much hope.'

'Thank God,' said Vikram. 'The world is a better place without him.'

'Correct,' said Anirudh. 'I wouldn't be comfortable with him on the loose. That's for sure.'

'Of course you wouldn't. Especially since you know where his dear treasure is hidden, right?'

Anirudh smiled mysteriously. Ignoring Vikram's pointed query, he changed the subject. 'We'll be reaching our destination soon. I should tell you that we're headed towards a stone. A big one; big enough to call a rock. But whatever you want to call it, the remarkable thing about it is that it is circular, a perfect circle you could say, and that it stands in almost complete isolation in the forest. It isn't only for its geometry that I'm taking you to the stone; it's also because it was there in my dream. The stone hasn't been shifted since those days, which is interesting in itself. It's been 150 years and it's exactly where it was. It could be because it's so big that it's impossible to move. Also, it hasn't been defaced. No one has broken it or even chipped at it, again something you wouldn't expect. But getting back to the dream . . . it was Irfan who loved that stone. He liked it because it was flat and circular and therefore a convenient place to pray from. He prayed a lot after his father died, and the stone was one of his favourite places. You might ask why I'm taking you to that stone. It's because the stone was significant to Rustom too. He valued it because Irfan loved it.' Anirudh paused, gazing ahead at the forest. 'We're almost there,' he said. 'Look, you can see Salim and Altaf.'

A hand waved amidst the trees ahead. Squinting, Vikram picked out two figures in the distance. Salim was easy to see as he stood in a shaft of sunlight. Altaf was a shadow beside him.

Vikram spotted the stone before they reached it. It lay amongst the trees to one side of the path. Even from a distance, the stone was impressive, chest high and a couple of metres wide. Arriving beside it Vikram saw that it was perfectly circular, as Anirudh had said, and also that its upper surface was flat and smooth.

'Neat, isn't it,' said Anirudh.

'Is it natural?' asked Vikram.

'Seems to be,' said Anirudh. 'There are no noticeable marks of it having been worked on before. I would assume it's natural.'

'It's all by itself out here.' Vikram looked around. 'That's odd.'

Anirudh shrugged. 'That's the way it is.'

'It is a special rock,' said Vikram. 'I can see why Irfan thought it a great place to pray from.' He paused, turning. 'So why did you bring me here?' he asked.

Anirudh smiled his infuriating smile again. He beckoned to Salim. When Salim started forward, Vikram saw that he was carrying something on his back. It wasn't the backpack he had carried earlier, Anirudh had it now. It was a sack and it was heavy as Salim's torso was tilted forward.

'Thanks, uncle,' said Anirudh, when Salim placed the sack on the rock. He turned to Vikram. 'Put your hand inside,' he said. 'Go ahead, it's open. Slip your hand in.'

All of a sudden Vikram's heart began to pound. Anirudh smiled broadly. Beside him, Salim too was smiling.

His hand shaking, Vikram reached forward and inserted it inside the sack. His fingers touched something solid and cold. The contents were bumpy and sharp in places. His hand, trembling now, probed the contents of the sack. For a moment, Vikram was reminded of barnacle-encrusted rocks. But he knew that these weren't rocks he was handling. The material had a metallic feel. It was heavy and smooth in sections. Tightening his grip Vikram withdrew his hand.

In the sunlight, the object he held sparkled yellow and gold. Stones embedded on its surface flashed vivid colours. Vikram drew a sharp breath when he realized what he was holding—a gold necklace encrusted with precious stones.

'It's real,' said Anirudh, speaking in a conversational tone. 'Genuine gold. The stones are sapphire and amethyst. I had it checked out in Bombay. There's a hoard of other goodies in the sack: bangles and brooches and earrings and chains and necklaces galore. Dig around and you'll find chunks of solid gold; idols carved from gold too. Have a dekko.'

The forest and the rock swam before Vikram's eyes, and he had to draw several breaths before opening the neck of the sack. The sack was stitched from thick cloth. Barely a sliver of light entered its folds, yet there was a glow from inside, as if it were lit from within. The colour of the inner light was yellowish, embellished with a fiery sparkle. Vikram dug his hand deep and grasping a fistful, he pulled it out. Then he opened his fingers, allowing what he held to fall back inside. Several rings, bangles and a glittering bracelet slipped out. Vikram submerged his hand again and repeated the manoeuvre. This time a diamond-encrusted necklace and a leaf-shaped trinket of gold trickled down. In a robotlike manner, Vikram kept dipping his hand inside, allowing whatever he gathered to spill back inside. Once he extracted a solid idol, a miniature of Lord Shiva. Another time he hefted a chunk of gold. But mostly it was necklaces and bangles, all solid gold.

Not a word was exchanged. Such was his enthrallment that Vikram forgot about his companions. The warmth of the sun drew beads of perspiration on his forehead, but he hardly noticed. Finally, it was a sharp birdlike call that snapped him from the trance the treasure had cast on him.

'Quick!' snapped Anirudh, urgency in his voice. 'That's Altaf. Somebody's coming. Let Salim have the sack.'

Vikram's hand fell away. Salim materialized by his side. He grabbed the sack and even as Vikram struggled to recover his senses, he loped away, the sack on his back.

'Run to the path,' said Anirudh. 'Quick.'

Vikram dashed after Anirudh, his head still spinning. Anirudh eased his gait to a fast march when they reached the path. 'The call is a signal that someone's coming,' he breathed. 'Walk fast. Act like a trekker, as if we're crossing to the next valley. Don't look back. Don't worry about Salim. He is quicker than a hare in the forest. No one will find him.'

Anirudh lengthened his stride. They walked fast, leaves scrunching under their feet. The area they were in was level and the path wove through thick forest. They had covered a couple of hundred metres before they heard the tramp of feet. Around a bend, they spotted a lone figure. As the figure drew closer, they saw it was a man wearing torn trousers and a patched sweater. His face was dark and bearded. There was an axe in his hand. Its blade winked in the sunlight. The man stared at them as they drew close.

'Ram, Ram,' greeted Anirudh.

'Ram, Ram,' replied the man, his face expressionless. He passed them, not breaking a step.

'A villager,' said Anirudh, when the man was out of earshot. 'It could be that he is crossing to the Krishna Valley. Or, he might have come to the plateau to cut firewood. The axe indicates so.'

'Well, he's seen us,' said Vikram. 'I could pass as a trekker. But you . . . you're the one who's known in these parts. Think he'll alert others of your presence?'

'Can't say,' said Anirudh. 'I've never seen him before. But we'll have to be on our guard from now on. Sorry, but treasure hunting is over for the day.'

Vikram's eyes glowed. 'I've never seen so much gold before in my life,' he bubbled. 'That must be worth a fortune. All those necklaces and bangles. Wow!' He laughed. 'And correct me if I'm wrong, but what you showed me isn't all the treasure, is it? There has to be more.'

Anirudh nodded. 'There is. There certainly is . . . but I have yet to find it.'

Vikram glanced back over his shoulder. The forest was empty and silent behind them. There was no indication they were being followed. 'Where's Salim gone?' he asked.

'To a cave he and I know of. It's the cave Rustom and Irfan lived in. We keep the treasure there. It's a safe place. He'll put it away and join us.'

There was another shadow on the path ahead. Vikram saw that it was Altaf. Though it was cold in the forest shade, Altaf had discarded his shawl, which was now slung about his shoulders. Balanced on his head was a long, yellow bundle and when they drew close Vikram saw that it was the straw that he and Salim had collected. Altaf smiled as they passed him and then fell in behind them. Anirudh upped their pace and they strode like seasoned trekkers. After an energetic fifteen minutes, they emerged from the forest on to a sloping grassland that Vikram recognized.

He shaded his eyes and looked about him. They had arrived at an edge of the plateau. The mountain terminated ahead and a deep valley was visible. The Dhom dam and the River Krishna were a blue haze in the distance.

Pulling up, he said, 'I know this place. This is where we split up the first time we were attacked on Koleshwar. That tunnel through the rock, isn't it nearby?'

'It is,' confirmed Anirudh. 'We're headed that way. I want to show you something on the lower section of the mountain.'

'Some more treasure?' asked Vikram.

'No,' replied Anirudh. 'I told you we are over with treasure for the day.'

'Are you ready then to tell me how you found the map?' inquired Vikram.

'What map?' said Anirudh, starting forward. He descended gingerly as there was gravel underfoot.

'So, you want to act pricey,' said Vikram, gouging footholds on the slope.

'I'm not acting pricey,' said Anirudh. 'There is no map. It doesn't exist any more. Except for Peter's set, all the jigsaw scraps that were handed down have been lost or thrown away. Palkhivala and Chaggan have both told me so. Their families either discarded their sets or lost them. Rustom's descendants—Palkhivala says—have also misplaced their sets. Even Ralph's family doesn't have theirs any more.'

'So you want me to believe that you found the treasure all on your own. You have prescient knowledge of the treasure, I see.'

'Yes,' said Anirudh. 'If you want to put it that way, I do have prescient knowledge.'

Vikram reached the bottom of the slope and turned and stared at his friend. '

Anirudh slid to a halt beside Vikram. 'I probably know this mountain as well as Salim,' he said. 'Not because I have spent more time here, that's not true, of course. It's because of my dream. The dream has gifted me insights on Rustom; the working of his mind, subtleties no one else can ever know.'

Anirudh resumed their trek, speaking as he walked. 'According to the manuscript, Rustom spent the final years of his life here. The Parsee Ghar was indeed built by Rustom and it was to be his final home. It was his intention to die here and be laid to rest on this mountain; in the same cave where Irfan's remains lie. His wish was fulfilled because when he died, Dagdu and Faradh placed him there, beside his best friend. As per the will we know that the treasure was exhumed and reburied in thirty different places. Rustom supervised the entire effort. The manuscript is silent on where the treasure was relocated, but it mentioned something that was a revelation to me. Only a few lines on the relocation subject, a paragraph . . . but that paragraph was crucial to me. Rustom apparently was very emotional during those final days. Irfan was constantly on his mind. For the reburial, Rustom selected only those places that were connected in some way with Irfan. To most people, the information was of no use. No one knows the connection between Irfan and Rustom . . . that is no one except me.'

A burst of comprehension flashed in Vikram's head.

Anirudh laughed. 'I see you've understood what I'm getting at.'

'That stone!' said Vikram. 'You said that it was one of Irfan's favourite places. That he prayed there a lot.'

'Yes,' nodded Anirudh. 'That's the reason I searched there. Salim and I dug in a circle around the stone and we found a cache of treasure, which incidentally, was our first find.'

They arrived at the rock corridor where Aditya and Kiran had held off their pursuers. Vikram couldn't restrain a gasp when he stared at the fissure that cut through the rock.

'It's amazing, isn't it?' said Anirudh, entering the fissure.

Black rock enveloped Vikram as he descended behind Anirudh. In the rains the rock had been wet and slimy, now it was dark and cold. The rock was ancient and smooth. Evidence, if any, that the passage had been hewed by hand, had long been erased by weather and time. It was impossible now to judge whether the corridor was natural or man-made.

They emerged from the rock in a forested area and Anirudh led the way down a twisting mud path.

'Where else have you searched and found Rustom's caches?' asked Vikram, descending behind Anirudh.

Anirudh negotiated a fallen branch that lay across the path. 'After our success at the prayer rock, I selected a spot on the western edge of Koleshwar, one that both Irfan and Rustom were struck by. For a period, when there was a break in the rains, they saw rainbows there. They popped up one after another every few minutes, even double rainbows sometimes. Oddly, one leg of those rainbows always seemed to hover over a flat-ish zone near the edge of the mountain. Irfan was fascinated by that flat area and its rainbows. You know of the saying of a pot of gold at the rainbow's end.' Anirudh grinned. 'I am a believer now because that's where we found our second cache.'

The path dipped, falling steeply, and talking turned difficult. The trees in this forest were taller than those on the plateau; consequently, the light that filtered through them was less. They emerged eventually from the forest on to a level expanse.

Glancing back, Vikram saw that Salim had joined them. Vikram waved, and Salim smiled. He walked beside Altaf, his back erect, no longer burdened by the treasure sack.

'Good,' said Anirudh, noticing Salim's presence. 'The treasure is safely tucked away.' He continued: 'I've only found two more caches, both in caves. The first was in the cave Rustom and Irfan lived in, the one where I'm storing our finds. The second was in the cave where I almost died. I had a hunch that Rustom would have stored some treasure there. Irfan's remains, after all, are there. It turned out I was right.'

The shelf of land they walked upon wasn't particularly broad. They quickly neared the cliff edge and the spread of the valley and the Krishna River lay before them.

'Does anybody else know about your discoveries?' asked Vikram.

'Just you and my mom and dad,' said Anirudh. 'I'm not telling anyone else.'

'Makes sense. You're not the kind who talks much anyway.' Vikram grinned. 'What may I ask are your plans for the treasure?' he asked.

Anirudh's gaze turned soft. 'You can have as much of it as you want, Vikram,' he said. 'You are my best friend.'

Vikram experienced a rush of shame at having questioned Anirudh's friendship earlier. He swallowed as he replied. 'Thanks, Anirudh,' he said. 'What you just offered is the nicest gesture ever in my life. I know you mean what you said. But the treasure is all yours.' He placed a hand on his friend's shoulder. 'All that I want of it is to run my hands through it again. It gave me a real high.' He laughed. 'Gold and jewellery slipping through one's fingers. It's difficult to beat that. But seriously, Anirudh—I have no need for it.'

'Don't be hasty,' said Anirudh. 'Take a while to think about it. Sure, at this time, you see no need for money. Nor do I. But what about later? You never know. The money can finance your higher studies in the best colleges of the world. Tell me and I'll keep some aside for you.'

Vikram shook his head. 'Thanks, Anirudh, but no.' His voice was firm. 'This money is yours. You found it. You experienced the dream. You deserve it. Do what you please with it, but keep me out of your considerations. I don't want anything. Let's not argue about this.'

Anirudh's lips creased in a thin smile. 'You are such a boring sort, Vikram. Predictable, like night follows day. I had expected this reaction from you. I knew all along you would say no.'

Vikram fixed a quizzical gaze on his friend. 'Then am I right in saying that you would have been disappointed if I had taken up your offer?'

Anirudh dropped his gaze.

'Of course you would. I'm glad you had expected me to say no. It shows you know me for what I am. That kind of understanding is essential for any true friendship. I know also that your offer is real. I know that if I ask, you will give me whatever I want. And that's no ordinary commitment. It's a mark of fine bonding—the kind that Rustom sought.'

Anirudh nodded. 'You're right there. Rustom would have appreciated our friendship.'

Vikram changed the subject. 'What are your intentions? What's your plan for the treasure?'

Anirudh shrugged. 'I don't know. I haven't given it much thought.'

'Oh, come on,' said Vikram. 'Save that line for someone else. Of course, you've given it thought. Plenty, I'm sure.'

Anirudh grinned. 'Okay, I have done some thinking. The problem is I haven't got anywhere. I have no idea how to use it.'

'Another question then,' said Vikram. 'How much of the treasure have you found?'

'I have no clue. And that's half the reason I haven't made up my mind. I still have to locate the remainder—twenty-six caches more, to be precise. It's obvious I won't locate all. Some have already been discovered. Salim found one. I know of another discovery seventeen years ago. There have to be other discoveries too. Years have passed. It's impossible to say how much of it I will recover, but it's certain I will come across more . . . a lot more.

'For now, the plan is to halt the search. What has been found is being put away in Rustom and Irfan's cave, and it's going to remain there for years. When I'm older I'll come back and decide what to do. Salim has been talking about opening a school for the children in his village. He's also spoken of a hospital; there are no medical facilities to speak of here. I'll be frank with you, Vikram. The way I see it is that I will use some of the wealth for my parents and myself, but the majority will be kept for Salim and the people who live here.'

'Wah!' exclaimed Vikram, patting his friend on his back. 'Noble intentions indeed. I'm impressed. But your generosity intrigues me. I can understand your feelings for Salim, but I can't figure out your charity for the villagers here. I see no connection.'

Anirudh halted beside a broken stone wall. 'Charity?' he queried. 'Does it need a motive?'

'No, but it needs a connection. Donors choose carefully whom they give to. Why the villagers? Aren't they the ones after you? Tracking your moves as you put it, expecting you to lead them to the treasure. Their conduct is not exactly deserving. Why them?'

'There's nothing wrong with their conduct,' said Anirudh. 'What would you expect of people who get a sniff of the possibility of a treasure? I should be counting my blessings that they are simple villagers and not greedy city hoodlums like Peter. Yes, the villagers keep an eye out for me, but they don't bother me or use strong-arm tactics. And you are mistaken about a connection. There is a connection. A strong rationale exists for giving to the villagers.' Anirudh gestured with his hands. 'It's so overpowering that I cannot ignore it. It's a one-in-a-million reason that cuts to the core of my existence . . . to my very being.'

Vikram stared. For no accountable reason, Anirudh's voice had turned emotional. His throat was quivering too.

He turned his back on Vikram, embarrassed at his display of weakness.

Vikram remained silent, uncertain how to react. He turned, looking for Salim. Possibly he could explain Anirudh's breakdown. But Salim sat at a distance, gazing out across the valley.

A minute passed before Anirudh turned. His face was set. He had collected himself. His voice was steady when he spoke. 'I'm going to tell you a story,' he said.

'You've told me several today.' Vikram laughed, trying to lighten his friend's mood.

Vikram's ploy worked because Anirudh laughed too. 'Yes, I have. This will be the last, I promise you. But again, before I start I have to request you to keep this to yourself. No one is to know.'

'Phew!' breathed Vikram. 'What's come over you? At this rate, you'll make yourself a candidate for the secret service. What's this latest intrigue?'

'There is no intrigue,' said Anirudh. 'It's just a story as I said, except that it's a true one and it concerns me. The story was told to me here; right here where we stand. Salim told it to me. My parents were present too. They had come up here especially for me. They wanted to be here when I heard the story. They knew I'd want their support, and they were right because the story shattered me. It turned my world upside down. It tore apart my notion of who I am. It changed my life forever.'

Vikram stood still. Dragonflies buzzed. Swifts sped sorties in the sky.

Anirudh pointed to the broken wall. 'You remember this place?'

They were standing at the remnants of what had once been a home. A hut had stood there, but now only its shell remained. Vikram felt a wakening in his head. It wasn't the ruined structure that jogged his memory, rather it was an association of sadness and desolation that he recalled.

'Yes,' said Vikram. 'This is where the rest of us caught up with you and Salim when you two sprinted up the mountain. I remember this place because you both had such sad expressions. We felt as if we were gatecrashing a funeral. For the life of me, I couldn't figure out why you had tears in your eyes. Then Salim explained that his brother had once lived there and that he was no more.'

'That's right,' nodded Anirudh. 'Salim spoke of a death in his family.'

Anirudh turned silent again. He pirouetted slowly, looking around him as if he were seeing the area for the first time.

The cliff they had just descended towered like a fort wall behind them, a natural barrier guarding the fastness of Koleshwar's plateau. The cliff was dry and black now, but when Vikram had visited last, a waterfall had flowed from it and living moss had added lustre to its dull surface. Thick mists had clouded the area then, heightening the bleakness of the place. The mists had gone now and the sky was a dazzling blue, yet the sorrow Vikram had associated with the area persisted.

Anirudh cleared his throat. 'There was something here that I could feel. I didn't know Salim's brother, yet I experienced a distinct kinship for him. I cried that day and I had no idea why. There was this extreme sorrow connected with this place.

'I returned here, as I said, with Salim and my parents. This was a month after Peter kidnapped us. The monsoons had just ended then. Water was still flowing from the cliff and everything was green and beautiful. It was really wonderful here, and I was happy to have Mom and Dad with me. Yet, in spite of having my parents, I couldn't shake off the sadness associated with this place. It clung like an invisible mist, especially to these broken walls. Birds were chirping, water was flowing, the area was a lush green and the view stunning, but the sadness refused to lift. Mom and Dad's attitude that day didn't help. Mom was nervous and fidgety and she refused to look me in the eye. She was wringing her hands continuously. Dad just stood there, not moving, not saying a thing. Then Salim sat me down and told me the story that changed my life. A story I didn't believe, but my parents corroborated his every word, and from that day on the world has never been the same for me.'

Anirudh wandered to the broken walls, entering the area where the hut had once stood. Salim was taking interest in them now. Vikram was certain that he was aware that he was the subject of their conversation.

Anirudh ran his hand over a splintered rock in the wall. 'The story is about Salim's brother Rafiq and his wife Zeenat. They were the couple that had once lived here in this hut. No one in his right mind would come and live here, especially if he had a home in the valley below. But Rafiq came to live with his wife. He did so because he had quarrelled with his father. His father had not approved Rafiq's marriage. Zeenat was from a lower status of society—so Rafiq's father believed—and he forbade the union. Almost all the male villagers here go to Bombay to seek work, and it was in Bombay that Rafiq met Zeenat and fell in love. In spite of his father's opposition, Rafiq married Zeenat, and as a consequence was thrown out of his home. So they came to live here, on this lonely verge of the mountain. Rafiq built this house, and he and Zeenat lived here as happily as was possible under the circumstances. In a few months, Zeenat was pregnant with their child and Rafiq decided to extend their tiny home to accommodate the baby that was to come. He set about excavating the area and found something that was to bring a premature end to his life and permanently alter the life of his unborn child.'

Anirudh's gaze flicked around the hut ruins. 'The place where the hut stands is another area that was special to Rustom and Irfan. They would come here with Dagdu to admire the view of the mountains and the valley. Later, this spot was chosen by Rustom to hide a cache of Wallace's loot. The cache buried here was found by Rafiq when he extended his hut for his yet-to-be-born child. They kept their find a secret, telling nobody, not even Salim—Rafiq's favourite brother and only friend. The child was born and yet they kept their secret till the day tragedy struck.

'Peter, yes our same terrible Peter, climbed to the plateau on a winter morning exactly seventeen years ago.

Peter was carrying the jigsaw pieces his father had handed down to him, and with a friend had come to search for the treasure. As was his routine every day, Rafiq had left the house early with his cattle. The child was a few months old then and to keep him quiet while she worked, his mother had given him a gold coin from the treasure to play with. Peter and his friends came to the hut and spotted the coin with the child before Zeenat could hide it. I don't have to tell you the effect the coin must have had on Peter. In his rough manner, he questioned Zeenat where she had found the coin. While Zeenat denied having any knowledge, his friend searched the house and found the treasure, which was stored in empty water jugs. They then immobilized Zeenat, tying her up. They took the treasure with them, leaving behind Zeenat and her infant child. But instead of returning to the valley, they climbed to the plateau, and Zeenat had been afraid for her Rafiq who was up there with his cattle.

'Zeenat's fears turned out to be chillingly real.' Anirudh paused here, swallowing. The tremor returned to his voice. 'Her husband did not return.' Anirudh lowered his head and Vikram saw he was having difficulty breathing. He drew several breaths before ploughing on. 'Salim visited his estranged brother often and it was he who found and freed Zeenat when he climbed up that evening. A search was launched immediately for Rafiq and the next day his body was found, crushed and broken below one of Koleshwar's cliffs.' Anirudh's voice dropped to a whisper. 'An inquiry into Rafiq's death concluded that it was accidental.'

Vikram drew closer, bending to catch his words.

'Zeenat never believed that to be true. Salim doubted the verdict too as he knew his brother to be an excellent rock climber. Zeenat was certain that Peter and his friend had murdered her husband, but there was no evidence to back her accusation.'

The tremor waned from Anirudh's voice, yet it remained soft.

'Poor Zeenat. Life as she knew it had come to an end. Her beloved Rafiq was gone. There was no point in staying on any longer. She returned to Bombay with her son. But her parents, who hadn't approved of her marriage either, refused to take her back. Zeenat was homeless. A friend of hers knew of a young naval couple who needed a live-in maid and Zeenat accepted the job.'

Anirudh paused to clear his throat. His eyes were wet, filled with unshed tears. He spoke fast now, as if he wanted to get the story done with.

'Zeenat worked for the couple for a year, during which time the couple was posted out of Bombay to the Andaman Islands and Zeenat went with them. The sorrows Zeenat carried with her were hard to bear. The couple she worked for was unfailingly kind to her, yet they say they rarely saw her smile. It was clear to them that she had fallen into deep depression. It seemed that she kept herself going only for the sake of her son. In those days malaria was rampant in the Andaman Islands and one day Zeenat was struck by the disease. She suffered fever and bouts of shivering and cold. The doctors treated her, but to no avail. The couple believes that Zeenat gave up on life, and when she died they were left with her infant son.'

Anirudh's face was like chalk now and his chest had started to heave.

'The naval couple was childless, the wife medically unable to bear a child. After Zeenat's death, the couple kept the child with them. They adopted the child and brought it up as their own. The child's original name was Irfan, but after adopting it they changed it to Anirudh . . . Anirudh Dongre. I, Vikram, am that child.'

Somewhere at the back of his head, Vikram had anticipated the story's conclusion, yet when Anirudh was finally done, he found it hard to accept what he had heard. As he stared dumbfounded, he saw Anirudh sag. The effort had drained Anirudh and his knees were buckling beneath him. Before Vikram could react, Salim rushed to Anirudh's side, supporting him with his arm and on seeing them together, Vikram was instantly reminded of the number of times he had been struck by the similarities in their features. The evidence was before his eyes: their short statures; their chocolate-coloured countenance; the same deep-set cheekbones and dark eyes. Though hard to believe, the story was true.

Anirudh gently detached himself and walking to the cliff edge, sat there. Salim made to follow, then hung back. He looked at Vikram. Vikram nodded and crossed to where Anirudh sat. Peeling off his final sweater, Vikram settled beside him.

Anirudh was staring into the valley. Choosing not to disturb him, Vikram looked down too. Like the mountains, the landscape below was chiefly brown. The only traces of green were in the deepest portion of the valley where a river had hollowed a trench. There were scattered pools of water in the riverbed, spread in giant puddles along its length. A patchwork of green fields hugged the riverbed, outlining its winding path. At the head of the valley, below where they sat, the fields narrowed, and near the last of the fields stood the ruins of what had once been Rustom's house.

Vikram glanced at Anirudh, wondering whether it was Rustom's cottage he was looking at. It was hard to tell, but the tilt of Anirudh's head seemed to indicate so. Vikram turned his gaze to the distant mountains and the sky, which was alive with swifts. He leaned back, observing their soaring acrobatics.

Several minutes passed before Anirudh finally spoke. 'Salim recognized me during that regatta when he came to rescue us,' he said.

Vikram dropped his gaze from the birds.

Colour had returned to Anirudh's face. 'Salim knew of the defects in my fingers and toes as a child. He too has identical disfigurations and so did Rafiq, my real dad. It was a genetic defect passed on by their father.'

'You have me to thank for Salim finding you,' pointed out Vikram. 'It was I who forced you to take part in that last race.'

'Yes, you did,' said Anirudh 'I never thought of it that way.' Vikram was pleased to see him smile. 'True, in a sense you are responsible. But don't get carried away as if it's all your doing. It had always been my parents' intention to level with me. They had let things be because they knew it would be hard on me.'

Vikram wagged a finger. 'They would have levelled with you one day. But that race and your rescue by Salim were crucial. You would never have worked out your origins otherwise.'

Anirudh smiled but did not pursue the topic further.

'I'm sorry for that show of emotion,' he said instead. 'I can't help it. I feel this churning inside every time I think about my true parents . . . especially about their deaths.' Anirudh dropped his head. 'It's such a sad story . . . such terrible hopelessness.'

Anirudh's eyes had filled with tears again.

Vikram spoke hastily. 'Your urge to help the villagers here makes sense to me now,' he said. 'You have roots here, deep roots. But tell me, when you learnt of those roots . . . was it a shock?'

Anirudh rubbed a sleeve across his eyes. 'Shock is putting it mildly. It was as if a bolt of lightning had hit me.' He sighed deeply. 'Every once in a while it did strike me that I was different from my parents. Our physical contrasts are hard to miss. Yet, even then, it never occurred to me that they were not my parents.'

'You didn't doubt Salim's story, did you?'

'No, I didn't. Not for a moment. Everything seemed to fit. There was a deep connection the very first time I set my eyes on this hut and its broken walls. It was crazy. I cried here that first day and I didn't even know why. Then later, when I returned with my parents, and Salim spoke, everything fell into place. The connection I felt on that first day was very real, as natural as it can get . . . an umbilical one. I was born here . . . in this very hut. My parents named me Irfan . . . on the very spot Rustom chose to bury a portion of the treasure. Salim's revelations turned my life and everything I knew upside down, but I didn't doubt him even once.'

'Phew,' breathed Vikram, shaking his head. 'You've really been through it, haven't you? I wonder how I'd feel in your place. It's like brain surgery.'

Anirudh laughed. 'More like a brain repair job, actually. But I've accepted it. Took a while, but I got over it. Funny, but you know at first I had thought I'd be ashamed of my humble origins . . . my underprivileged background, but I'm not. It doesn't bother me at all.'

'It had better not,' said Vikram. 'I'd have been ashamed of you if it had.'

'You don't have to worry.' Anirudh grinned. 'I'm proud of my background.' He swept his arm. 'And of my beautiful home in this corner of the Sahyadris.' Then his face clouded. 'But there's one thing . . .'

Vikram gazed inquiringly.

Anirudh's expression had undergone a change. It was troubled now, deeply so.

'My religion,' he said. 'I'm horribly confused . . . Am I a Hindu or a Muslim?'

'Oh, come on, Anirudh,' said Vikram. 'That's the very least of your worries.'

Anirudh turned red. 'Oh yeah,' he said, anger evident in his voice. 'It's easy for you to speak. You're not the one who underwent brain repair surgery. I come here so often, to this hut, to this only home my parents ever knew, and I want to pray for them. I dearly want to . . .

but I can't. I cannot because I don't know what is right. My parents are Muslim. I want to pray . . . but all the prayers I know are Hindu.' Anirudh wrung his hands, the way his mother did.

Vikram looked searchingly at his friend. 'It's true,' he said. 'This really bothers you. You need straightening out, Anirudh. I have to rid you of these dumb thoughts.'

Anirudh gazed hotly at Vikram. He started to speak, but Vikram shushed him.

'Tell me,' said Vikram. 'Have you ever harmed anybody?'

Anirudh stared. 'I don't see what my harming anyone has got to do with religion.'

'Just answer my question, Anirudh.'

'No . . . I haven't harmed anyone.'

'Good,' said Vikram. 'I suspected you hadn't. Now tell me, do you go to the temple?'

'Yes, I do,' said Anirudh. 'Not often, I admit. Only when Mom takes me. But if you want to know I say my prayers every night.'

'All the better,' said Vikram. 'Now . . . the next question. When you go to the temple do you look around and see the faces of the people there?'

'I don't. I go there to pray.'

'Well, the next time you go spare time to look around. When you do you will notice a strong sense of faith there. The faces you see will reflect love, reverence and humility. My dad pointed this out to me. He also took me to a church one day and asked me to look around. The faith I saw in the peoples' faces was identical. So also the reverence, the love and humility. We went to a mosque another day and I saw that it was no different.'

'You're speaking in riddles, Vikram. What has all this got to do with me?'

'I'm only pointing out that at a very fundamental level all religions are the same. They tell you to do good things, and they inspire faith and love and kindness. You say you're all mixed up, Anirudh. You say you don't know whether you are a Muslim or a Hindu. I want you to ask yourself what have you got to fear if you pray, if you have faith and you have never harmed anyone.'

'You're not getting it, Vikram. I'll spell it out for you if that's what you want. I was born a Muslim and I have lived my life as a Hindu.'

'No, Anirudh. You're the one who's not getting it.' Vikram paused. 'I want you to forget about everything for a moment. Just look inwards . . . at yourself. You are blessed with good character. You have faith and love and reverence. And you possess another exceptional quality— charity and selflessness. You want to give away your riches to the needy.'

Vikram leaned forward, gazing intently at his friend.

'Now, switch perspectives, Anirudh. Try looking beyond it all . . . to God. Hindu or Muslim is a big thing for us humans, especially to politicians my dad says, as it suits their purpose. But perhaps to God, religion is not the issue; perhaps it doesn't matter at all. It could be that God sees beyond religion, that He delves deeper, to the very soul of the person in question. That's what you need to get in your head, Anirudh . . . that maybe to God the language of prayer is irrelevant; that to Him your deeds and your goodness, and the purity of your soul, is all that matters.'

Anirudh stared at Vikram.

For a long time, he sat very still. Then he rose and crossed to the remains of his parents' hut. Vikram watched as he knelt beside the broken wall. Anirudh bowed his head and his eyes turned wet, flashing like pearls in the sunlight. Then his lips moved in prayer.

ACKNOWLEDGEMENTS

Sharda Dwivedi was a noted Bombay conservationist, historian and friend. This book would not have been possible without her encouragement and support. Deepak Rao is a Bombay historian and an expert on the history of Mumbai's police force. His guidance and assistance were invaluable. My thanks also to Saaz Agarwaal, for her literary inputs and encouragement.

READ MORE IN THE SERIES

Sahyadri Adventure: Anirudh's Dream

Once upon a time, there were fields in the city of Mumbai. In its heartland were forests where panthers roamed. In those days, the seas flooded the channels that separated the seven islands of the city. On one of those islands was a fort guarded by cannons that bristled from black ramparts.

Vikram had no idea of the existence of this fort. Nor did his friend, Anirudh. But in a cave, on a windswept Sahyadri mountain, Anirudh had a dream. He dreamt of a boy named Irfan who once lived in this fort.

Journey to the Sahyadris in the first part of this riveting tale where history meets adventure in one of the most beautiful locales of India.

READ MORE IN THE SERIES

Ranthambore Adventure

THIS IS THE STORY OF A TIGER

Once a helpless ball of fur, Genghis emerges as a mighty predator, the king of the forest. But the jungle isn't just his kingdom. Soon, Genghis finds himself fighting for his skin against equally powerful predators but of a different kind—humans.

The very same ones that Vikram and Aditya get embroiled with when they attempt to lay their hands on a diary that belongs to a ruthless tiger poacher. Worlds collide when an ill-fated encounter plunges the boys and their friend Aarti into a thrilling chase that takes them deep into the magnificent game park of Ranthambore.

Journey through the wilderness, brimming with tiger lore, with a tale set in one of India's most splendid destinations.

READ MORE IN THE SERIES

Snow Leopard Adventure

Vikram and Aditya are back in magnificent Ladakh. Having finally freed their young friend Tsering from the hands of dangerous men, they've set themselves up for an even greater challenge: to track down the grey ghost of the Himalayas, the snow leopard. The boys join a team of ecologists and explorers in their search for this rare and beautiful creature.

Here, Vikram befriends a troubled and unhappy girl called Caroline. The soaring peaks of the Himalayas hold no attraction for her, yet she is driven by an overpowering desire to spot a snow leopard. Set amidst majestic mountains and plunging valleys, *Snow Leopard Adventure* is a satisfying finale to a chase that began in *Ladakh Adventure*.

Journey in search of the elusive snow leopard with an enthralling tale set in one of India's most splendid destinations.

READ MORE IN THE SERIES

Lakshadweep Adventure

Far out in the Arabian Sea, where the waters plunge many thousands of metres to the ocean floor, lies a chain of bewitching coral atolls—the Lakshadweep Islands. Vikram and Aditya dive into lagoons with crystal-clear water and reefs that are deep and shrouded in mystery. But when they stumble upon a devious kidnapping plot, their idyllic holiday turns into a desperate struggle for survival.

Forced out into the sea in the eye of a raging storm, they endure a shipwreck, only to be marooned on a remote coral island.

Journey through these breathtaking islands with a tale of scuba diving and sabotage, set in one of India's most splendid destinations.